An Innocent Secret

UNCOMMON LORDS AND LADIES

BOOK THREE

Margaret McGaffey Fisk

TTO
PUBLISHING

Cover created by Margaret McGaffey Fisk

TTO Publishing logo design by Blue Harvest Creative
www.blueharvestcreative.com

An Innocent Secret

Published by
TTO Publishing

ISBN-10: 1-63139-018-X
ISBN-13: 978-1-63139-018-0

First Print Edition

Chapter One

Georgiana Ferrier had all but given up on the chance of seeing her friend for yet another day when she heard his thundering footsteps through the underbrush. He'd turned eighteen this very April, and though she had no brothers, she'd seen enough among her father's farm hands to know such an age changed things. She'd begun to fear he would lose interest in their friendship.

"There you are," Frederick Hathwell said as he burst through the bushes surrounding their spot, light brown hair tousled from his journey. He looked nothing like the heir to a small but respected barony should, but exactly as she expected her friend to appear.

Georgie shook her head. "As if I'm the one who's been missing. I've come looking for you every single day since the last on the hope you'd be here. And you never were."

"I'm here now." Freddie shrugged as if his absence meant nothing. "Though not for long. My father has me working on the estate. Mother was less than pleased with his decision, but he wouldn't have me as ignorant as he had been when the barony fell to his shoulders."

"So your promises to me have little meaning now that you're a man grown?" She hadn't meant to scold him, but the careless way he mentioned leaving so soon came too close to her own fears.

He moved forward and laid a hand on her shoulder. "Don't ever think so. You know how important you are to me. I've outgrown my tutors is all, and I have more responsibilities. I am a baron's son in the end."

Georgie's eyes narrowed as she stared at him. "And my work isn't as important? You might be titled, but it doesn't make you better than any of the rest of us. We all have important work to do."

"I didn't mean it that way. It's just harder now to sneak out and come to you. I can't have my father discover what we've been doing."

His apology only made her anger rise. She stamped a foot, caring not one whit if it might make her seem younger. "And what have we been about that your father would care? You don't want him to know you couldn't even catch your own supper when I first came upon you, do you? Or is it that you're spending your time with someone who's beneath you?"

"Georgie, it's just how my father and mother will see it. They won't understand." He frowned and shook his head at her.

"Well I don't think I understand either." She sent him a fierce scowl in return. "Go on with you, Mr. Hathwell, heir to the Lord Brookway. Go see to your important duties. I'd best help make sure there's food on my father's table when he gets done with his unimportant labors."

She twisted and marched off into the forest, even in her anger keeping her footfalls soft so he could not follow her. The brook had fallen far behind before her pace slowed and her feet dragged.

He didn't say anything she hadn't expected, but Georgie had not anticipated how his clear change of focus would affect her. He'd been her friend through so many major changes in her life. She'd thought he would always be there at her side. The idea of losing him now, of having him wander off into the adult world without her, made her chest ache.

Georgie had heard him coming after her for a bit, but he gave up all too soon, a further sign her concerns were grounded in nothing less than fact. If he'd called out to her, she would have gone back.

Tears gathered at the corners of her eyes, but she wiped them away, unwilling to give him even so much. "If he's only concerned with his title and the property that will come with it, I'm better off without him. He doesn't know much else besides what I taught him in any case."

Her sharp words offered little comfort and even less truth.

Georgie sank to the forest floor, her back braced against a broad oak tree. She longed for the shelter of his arms, the one place she'd found comfort when life became too hard. She had no one to help her suffer this loss. Her family didn't even know why she sought out the forest and would be unlikely to mourn if they had.

It had once been a place away from the farm and three sisters who all thought they knew better than she did simply from the order of their birth. But everything changed when her favorite spot along the brook had been invaded by an ignorant boy.

How she missed that boy.

He read her lines of poetry and told her of the arguments found in his studies, but he'd looked to her for everything governing real life. Now, though, he'd grown beyond her teachings and cast her off as easily as he'd outgrown his tutors. He'd become just another one of the arrogant lordlings her father complained about when reading the London papers.

Georgie clenched her fists in the moss on either side of her, wishing Freddie could be as easy for her to forget.

She had other friends in the village. She had her sisters. She couldn't figure out what made him so important, or why the way he dismissed her own value hurt so much.

Georgie's expression haunted Freddie all night and continued to throughout his morning tasks. He'd given up the chase when he lost her trail, choosing to return to his tasks even though he hated leaving things unresolved between them.

He hadn't been pretending when he told her how important his new responsibilities were, to her as much as to him. But he hadn't expected her to run away without giving him the chance to explain.

Yesterday, he'd been angry. Today, he ached as if the place where their friendship had nestled close to his heart now stood empty.

She was still so young.

He hadn't thought her ready to hear what he had to say. Yet, he hadn't considered how she might hear his words without knowing why his father's opinion held such weight, why it was so important he performed his labors well.

When the time came to gather for luncheon, Freddie slipped into the kitchen and asked Mrs. Baker if she could put together a basket for him. He planned to go inspect the far fences, or so he told her. He knew the particular section better than any other because it abutted the edge of the forest and the trail he'd first learned of from the family coachman when just a boy before his mother put a stop to their rambles.

His gaze fell upon his mother's garden as he crossed to the stables with a heavy basket slung over one arm. The flowers would have won prizes had they still been in London, his mother said, but they could serve another purpose as well, one Freddie had need of.

He took out a knife, and paying little mind to the thorns that scratched his skin, he cut ten roses, the flowers bursting with many beautiful colors at the end of their short, thorny stalks. These he laid on top of the cloth protecting his food and continued on his way. He had no idea if Georgie would be at their special spot, but he had to try.

Their place seemed too quiet when he arrived.

Shoulders slumped, Freddie put the basket on the ground and contemplated leaving the roses for her to find. Would she understand from the gift how he regretted his words? Would she even return here? He feared he lacked the courage to find her at her home when he couldn't be sure of his reception.

A slight movement in the corner of his eye caught Freddie's attention and distracted him from the disheartening thought. He turned, startled, to meet bright blue eyes staring over her rock much like the first time he'd seen her eight years before.

"I didn't expect to find you here," he said without thinking.

"I didn't think you'd return."

Her voice came out soft and quiet, holding neither the sharp anger of the previous day nor her usual delight. It reminded Freddie all too well of when she'd mourned her mother so long ago.

He turned and knelt, both to hide the guilt in his expression and to collect the flowers. It was little enough to repay her for his arrogance, but he could hope she'd understand.

Freddie bit back a curse as one of the thorns pierced deep into his thumb, his focus more on her than his actions. He winced and thrust the finger between his lips even as he smiled around it.

The roses were much like his Georgie. Sweet and beautiful on the surface, but with sharp defenses when provoked.

Georgie came around her rock and pulled his thumb free, stroking her finger over the injury. "You might think you're all grown up," she said, "but underneath, you're still a sheltered boy."

He would have torn open every one of his fingers if it brought her spirit back.

She shook her head as if aware of his thought. "Wildflowers might make for a better apology next time. Your mother will know from the look of your hands just who stole her prized roses."

Freddie turned his hand in hers until he could clasp her fingers and pull her nearer. "I could hope they'd never be needed a second time."

When she laughed, he knew he'd been forgiven. Georgie was not one to hold onto her anger, whether or not her response had been warranted.

She looked at him then with a contemplative expression, and glanced between the flowers still in the basket and him. "Flowers are a courting gift in London, are they not? So my sister said."

He'd thought her too young to know or care about courting. From the blush pinking her sun-kissed cheeks, he'd been mistaken.

Freddie stared down at his hands then turned to pick up the roses. This time he lifted only one and used his knife to trim its thorns.

"And what are they here?" he asked, raising the first one toward her.

The faint hint of color in her face deepened until he had no doubt of her blush. Her gaze fell to the dirt between them, lashes casting shadows across the top of her cheeks. "An apology from how you're using them," she said, her voice once again soft.

Freddie rose from where he'd been kneeling and stood beside her. "And what if it could be both?"

Her head came up then, a smile trembling on her lips. "It would be surly to refuse them."

Her words did not answer the question he'd carefully not asked, but he chose not to press. The blush had told him enough to know, while she might still be young and boyish, she was not as unaware of him as he'd expected.

"Does the same courtesy extend to sharing my luncheon?" He could feel the tension in the air lightening and gave a long-suffering sigh to encourage the change. "Mrs. Baker always packs too much. She'll be offended if I come back with any of it."

Georgie shot him a grateful glance as she sank to the ground and arranged her skirt around her. More than almost anything, her care with her clothing told him how much she'd grown past the wild child he'd first discovered in these woods. Perhaps he would not have to wait as long as he'd thought before getting a truthful answer to the question he'd yet to ask.

She lifted the rest of the flowers free, careful not to be scored by the very thorns that had marked him. "So what did she pack for you?"

Freddie dug into the basket and lifted a loaf of bread free. He put discussions of courting and their future aside in favor of sharing a meal with the young woman who had captured his heart.

Chapter Two

Georgie crouched behind the same rock where she'd hid three days earlier as she watched Freddie. She hadn't seen him since their picnic, as much because of the preparations for her sixteenth birthday as his own absences. She shouldn't be here now, either, but her sisters had shooed her away from cleaning up the celebration, and Father and the farm hands had returned to their work.

Freddie hadn't noticed when she'd slipped from the cover of trees to behind this rock. His woodcraft had improved a lot over the years, at least when he paid attention, but not enough to know when he'd been spotted.

She watched him, studying his form even as she remembered the look in his eyes when he'd handed her those flowers. Her cheeks heated, as much with the memory as with the curve of his fine calf when he stepped forward to release a stone.

The water kicked up in a sharp curl as he failed to skip the stone he'd tossed.

She proved just as unsuccessful when she tried to contain her laughter.

Freddie jumped to his feet, staring around wildly before he stopped, grinned, and turned to face her.

Georgie scowled back. "You knew I was here all this time?"

He shrugged, not denying the charge or the playacting in his pretended surprise. "I had a good teacher, and you were never one to hold in your humor when faced with some folly of mine."

She glanced out at the water, realizing she'd been flushed much like a quail. His rock had plunged not by accident but by intent. "So the fancy nobleman has learned some tricks after all."

Georgie sauntered free of her shelter, the dress she wore a new one in honor of her birthday. "Only I know you're still a runaway boy at heart."

The look he gave her seemed full of meaning, but he never said a word no matter how much she grew. Always the gentleman. She'd have sworn he liked her, but he kept his thoughts to himself.

"You're dressed a bit finely for fishing," Freddie commented, waving at her in an offhand manner. "Only I know the dirt-encrusted urchin you seek to hide."

Her annoyance melted away into laughter, Freddie always able to bring out the joy in her.

"I'm afraid that secret is all too poorly held. The tavern in the village is full of tales about me. A wild child, sometimes even hinted a changeling, but never in my father's hearing, or so I've been told."

"Well, then, at least I've given you a secret even the tavern folk don't know."

What he meant beyond the obvious, she could not tell, but from his intent gaze, he meant something. If only he would speak plainly for once. All the poetry he'd studied had gone to his head.

"No one will discover our meetings here," she said after a pause, wondering if he still feared his father's wrath, or more likely his mother's. "At least not from my lips."

"Someday that might change."

He turned away before she could ferret out what he meant by such a statement.

"In honor of your sixteenth birthday, I had Mrs. Baker pack a basket."

"You told her of us?" Georgie didn't know whether to be cheered or worried.

Freddie spread a blanket on the rough ground and patted it once to indicate she should join him. "No. She would be the last to keep our secret. I merely said I was checking the far fields—which I did, so you needn't tease about the lie—and thought I'd have my midday meal out there. She's forever pushing food at me as I told you, so it took little coaxing to get her to pack extra. I thought we should celebrate."

Georgie dropped to her knees on the blanket, much closer to him than he'd expected from how he jerked, but he did not move back, not even when she met his gaze with a loving one of her own.

"You were lucky I came today. It is my birthday after all." She grinned at him, a thrill rushing through her at his decision to plan a celebration even when she might not have been able to get away.

He didn't know she'd been planning something of her own for weeks.

The farm hands had grown used to her over the years. They hardly noticed her presence, and so she'd been privy to many a conversation they'd never have continued around any other Ferrier daughter. About what went on between a man and a woman. She'd learned at a young age no one could be sure how many years they'd walk the earth, and she wanted to experience all life had to offer.

But most of all, she wanted to experience life with Freddie.

Instead of settling, Georgie moved forward and straddled his lap much like she would a horse, her skirt billowing around her.

"Kiss me," she demanded, never one to use pretense when she knew what she wanted.

Freddie caught her arms and went to push her away. "It's not proper."

Georgie threw back her head and laughed, the response surprising him enough to loosen his hold.

"As if any of this is proper? Even if the impropriety could be brushed off when we were small, there's many a girl younger than I am who's already married off with a child on her hip."

His hold tightened again as he stared up at her, a position she'd rarely achieved with his significant height.

"You're not a farm girl as much as you like to pretend so. Your father is respected and he'd want his daughters to act accordingly."

She twisted off his lap and sank to the blanket. "When have we ever been worried about such things?" Her breath huffed out as she stared at the blanket weave.

Freddie caught her under the chin and raised her face to meet his intent gaze. "Since you became a woman. I won't be the cause of soiling your reputation, Georgie. I care too much for you."

She stared back, meeting such a tortured look her heart skipped a beat and took up a faster pace.

His lips twisted into a smile as he moved back. "Which is why we'll have a nice picnic and go our separate ways."

Frustration threatened to overwhelm her, and Georgie surged up to kneel at his side. "There's no harm in kissing. It doesn't ruin a woman, or so the farm hands say. I want you to, and I think you want to as well. I can see it in your eyes as you must in mine. So kiss me. Give me this gift for my birthday when I have no others."

She caught his arms in turn, holding him fast so he could not move away.

He looked about to argue, but then his features twisted in a momentary agony. He leaned in to close the small space kept between them.

Georgie almost pulled herself away, unsure now with him having given in to her demand. Before she could decide, his warm, strong lips lay across hers, and her body flushed with a wave of emotions ranging through her.

She gave a slight sigh, and he pressed closer, his arms twining around her now. She'd released him when her muscles relaxed.

Whatever she'd imagined from overheard conversations among the farm hands, nothing prepared Georgie for the way the touch of his lips sent a shiver through her whole body. Firm, yet soft, confident, but not demanding, he sipped at her very essence, and she wanted the kiss to last forever.

The kiss ended as abruptly as it had begun with Freddie lifting her up and away from him.

She opened eyes she had not noticed closing, but could not voice a protest as she saw the longing still marking his features.

The silence between them grew.

A flush reddened his skin before he found the voice to say, "I should not have done that, Georgie, no matter how much you teased, but I cannot say I'm sorry for it." He frowned. "Only, don't go asking any others."

Her hand met his cheek with a stinging slap before she'd decided to move. "As if I would. I thought to share something special with you. Clearly you didn't find it so."

She struggled to rise, her pretty dress tangled around her legs.

Freddie caught her arm with a tight grip that yet did not hurt. "I didn't mean you were so wanton. I swear I didn't. I just don't want you thinking this has no meaning. We're too young as of yet. My parents, your father, will fight any bonds we seek to make, but our future lies together. I've known it for almost as long as I've known you, and yet we could lose everything if we're not careful."

His words sank in slowly, her anger softening to a much deeper emotion.

He did care. He more than cared.

She turned back to face him, her quiet smile coming from a place much different than the grins they usually shared. "I only ever want to share this with you as well, Freddie. I thought you didn't see the woman I've become."

A deep chuckle escaped him as he shook his head. "If only you could know how long I've suffered these pains. You are much too innocent."

"And you are much too proper." She brushed a hand against his cheek where she'd left an imprint. "I'll wait for you to decide when to tell our families then."

Though he looked to offer his thanks, she held up one hand and a more usual grin pulled at her cheeks. "Only I won't wait on more kisses like that one."

Rather than give him time to argue, she spun on her heel and left him to his picnic.

She didn't return home straight away, but instead went deeper into the woods to where no one would find her.

Everything had changed, though from his words, it had been changing all along. She wanted to savor their first kiss without concern for what would come, and she refused to give him the chance to express a single regret. Freddie had to come to terms with the fact that she'd claimed him, and no one, not his family or hers, would keep them apart.

She tipped her head to one side, listening to the rustling of the forest.

Sometimes she imagined she could hear her mother's voice in the sounds. Would her mother be happy or scold her for her wanton behavior? Either way, she'd have given anything for her mother's advice.

Charlotte would never have understood for all her older sister had taken on a mother's role.

FREDDIE STARED AT THE BASKET beside him, the abandoned remains of the simple birthday meal he'd hoped to share with her.

He should have expected something like this. Georgie had never been shy about what she wanted. How he'd missed the moment when she began to see him as more than a friend, though, he couldn't quite imagine.

She called him too proper, but someone had to be if they were to make a life of this. For her to call him proper when he met with her in secret and even laid his lips on hers seemed a wonder almost as great as how her acquiescence had set his heart to thudding and the blood roaring through his body with the demand he lay claim to her for all to see.

He stood and gathered up his things, but his mind focused not on the task but on what had just occurred, and what had to next.

The trip back to his horse and then to the Brookway Manor seemed to take a mere beat of his heart before tossing him down at his father's study door, one hand raised to make his presence known. He could wait no longer to prove at eighteen he'd reached an age of maturity.

Once his father accepted his rank among men, he'd be able to reveal his decision where Georgiana Ferrier was concerned. Whatever objections his mother might marshal would fall on deaf ears if his father supported the plan.

"Come in."

The irritable tone in answer to his rap marked this a poor time for his request, but Freddie could delay no longer. Even if he were willing to put aside kisses until much later, Georgie had already made her intentions clear. He would not risk her virtue or reputation when he meant to do the proper thing, and if that made him too proper in her eyes, she could very well tease him about it until they were old and gray.

"What is it then, Frederick?" Lord Brookway asked as the door swung wide enough to reveal Freddie. "Have you come to tell me half the fences are down and the sheep scattered? It best be something so significant for you to disrupt my work."

A glance at the books before his father almost made Freddie want to back down, but paying the tradesmen always made his father irritated. At least they had a steady income from the barony and had the funds to make those payments, unlike some.

"No, Father, the fences were fine and the flock still within them. I came to ask for a section of the farm to manage on my own. I've been checking the fences, talking to the farmers, and doing all manner of studies. I think I'm ready to take some of the burden from your hands."

Lord Brookway's expression lightened, and he waved Freddie over to the companion chair. "What brought on this sudden concern? Don't think I haven't noticed how you wander about and use my tasks for excuses to roam even further. Seems to me you have more interest in taking your exercise than in exercising your education."

Freddie sank into the chair and stared at his linked fingers.

He could not explain the true cause without revealing his indiscretion with Georgie, and no one, not even his father, would believe they'd met in pure innocence all these years until this very day. Nor would they believe he'd stopped at a simple kiss when none would be the wiser unless she swelled with his child.

Lord Brookway gave a deep sigh. "How much do you owe? I should have guessed you'd spent your time down at the tavern. I had hoped when I heard nothing of the sort… I suppose they thought to protect me from the pain of your nature, but my men did me no favor in doing so."

It took a moment for Freddie to understand his father's meaning, but less than a fraction of that time to jerk back to his feet.

"I have not been gambling. I come here to be counted a man, not a spendthrift. I'm done playing at being mature by running what little tasks you're willing to give me while keeping me sheltered from the true work. Would you have me wait until I'm grown and settled in my ways before preparing me to assist you here?"

Anger at the accusation made his tongue too quick, and from the pained look on his father's face, his mark struck home.

His father had done nothing but live on the gratitude of Freddie's grandparents all the years they'd lived in London. When it came time to take over the barony, he'd had little knowledge and no training to bolster his position as their lord.

Rubbing a hand across his brow, Lord Brookway said, "I have no reason to assume my own weakness exists in you, but I've never seen you take on anything more taxing than to ride the fences." He held up a hand when Freddie would have protested. "I know I have your mother to thank for that, though you could have helped me with the ledger had you shown any inclination. Your tutors gave good reports of your calculating skills. Still, you are young yet. Enjoy your youth before the pressures of marriage and property come swallow you whole."

Freddie stared at his father, seeing him in a very different light.

He'd avoided the study because the work always put his father in a foul mood, and he hadn't thought his inexpert efforts would improve the situation. Now Freddie regretted his cowardice as he realized his mother was not the only one to suffer their retreat to the country.

"Father," he began in a softer tone. "I am not like you. I love it here. I love the country, I love the animals, and I'd be happy to take some of the burden from you, whether it be checking the fences or doing the figures. As you said, my tutors have had little complaint regarding my work." His absences were another issue all together, but as none of his tutors saw fit to inform his parents of how easily he slipped their charge, he saw no reason to raise doubts when it seemed he'd come to this moment for more than just Georgie's sake.

Lord Brookway stared up at him, a frown pinching his brows as he searched Freddie's countenance, though for what Freddie had no idea.

The silence stretched long enough to become uncomfortable, but Freddie refused to undermine his efforts by fidgeting. He held his father's gaze with one clear of hostility but full of determination. He would convince his father he could be of assistance both for his own future and his father's.

Finally, Lord Brookway broke the contact with a laugh. "It seems you have earned what I never did despite your mother's attempts to keep you untainted by the country life. She'd always hoped we would reach a point where we could return to town, though I haven't the skills to improve our income to such an extent and we cannot forever live off her father's bounty. Your tone showed the reasons against it clear enough even had I been willing to entertain the thought."

A flush heated Freddie's cheeks at the reminder of his harsh words, but his father waved off the apology trembling on his lips.

"Give me a portion of the land to manage on my own then," Freddie said. "If I prove talented, perhaps you and Mother could take to spending some of the year in town as it seems both of you would prefer."

"And I suppose you'd stay here all on your own? I doubt your mother would agree to the plan. She'll want you at her side."

Freddie sank back into the chair so he was of a height with his father. "I am a child no longer and have little need to cling to my mother's hand no matter what she might prefer. Soon I'll have a wife of my own to tend."

Lord Brookway shook his head. "You're all in a rush to reach maturity. You won't know what you've lost until it's too late to reclaim it. Still, I can see your mind is made up. The stubbornness comes from your mother's side, not mine, and I've no strength to stand against it."

"I speak nothing but the truth," Freddie protested.

He did not mean to be stubborn or to reject his mother's concerns, but neither did he think Georgie would look kindly on bowing to his mother's rule, nor would he want her to. Lady Brookway would be quick to condemn all that drew him to Georgie and would do her best to weed those aspects from her character. Somehow, he didn't think Georgie would be the one to come out the loser in such a contest, but neither would any of them win.

Unaware of how Freddie's thoughts had wandered, his father only nodded. "I should have guessed this day was coming. First you ask for duties on the farm, and now this. It may just be you've grown more than either your mother or I suspected. I'll give you the south-western strip to manage as you see fit, whether in crops or flock, and you're to spend the hour before dinner here with me each day learning the accounts. If this is the life you imagine for yourself, better you know the full of it."

"Thank you, Father. I promise I will not disappoint you."

Lord Brookway gave a short laugh and waved Freddie to the door. "Enough. You've won your case. Get on with you to savor the victory while I figure out just how to tell your mother she's begotten a farmer despite her best efforts. You can begin in the morning. You'll have little enough to do for this year beyond choosing the time of harvest, and you'd best speak to the men before making any decisions. They all but run the place anyhow."

Following his father's directive, Freddie quit the study and headed for his rooms to manage a wash before dinner. He needed a much different approach if he wanted his mother to accept his maturity. Coming to eat with the whiff of dirt and horse would do nothing to help his efforts.

Chapter Three

S lipping away after her morning chores the next day had never carried with it such a weight of expectation before. Georgie touched the tips of her fingers to her mouth even as she strode for the forest edge.

She took care to complain often about the distance so Charlotte might not realize how quickly she could cross it, but Georgie wondered if perhaps her sister chose not to make a concern out of the absences more to give Georgie a little freedom. Or maybe the wandering reminded Charlotte of the mother they'd all lost and made her spirit seem a little closer. It certainly had that effect on Georgie.

Georgie stumbled on an outstretched root, her thoughts wandering back to the days when her mother would seek her out here in the forest. They'd both known her scolds to be half-hearted, a nod toward conventions neither welcomed.

"You would have liked him, Mother," she told the spirit that lingered for her here in the forest's shelter. "He has a bit of the wild in him for all he comes from London stock."

"A bit of the wild?"

Georgie stared around, her eyes wide. For a moment, it seemed her mother had spoken to her from beyond the grave after all. She pressed a hand to her chest and told her heart to stop hammering.

"You startled me," Georgie accused Freddie, who stepped free of the path.

"It's only fair. How many times have you come upon me through stealth?"

She shrugged, conceding the point though she had protested more to give herself time to regain her composure than out of true anger. Her thoughts went again to her mother and she warmed as though she felt her mother's approval of her choice.

"What are you doing out here? Did I catch you on your way home?"

Freddie shook his head. "I wasn't sure you'd come, and if not, I'd hoped to draw you away from gathering with your sisters. I need to have a word with you."

His expression turned serious, and her heart sank.

While she'd been anticipating more of those wondrous kisses, he'd decided she had a bit too much of the wild. Good enough for friendship but nothing more.

When he reached for her hand, she shook it off. "I'm here now. You might as well tell me and get it over with."

He gave her an odd look then crossed his arms as if to prevent them from reaching for her again. "Your sisters are about after all?"

She shook her head, mutely demanding he speak and let her get to mourning their friendship as much as the path they'd started down. She could not see herself turning back to the way things had been, not now, and not for some time if she were being honest.

His arms fell to his sides, and he gave her a grin. "Then I have you all to myself."

Georgie held still as he moved closer, his words having little in common with what she'd feared would come from his mouth. Neither did his actions as he ran his hands down her arms until he captured not one but both of hers in his own.

"I've spoken to my father."

Her eyes widened once again, though not in fear, as she squealed her delight and surged forward into his embrace, her hands pulled awkwardly behind her as they lingered in his grip. She lifted her face to his, expecting kisses along with the declaration she'd just received.

Freddie stepped back.

"It's not what you think, or at least not entirely."

His words drained the excitement from her along with the hope he'd seen fit to end their secret so he could court her properly.

"What then?" she asked, turning away to sink onto a fallen tree.

Freddie dropped to her side, catching hold of her hand once again. "I've asked to manage a portion of the property. My father has agreed to it. If I can prove I'm capable of such responsibility, he's sure to listen when I tell him of you. I've already laid the ground for it in my discussion with him."

Suddenly shy when she'd never felt so before, Georgie twisted to look at him through the strands of blond hair that had slipped free of their bindings as they always did.

"You did this for me?"

He shook his head. "I did this for both of us. And for me as well. I cannot forever be the boy traipsing around the forest with no means of support beyond my father's good will. How can I make a future on that basis?"

"My father would respect a farmer."

Freddie laughed, a soft, gentle sound that caressed her skin. "I'll never be a farmer if my mother has any say in the matter, but I will be a man grown and one with prospects. Should I succeed in this, I plan to take over management of the barony from my father so my parents can return to London."

He sounded so serious and so mature, Georgie didn't know whether to be impressed or mourn the loss of the boy she'd known and loved.

"And what of you? Do you want to be a farmer, or do you long to return to London yourself?" She held her breath, waiting on his answer.

A slow smile stretched his lips as Freddie looked down on her. "Ever since I met the loveliest urchin in the forest, my dreams have been tied to this place. I plan to make my life here and become a sheep farmer like my grandfather."

"A far cry from the boy feeding fish I first discovered in these woods." She poked him in the arm and leapt up to race into the forest. As much as this talk of the future made her heart swell, she could hold still no longer.

Where once his blundering would have given her warning long before he came upon her, when Georgie reached their glade, Freddie was only a stride behind.

She jerked to a halt at the sight that greeted her, and Freddie slammed into her back, wrapping his arms tight around her so they wouldn't fall.

"You made a picnic once again," she whispered.

Freddie turned her slowly within the shelter of his arms, and his gaze was tender. "We never did have the chance to celebrate your birthday properly, and now there's more to toast than yesterday."

"A toast to you becoming a farmer." She'd meant to tease, but the words came out breathless as his gaze sharpened with something she didn't know and yet recognized with all her being, a languid heat rising within her.

"A toast to becoming a man." He whispered the last against her lips as he drew her very soul into his keeping.

Minutes passed before he pulled away, though she couldn't have said how many. The touch left her breathless and dizzy. Georgie leaned forward, hoping he'd restore their connection.

Freddie raised her hand and laid a kiss on its back that had little in common with the one still tickling her lips. "And now we eat."

Georgie gave him a dazed look, but followed his directions as her mind caught up with her sensations.

She might not have the experience of the farm hands, but she knew well enough what they risked should they go beyond kisses. She teased him often for being proper, but her Freddie would always be thinking of her reputation before the heat flowing between them, a fact that should have brought forth gratitude instead of frustration.

She pressed a finger to her sensitive lips and gave a quick laugh. "All of a sudden, I'm starving."

FREDDIE CUT A SLICE OF pie and held it out to Georgie. "Mrs. Baker makes quite delicious fruit pies. You have to try some."

"Oh, I couldn't. Cook would think me ungrateful."

He waved the piece back and forth in front of her, the buttery crust flaky and the berries firm. "How would she know? You've told no one about us, or have you?"

"Of course I told no one," Georgie said as she took the pie from him. "It would bring nothing but trouble."

"But surely your father would not object. Not once he learns of my plans to be a farmer in truth. Unlike my mother, I doubt he would object to my parentage, though from what you've said, it doesn't seem as if he intends to raise your standing through marriage at all. He seems interested more in the peerage's eager desire to purchase his horses."

The sight of Georgie dissolving into laughter warmed his heart, and for just one moment, he wanted to convince her. He wanted her to tell her family about him so he could meet them properly.

"We should." The statement burst out before he could think it through.

She stopped laughing and shot him a confused glance. "Should what?"

"Should tell your father. My family may not be ready to hear, but surely yours could. Then we wouldn't need to hide. And you wouldn't feel guilty for obscuring the truth."

She shook her head so hard she almost dropped the pie. "No, Freddie. No. As much as I want to end our secrecy, all that would accomplish would be my father dragging us before your parents. I refuse to have the first introduction to your mother be in the midst of him accusing you of despoiling me. It would do your claims of maturity no good either."

Freddie let a sigh escape. "It's just I'm tired of the situation we're in. I don't want to chance my parents making life hard for you and your family either. If we could have your father's support, it might make our case stronger." He frowned. "But I can see you're right. He has no cause to be on our side—on my side. We've hardly been the model of propriety."

Georgie tipped her head to one side, her eyes glittering with mischievousness. "And what behavior makes you think so? The fishing?

Or sharing of this pie?" She shifted closer, a grin on her lush, berry-tinted lips. "Perhaps you should show me."

He laughed then and leaned in to brush a light kiss on her mouth. "It must be the pie. Cook would never forgive you."

She slapped him lightly on the arm, careful to use her free hand. For all her protests, it seemed the bites she'd taken had won her over. She would no more waste any of the pie than he would.

As much as he wished it were different, Freddie accepted the time it would take before he could declare his intentions to all and sundry. Her family might not have the title, but that didn't mean they were unaware of proper behavior. If only his parents showed any interest in engaging with the local folk so they could meet in a more formal setting. It wasn't as if a farmer could hold a grand ball.

Even the Pendletons, who had returned from London last year, kept separate from the local gentry and landowners. Though his father had spoken to Lord Pendleton a time or two, there'd been no social calls, much less something large enough to include a landowner like Mr. Ferrier.

Freddie pushed his concerns aside to enjoy this moment. There would be time enough for the formalities once he knew there would be no barriers to their engagement. He would not risk losing the regard of Georgie's father any more than he would chance that of his own. And what they had was not so poor he would give it up rather than be patient.

"I fear this luncheon has been too vast. I cannot finish my portion."

He glanced up to see her raising the remainder of her pie toward him. When he took it from her, his fingers tingled where they brushed against hers. "You'd best go to the brook and rub away the berry stains if you hope to keep your cook happy. Otherwise, she'll suspect what you've been doing out here in the forest."

She pushed up from the blanket, but at the last moment, she glanced back to say, "My Father would be the most perturbed at the sight. He'd think I found a patch and ate them all myself."

"Because you do this often?" Freddie asked as he admired the curve of her backside with her bent over the rushing brook.

He had no time to duck the splash of water she tossed with her cupped hands, her laughter as delightful as the water was wet. He could wait a lifetime if it meant more hours spent in her presence.

Chapter Four

Georgie returned home in time to hear her father read out a letter about her cousin Barbara who would be arriving shortly. She had not been to visit them in some five years. The reasons behind her coming were perhaps not as happy as they could have been what with Lord and Lady Whitfeld sending their daughter away in disgrace, but her sisters shared Georgie's delight in the event in any case.

If some of Georgie's smiles had more to do with thoughts of earlier in the day, they went unnoticed in the general cheer.

Cousin Barbara arrived the next morning with Sarah, her companion. Barbara slept the day through, but Charlotte kept them all close to show Sarah about the farm while they waited for their cousin to rise.

Barbara did not wake for dinner, but even with plans delayed until she could join the discussion, it became all too clear the addition of two members to their household would make it much harder for Georgie to slip away. She'd be called on to entertain when they were not busy with chores. Besides, extra eyes just might draw attention to her absences where her sisters had grown complacent.

The knowledge soured her good mood, and she struggled to keep up the appearance of delight in the visit so no one would know what this cost her.

Part of her railed at the timing. Why now when Freddie had at last made his true feelings known? She longed for his presence and to share in his delight as he took on the responsibilities he craved. So much had changed, but she stood apart from the differences, unable to do more than guess at their nature.

Luckily, talk of London and the doings in the Whitfeld household kept her family too entertained to notice her distraction as she laid the groundwork for her plan. Come the next sunrise, she was ready to put it into effect.

Georgie rose even earlier than any of her family, sneaking out of the room she shared with Jane so she could steal down to her father's study undetected. This missive needed more than the scraps of written-over paper she used for simple notes she left her Freddie, nor would the stump of pencil serve.

My Dearest Freddie,

She paused, unsure how to continue. She couldn't very well tell him how her cousin had come to be sent down in the middle of her season. The secret was not hers to reveal, but neither did she want Freddie to think her so fickle as to ignore him after what had gone on between them.

Georgie stared at the paper, for once wishing she'd had tutors like Freddie's to teach her eloquence and poetry rather than her sister Charlotte schooling her in the letters to allow for simple missives and instructions to the more educated tradesfolk.

The sound of voices from where the farm hands took their rest startled her. More time had passed than she'd thought.

Georgie glared at the mostly blank page before dipping the quill back in the ink. Then she wrote in swift, confident strokes the following message:

My cousin has come down from London for a visit. With her presence, it will be more difficult to get away. As much as I long to see you, I fear it is beyond my abilities. I will leave you a note in our tree whenever I'm able and will look for you when I can. Know I love you more than I can say. Work well under your father's hand so soon we can be together without secrecy to maintain.

Yours truly,
Georgiana Ferrier

She glared at the short message, wondering if it had warranted the risk of her father's study after all. And just how would Freddie see her formal signature? But she had run out of time. It would have to do. Georgie dusted the page with sand and carefully set her father's desk to rights before tucking the folded cloth into her chemise.

"Good morning, Georgie," Cook said as Georgie stepped into the kitchen on her way to the back door. "You sure are up and about early."

She lifted the basket she'd collected from the cupboard in the hall. "I thought I'd gather some wildflowers for the breakfast table. It will be Cousin Barbara's first true day here, and she might enjoy them."

"You may be half rapscallion, but you've a good heart. Get on with you then. There's not much time before breakfast will be ready. Though whether your cousin will rise in time for it remains to be seen."

Georgie stepped out on the heels of the last, the murmur not meant for a response.

Cook had put some effort into the meal the night before, thinking to serve nobility. That Cousin Barbara slept right through it obviously rankled. Unlike the sisters, Cook had not been privy to the reading of her uncle's letter and so could not have known just how busy their cousin had been during her season. From the sound of things, the poor girl had gone from suitor to suitor with hardly a breath between.

Georgie chuckled at the thought, amazed at how different their lives had been. She'd met Freddie not so many years before Barbara's last visit, and even then she'd wanted a life at his side.

Cook's warning sped her steps all the way to the forest, and though she checked for him, had Freddie been there at this odd hour, she would not have been able to stay.

Georgie thrust the note into their tree, disappointed beyond reason at his absence.

"I'll be back as soon as I can," she promised the tree when Freddie could not hear her.

Surely their affection could last a few days apart. Their friendship had done so often enough when he'd been taken to London to visit his grandparents. She just wished it weren't necessary.

Georgie came within sight of the farmhouse before she remembered her promise of wildflowers. The empty basket served as an accusing reminder of her plan to trick her family once more.

Luckily, with the heavy rains in spring, they had all sorts of flowers growing wherever the plants could find a patch of soil. She made short work of filling the basket to the brim, tucking the last few stems in at the top with just enough room to lace her arm beneath the handle.

She burst through the kitchen door when she should have waited for her breathing to settle, sure she'd been much too long in her task.

The kitchen table stood empty, only Cook present when she'd expected all of them.

Cook glanced up from where she stirred a pot on the woodstove and shook her head. "Your porridge would have gone cold had everything been as it should. Instead, you're the first beyond young Sarah to come down. Her I have getting some fruit from the pantry. You might as well make yourself useful and set the table once you've found jars for all those flowers."

Georgie knew better than to argue or ask more questions. If the others were not down as of yet, more likely they pestered Barbara. Cook would vouch for her presence better if she helped set the table rather than annoying the woman. Besides, the jars for flowers were right next to the bowls and plates so she could just gather them all at once.

As if she could read Georgie's mind, Cook warned, "And don't you be piling them dishes too high. We have none to spare with so much company."

Chuckling, Georgie took the care she might otherwise have failed to. She had no wish for cold porridge nor the first of the tea before it had steeped. Of course, from the grumbles, she suspected the tea would be dark and bitter for everyone, standing as it had so long.

Chapter Five

reddie tethered his horse on the edge of the forest nearest to his section of the barony. He strode under the leafy branches with a new sense of confidence and pride. He couldn't wait to tell Georgie of everything he'd done in the three days since he'd seen her last.

She'd scold him first for not coming at least long enough to leave a message, and she'd be right to do so, but his father had taken his request quite seriously. When he'd returned to the manor after the picnic with Georgie, his father had called him in to work on the ledger and before he had a chance to catch a breath, Freddie had a schedule starting with the farm hands in the day and ending with his father's papers each night.

He'd eaten with the men at midday and his parents for breakfast and often dinner. If he'd tried to slip off to the forest at any point, he would have undone all the good he'd been trying to achieve.

The labors had been intense, even when he spent most of his time listening.

Only his forest rambles kept his feet from aching after days of standing in the fields while one man after another explained how things worked. He learned about crop rotation and when to let the sheep graze or when to keep them as far away as possible or they'd graze down the harvest. The farm boys knew more than he did, though some of them had fewer years, and he listened carefully to the herders as well. A good bit of the barony income came from the wool sheared from their flock, so neglecting this aspect would be foolish.

He smiled at the memory of the herders offering their insincere regrets that he'd missed the shearing by a few short weeks. But they'd be sure to put a shearing blade in his hand come next May, or so they promised him.

They didn't realize he'd found a good hiding spot and had watched their work for the past two years. Sheep were neither docile nor cheered at the thought of casting aside their heavy wool with the days growing warmer. He'd let the more experienced farm hands do the work if he wanted the poor sheep to survive the process without blood loss making them good for nothing but the stew pot.

He'd followed the hands down to the tavern the previous evening, standing them a round of bitters in return for more tales of the good years and bad. He kept to stout, leaving the lighter beer to the others as it lived up to its name a bit too much for his taste. Freddie wouldn't give up his time at the tavern, though. The folk wisdom he'd absorbed, along with the chuckles such stories often provoked, proved valuable.

Smiling at a particularly fanciful tale he couldn't wait to share with Georgie, Freddie burst into their glade. He'd been so confident she'd be waiting for him, he thought for a moment he saw her standing there, her blue eyes glinting with suppressed humor.

In truth, the space stood empty, and why shouldn't it? She had no way of knowing he'd break free today if only long enough to tell her why he had not come before.

Despite that truth, disappointment made Freddie's steps heavy as he moved to the tree to leave a note he'd prepared in case she had not waited for him. Or perhaps she'd spent the past three days waiting, long hours when she could have been missed from her chores, and had only then given up.

Freddie shook his head.

He did not wish trouble to come to her because of him no matter how much the image of Georgie waiting here, desperate for his company, made his heart beat a little faster. Still, the glimpse of a folded sheet of paper nestled in the tree provoked a grin.

Freddie tugged hers loose, shaking it open almost before his hand cleared the tree's opening. With the other hand, he pushed his own note into place before he skimmed the short missive once then read it slower as he took in the meaning.

She had come for no longer than he came now, and rather than waiting for him at every opportunity, she'd been too busy to stay at all.

His breath pushed out in a huff then he followed the annoyed sound with a laugh.

Here he'd been worried she'd pined for him and the kisses they'd shared half as much as he had. Instead, she'd most likely been too employed with entertaining her cousin even to notice he hadn't picked up her note. The damp edges offered proof enough it had been there for at least a day already.

Freddie glanced at the note again, lingering over her words. Any irritation faded as quickly as it had risen in the face of her affection.

He didn't need to see her pining for him to know how she felt. She'd told him so herself, both before and within her message, one he'd do best to find a safe place to hide. Though he'd do better to leave it here where no one would think to look, her declaration would give him the strength he needed to stay true to his path. He had much to learn and little time to learn it in if he wanted to prove himself worthy of her hand.

For all he knew, her father had plans of his own with her now reaching marriageable age. From his reputation, Freddie suspected while Mr. Ferrier would look for something more than a farm hand to claim his daughter, he would not find the simple fact of a title, and one Freddie hoped not to inherit for some time to come, reason enough to look kindly on Freddie's suit. Even if he did welcome Freddie's interest, any expectation of success assumed Freddie's parents wouldn't stand in the way either.

No, he needed to turn his focus to becoming more than just an idle lordling so he could prove to all of them he had both the maturity to choose his wife and the ability to support her.

As much as he longed to tell Georgie everything—and yes, longed to feel her lips meeting his, her breath mingling with his own—he should be grateful she had something to keep her entertained. Concern for her comfort could not be allowed to distract him from the process of becoming a valuable member of the farming community rather than a sheltered boy good only for a laugh when he attempted shearing next year.

Chapter Six

Georgie's first opportunity to slip away came one afternoon when they'd spent the morning working in the kitchen garden.

Charlotte had gone down to the village, and taken both Barbara and Sarah with her. Georgie stayed to help Cook make preserves from the berries they'd collected, but when she came close to dropping a jar the fourth time, Cook waved her out of the kitchen.

"You're no good to me with your attention on the fine weather we're having. Go on with you."

She didn't need to be told twice. Georgie grabbed a basket just in case, though what she'd put into it, she had no idea. She'd been absent so often, and her note told Freddie not to expect her, so the chance of catching him in their special glade seemed unlikely. Or maybe it was all the more likely as he took every opportunity to see if she'd managed to get free.

Perhaps he'd taken to haunting their spot down by the brook in the hopes she'd appear.

Her feet pushed off the rough ground a little faster the nearer she came to the forest edge. She crossed from the sun to the leaf-covered shadows, laughter threatening to burst free. As much as she enjoyed her cousin's visit, she'd missed the woods, and not entirely for the friend she met there.

The brook, when she reached their spot, merrily chuckled its way past, but no rope cut through its surface nor did a blanket cover the soil.

Georgie sank to the top of her rock and tried not to be disappointed. After all, he'd had no idea she'd be coming.

The sound of hurried steps, as rushed as hers had been, brought Georgie to her feet. She clutched the basket before her as proof of her purpose, though it's woven curve held nothing as of yet.

Rather than one of her sisters, Freddie burst through the bush covering their entrance.

Her cheeks ached with the width of her grin at the sight of him. "You came after all."

Freddie laughed. "I'll have to concoct some wild tale for the others, but when I caught sight of you from where I was working with the farm hands, I couldn't miss this chance. I just grabbed my horse and ran."

She shook her head, but could not come up with the words to reprove him. Nor could she regret his presence.

Not that he gave her the chance.

Freddie caught her up into his arms and spun around in a circle before laying a quick kiss on her lips.

Georgie stared up at him with a quizzical look. "I haven't been gone that long for you to miss me so. You've been off to London for longer many a time. And I left you a note."

He brushed some loose hair back from her face and grinned down at her. "You might not think much time is passed as busy as you've been with your cousin, but a lot has happened in the week since she arrived. I can't wait to tell you all of it."

"So tell me then," Georgie said with her normal impatience. She caught hold of his hand and pulled him over to the rock so they could settle close.

Freddie lifted her once again, this time to sit her on his lap rather than next to him. "My father agreed to give me a section of land to manage as I told you, and he's wasted no time in making it happen. I've been working with the farm hands, talking to the herders, and learning all manner of things. I've been working with him as well, keeping his papers in order. I doubt he had any idea the assistance I could provide."

"I doubt you had any idea either." Georgie widened her eyes, pretending to be shocked. "Do you need me to come and teach you a thing or two like I did with the fishing?"

Freddie straightened his back, pulling away from her though he couldn't go far with her still nestled on his lap. "Did you think I spent all my time with the tutors learning other languages and grand philosophy? Do you think I did nothing to prepare for the life ahead of me?"

She frowned, worried this time her teasing had gone too far until she saw his lips begin to twitch.

Leaping off, she planted both fists on her hips. "You are nothing but a scoundrel," she charged. "Making me worry you believed I thought less of you."

"But you should've seen your expression. It was precious."

He laughed so hard he toppled from the rock and landed with a quiet grunt.

She dropped to his side to check on him, running fingers through his hair to find any injury.

His arms came up to surround her, and he rolled, one hand tucked behind her head to cushion it. She wouldn't have protested, but he gave her no chance either as he leaned down to press his lips against hers.

This time, the kiss felt as deep as ever she could have hoped.

When at last they came up for air, Freddie brushed a finger across her reddened lips. "I'll be in for a lifetime of teaching you proper behavior if I go ahead with my plan. Perhaps I should choose to be a gambler instead of gaining my father's approval."

Georgie laughed up at him, not believing for one moment he meant his words, not with the force of their kisses behind her and his wish to please her father. "You plan to love every minute of it, paying me back in droves for the wisdom I've given you."

"And what wisdom is that? You've taught me the ways of the wild. Few would consider such wise."

"I would not attempt to argue. After all, your tutors are sure to have taught you the way of debate along with philosophy and poetry."

"I'd guess your sisters taught you even better, but had I the choice, I'd spend forever crossing words with you."

She gave him a saucy look. "Only words?"

He dropped a kiss on the tip of her nose before pushing to his feet and pulling her after. "I plan to earn the right to much more than words or even kisses, but to do so, I'd best be off. If my father catches me out wandering instead of working the land, it won't be maturity he suspects me of."

They dusted each other free of evidence then Georgie perched upon her rock to watch him go. It seemed nothing more than a dream to have him striving for the chance to speak with her father, and yet he did just that.

It took some time before she bestirred herself to return, but then she delayed only long enough to gather some kindling for the fire. It would not provide much of an excuse should Charlotte catch her coming from the woods, but she didn't want return with an empty basket and a smile on her face.

She would not be the one to endanger their future by making her family suspicious.

Chapter Seven

rederick, there you are. I've hardly had the chance to speak to you in days what with you taking some meals down the tavern and others in the fields."

Freddie turned to see his mother standing at the door of the morning room. His fingers tightened on the baluster for a moment, having just returned after the end of a long day checking the flock alongside the herders. He'd never really considered all the steps necessary to make sure the sheep were healthy until now.

He forced his lips into a tired smile. "Mother. I'll be right down after I've had a wash."

Though her nose wrinkled, Lady Brookway waved a hand to dismiss his words. "If you don't come now, you'll just be locked up in your father's study until dinner. I can suffer your scent."

He had no choice but to follow her, though he stood at the fireplace rather than chance soiling the furniture. "What is it you want to talk to me about?"

She gazed up at him with an expression he couldn't quite place, but Freddie knew well enough to tense.

"Your father has told me what you've taken on. I find it wonderful to discover you have ambition for all it would've been better if your interests had taken a turn towards something more fitting for your station. Politics for example. Still, clearly this shows you are mature enough to take a bride."

Freddie's eyes widened as he stared at his mother. All this time, he'd thought he needed his father's support to bring her to this point.

"I'm sure my family can help find some girl willing to make a life out here as long as you bring her to London on a frequent basis. I'm afraid the chances of such in a girl with claim to an improved title are slim, especially for one able to pass the title to her children, but a viscount's daughter as I was may be possible. You are a handsome enough boy. It will help."

It took Freddie a moment to catch her meaning as she continued to speak, but when he did, all his strain returned.

"Mother, the times have changed. I plan to choose my own bride."

Lady Brookway laughed. "What could you possibly know about such things? Why, you'd be as likely to choose someone of common stock. One of the farm girls I caught you watching when they go to do the milking. No, I'll have to have a hand in it if you're to do anything suitable. Don't you worry. It seems you have enough to do with your responsibilities, and I certainly did not mean to put this on your shoulders. I thought only to tell you I plan to initiate the search."

Freddie bit his tongue. Any response he could muster would only harm his attempt to prove mature. Nor could he present Georgie now, because though she was the daughter of a respectable landholder, she was, indeed, common.

If not for the reason he'd suspected, Freddie still needed his father to see him as a man capable of making his own decisions. They might have their differences, but his mother listened to Lord Brookway where she'd never listen to him.

"If that is all, Mother, I will go wash the stench of the fields from my skin before dinner." He offered a stiff bow and moved toward the door.

She caught his arm when he went to pass her. "Now Freddie, don't be that way. I have only your best interests at heart. You are not to be expected to understand the complexities when it comes to marriage. Certainly not in your case where you have both ties to those in society and a lifetime spent mostly beyond it. I did not mean to offend you. Any young man's eye would be drawn to the hearty shine of the farm girls. There's no harm in it, but there's no good marriage in that direction either. Just imagine bringing one of them to your grandfather's house. Why his housemaids would look down on her, and you'd be the mockery of all your cousins. You can't want to court such a thing, can you?"

He couldn't tell if she meant his cousins' scorn or scorned the farm girls with the last, but his tongue could be restrained no longer. "I haven't stared at the milkmaids as you describe since I was but a boy. And I stared at them because their lives seemed better than my own not for any lustful purpose." His words came out tight and bitter.

Lady Brookway's hand fell away to press against her chest. "Frederick, I know you expected more from our life. I did as well. But I've done my best with what we had. I've given you many opportunities to spend time at my father's house and made sure you did not adopt the habits of those in the lower ranks. It hasn't always been easy, but as you grow older, you will understand my reasoning and come to thank me for it."

This time Freddie kept his mouth sealed. Without even a gesture to recognize her words, he strode from the room and up the stairs.

If she'd succeeded in her efforts, he would never have met Georgiana. He would never have found the one woman who held his heart. As much as he strained at the cost of their secrecy, he regretted his escape not at all. Had his mother not been so focused on London, had she made friends among the local gentry and those of modest wealth, they might have met in better circumstances—better to his mother's mind that was—but she'd have been no more likely to accept his choice even so.

Perhaps Georgie had done exactly what his mother feared. Perhaps her teaching him the simple joys of fishing and woodcraft led him to crave the countryside over the delights of London. Still, he suspected his inclination for the country had been set much earlier, and meeting Georgie in a more formal setting would not have changed his plans. Though he found the trips to London a greater burden now for the separation from Georgie, he'd rarely considered the beginning of one such trip with the same eagerness he'd felt upon coming home.

Chapter Eight

Georgie laughed with the others as Barbara gave a delighted shout, calling all of them to see what she'd found.

When Charlotte discovered their cousin didn't remember collecting fresh herbs at all, she'd declared all the seasoning for tonight's dinner would come from Barbara's hands. Though their father had sent them out after medicinal herbs for Grannie, there'd been time enough to find savory ones as well.

The meal would likely be bland but Charlotte held to her decision. Georgie's basket held as many cooking herbs as any of her sisters. Barbara had few. Even Sarah had discovered more seasonings. Perhaps Barbara had found a wild carrot or two. At least the root vegetable would offer some flavor.

Not that it mattered.

Georgie hadn't been so eager for this outing because of dinner.

She brushed her fingers against the front of her dress and felt the reassuring crinkle of paper. This message said nothing of importance beyond that she missed him, but she couldn't bear the thought of him sneaking away only to find no evidence she'd been there since he'd seen her two days earlier.

Charlotte waved the rest of them over, but while Marian and Jane answered the call, Georgie pretended she'd made a discovery of her own. Whatever Barbara found seemed big enough to require all of their attention, giving Georgie the best opportunity to slip into the forest.

She kept her attention on every nearby growth because she would need something to show for her distraction, but still she made good time down the familiar path.

THOUGH HE'D MEANT TO FOLLOW the farm hands to the tavern after a long morning haying, his mother's parting words at breakfast continue to eat at him. She'd waved a letter, saying it held all of his hopes and dreams come true. She'd planned to send it to London that very morning.

If he'd had any doubts of the contents, she'd been quick to reassure him it contained the request for a list of potential brides.

Freddie sought out the glade by the brook for once with no hope of finding Georgie there. He looked only for a place where he could rail at the injustice of his life. How his efforts to make his parents see him as an adult now threatened the very reason for the desire.

His feet pounded the forest floor, making no attempt to move silently as Georgie had taught him. Her very teachings only compounded his issues, one more sign of her state as a wild farm girl and exactly the bride his mother feared he would choose.

Lady Brookway would never understand what drew him to Georgie. She'd never see the quick intelligence and bright spirit which kept him coming back even once the need to escape his tutors had ended.

He racked his brain for any way he could introduce the two of them that would not make Georgie's unsuitability so obvious his mother would never be able to see beyond it.

"Freddie!"

He jerked his head up, stunned to see Georgie there waiting for him.

As he looked at her, though, he noticed the piece of paper she clutched in one hand. She'd been leaving him a message.

That one simple act, the way they communicated through secret messages and saw each other only by chance, threatened to destroy the last of his restraint.

"I didn't think to see you here. I can't stay. The girls are gathering in the meadow beyond, and they'll miss me."

Freddie caught her by the shoulders and stared deep into the blue eyes he'd grown to love. "My mother has decided it's time to find me a bride. She's already sent out letters seeking appropriate candidates."

Though she'd been about to pull away, Georgie froze, a tremor going through her shoulders where he held her. "You can't let her do this. You have to tell her."

He thrust Georgie away from him and scowled at their tree. "Tell her what exactly? That I've brought her fears to life and chosen a wild farm girl? She'll just move all the faster, and without my father on our side, I'll be married off before I can blink."

His arm ached with the force of the punch she landed on his shoulder.

"Is that what you think I am? Some simpleton wandering the forest? Are your words of love just lies?" Georgie's scowl had never seemed as fierce. "And to think I'd been about to tell you about my lessons."

Freddie had been too caught up in his fears to think of how his words would sound, and this knowledge came too late to mend the hurt he'd laid on her. "I meant only what she would see. I love you as you are. Barefoot and dirt-smeared makes no difference. But to my mother, standing is everything."

"And I have no standing. It's as simple as that?"

Freddie pressed a hand to his forehead, feeling an ache beginning. "Nothing is simple. If only we could put forward even the pretense of a usual courtship, but every aspect of our connection only worsens our case. Surely you can see that?"

He jerked when she touched his arm even though this time she used a gentle stroke. He hadn't expected her to understand.

"If your mother will never accept me," she said once he met her gaze, "then we have no choice."

"I won't believe that. I will not let her choose some other bride when I have found the one for me."

She laughed, the sound so unexpected he could only stare at her even as she began to shake her head.

"You misunderstand me. Oh, Freddie, I will not give you up for anything, not even to save my father from the pain of knowing I have married without his permission."

His eyes narrowed in confusion. "We're both too young to marry without it, and I will not disrespect you enough to force their hand."

"We can't marry here. But there's always Gretna Green."

He had no idea how she came by this knowledge, and the very fact that she possessed it stunned him, but then she'd always amazed him with what she knew and what she could do. It didn't matter.

His head began to shake even before he could marshal the words to explain. "I will not start out our life together with my mother and you at such odds."

She put both fists on her hips. "Then you won't start our life together ever. You'll end up married to some titled girl who knows nothing of country ways. A girl just like your mother. Is that what you want?"

Freddie smoothed down the tension in her arms and enveloped her hands in his. "No, I will not accept such a result. I will figure this out. You just have to give me time."

From her scowl, he could tell she found his request hard, but after a moment she gave a stiff nod. "If you think it's best, then who am I to tell you any different? Just remember what I said, and what I was willing to do for you, for us."

He met her frown with a gentle smile. "I will remember. And I will find an answer that won't cause a rift between my parents and the one I want to claim as my own. The only wife I will have is standing right before me."

Her expression softened, and he leaned down to press his lips against hers.

She jerked away.

He opened his mouth on a protest, but her panicked look held him silent.

"I was only supposed to be gone a minute. They'll be coming after me. They can't find you here."

Freddie understood the reason behind her rejection, but he stole a quick caress anyway. "They won't find me. I've been taught how to navigate this forest by a master."

Even as he heard the sound of her name being called through the branches, Freddie used every skill she had taught him and slipped back into the trees on his way to his own lands.

He'd come here for the privacy to shout out his anger at his mother's scheming. Instead, he'd been reminded of just what he fought for and why. Whatever it took, he would face the future with Georgie at his side.

A grimace pinched his features. He'd do best to stay within England's borders as he won his bride no matter what Georgie might think.

Chapter Nine

ord Aubrey joined them in the afternoon, and graciously agreed to help them practice the dance lessons as they'd promised Lady Pendleton they would. Georgie had intended to tell Freddie of her efforts to gain some refinement earlier, but first she'd been too annoyed with him and then much too distracted.

When Charlotte called a halt to their play, he stayed to help with the herb gathering, though from Barbara's sharing of wisdom earned just that morning, he had little knowledge of greenery. Georgie cast an envious glance their way more than once as the lord courted Barbara openly with Charlotte's unspoken approval though he thought their cousin a farm girl like any of the rest of them. She couldn't imagine him bowing before his mother's schemes.

Georgie frowned at the unworthy thought.

Lord Aubrey had years of experience over Freddie, and yet the man had not gone to speak with their father, in lieu of Barbara's parents, any more than Freddie had.

"While I've no doubt Barbara has made a conquest," Charlotte said, catching hold of Jane's arm, "What begins in falsehood rarely ends well, so don't you go concocting stories to trap the local men."

The statement pulled Georgie from her thoughts, her cheeks burning as bright as Jane's should anyone bother to look. Charlotte's words lingered as they returned home. Though there had never been falsehood between her and Freddie, their whole existence seemed built of them, delusions no less dangerous than those between Lord Aubrey and Barbara.

That realization haunted Georgie through the next two days as she worked with the others preparing the herbs for next winter.

Charlotte had discovered the whole gather a ruse to separate Barbara from her suitor and she took her annoyance out on all of them. If Grannie had no need for the herbs, Charlotte would teach all five of them how to store the excess properly. It served both as a just punishment for Georgie's wandering off in the morning and a necessity when they had so many herbs to prepare, or so Charlotte announced.

In the late afternoon of the second day, Charlotte declared them free to choose their own pursuits at last. Georgie wasted no time, eager to stretch her legs and wanting to explain her new understanding to Freddie. She paused only long enough to collect some bread and cheese, wrapping it in a cloth as she strode for the forest. With where the sun rested in the sky, her chances of finding Freddie were already low, and she didn't want to make them worse.

She tried to remind herself he had more to do than wait on her, but she needed to know what had gone on with his mother. Georgie might have conceded his point about eloping, but if he wouldn't stand up to Lady Brookway in this, for all Georgie knew, he could have already been promised to another. Their falsehoods weighed heavily on her. They'd been living their lies for far too long.

Freddie twisted to face her as she came through the bush, a half-hearted smile curving his lips. "I hoped you'd come, but my hope has been false often enough of late."

Georgie couldn't see a way to introduce the topic of falsehoods without returning them to anger, so chose a different truth.

"Charlotte had us working the herbs. There was no time to leave a message, and certainly none to come out here to stay a while."

He frowned. "I did not get you into trouble by delaying you, did I?"

The worry in his tone banished her lingering annoyance, and she laughed. "No, you did not. I've told you before. My sisters see me as half wild. They expect this of me."

If anything, his expression grew graver.

She crossed the short distance between them and placed a hand on his shoulder. "What is bothering you? It can't be just my absence. You are no more jolly with me here." She bit her lip to keep from asking after his mother when he already looked glum.

His shoulders slumped and Freddie stared at his hands, the fingers twisted together so tightly it could not have been comfortable.

She bumped him with her hip in silent encouragement.

He turned his gaze on her, the look full of confusion. "My mother heard back from her family. She has a list of potential matches and plans to approach them. While nothing will go forward until we meet in person, I do not believe she will withhold her assurances, putting both her honor and mine in the mix."

Georgie stepped back to jam both hands to her hips as the effort to keep from reviving their argument failed. "Then it's time to tell our parents. You cannot mean to raise expectations when you know you will marry none of them. What is it you worry about? You have only to stand firm against your mother."

Freddie leapt to his feet. "Do you really think it will be that simple? You do not know my mother. I must have Lord Brookway on our side, and even then it's likely to be a battle." He scowled down at her. "You don't make it any easier."

"And just what do you mean by that? Should I stand by and watch you be married off to another?"

"No, you should not, and neither will I." He thrust the fingers of one hand through his hair, making it stand up in all directions. "It's just you take such pride in being thought wild. My mother will never accept you as some wild woodland creature. She'll have a hard enough time with you as you are."

Georgie stared at him. "Is it really your mother you're worried about? Are you ashamed of me? Is this why we've met in secret all these years?"

"How can you think such a thing?" He caught hold of her shoulders and stared deep into her eyes. "I have little care to your standing, and your very wildness drew me from the start. I fear only for your future. My father's property is not so grand that we can live apart from my parents, and my mother has it in her to make our lives— your life—miserable."

Her anger melted away at his words.

Georgie went up on tiptoe to close the gap between them and pressed her lips to his, murmuring against the contact the surprise she'd longed to share the other day. "I'm not as wild as you might think. I swear I can act the civilized lady for your mother." She pulled away to twirl in a circle. "I'm even taking lessons."

This time when Freddie stared at her, his eyes grew wide and his eyebrows rose. "Lessons?"

His expression drew a laugh from her. "Yes, even out here in the country a young girl can learn how to be proper. Lady Pendleton has been giving us dance lessons, and Lord Aubrey was so kind as to help us in our practice."

"Lord Aubrey?" Freddie did not seem to find her news welcome.

Georgie laid a soft hand on his arm. "Yes, Lord Aubrey. Surely you must have heard of him. He's a nobleman visiting at the Pendleton Manor. But you needn't worry. His heart is set on none other than Cousin Barbara."

He tried for a smile, but she could tell his discomfort lingered.

"Oh Freddie, do you know me not at all? I care little for titles, and if I did, you will have one as well in time. Do you need me to go about calling you The Honorable Frederick Hathwell so you will be confident in my affections?"

That drew forth a smile, and a true one, if filled with embarrassment.

"I'm sorry. It's just hard to think of you enjoying another man's presence openly when you cannot be so in mine."

Her laughter rang through the trees. "Then you should find it all the more reassuring to learn he comes to us no more formally. He courts my cousin without my father's permission and lacking hers as well."

"And would you have me believe Lady Pendleton teaches you in the meadow?"

Georgie took up the first position of one of the dances they had learned and waited for Freddie to follow suit before she spoke. "You can teach me here under the trees if you so wish. I'll enjoy the practice more with you as my partner, but Lady Pendleton teaches us up at the manor. Her manservants stand in for the gentlemen."

Freddie took her hands and moved through the motions of the dance with precision and an elegance she admired.

At the first pause, though, he arched one eyebrow and said, "I don't see how I should be happier you spend your time dancing with manservants than with another lord, especially as you say titles factor little in your affections."

She grinned at him despite Lady Pendleton having told them to suppress anything more than a gentle smile. "As much as you work to prove yourself to your father, I seek to gain the approval of your mother. The sooner you see me as capable, the sooner we can be open to both our families."

He broke the step to draw her against his chest. "My mother is sure to appreciate your efforts, but don't become so proper that you cast me aside."

She gave him a saucy look. "I never would. Where else could I find a nobleman willing to take his schooling from a woodland creature?"

His shout of laughter was everything she could have hoped for, or so she thought until he bent to lay a deep kiss on her willing lips.

GEORGIE RETURNED TO THE FARMHOUSE to find the others gathered around having tea and doing some repair work in the rapidly dimming light. She hoped the blush on her cheeks had faded enough to remain hidden beneath the oil lamp's glow as she lifted a chemise from the basket and bent her head over the sewing.

The discussion soon turned to the possibility of a ride in the morning, and Georgie let the words wash over her, her thoughts focused more on Freddie's promises. And his sweet kisses.

When she glanced up, though, she caught Charlotte watching her with something like speculation. Not for the first time, Georgie wished she'd kept silent the other day, when they'd first met Lord Aubrey, instead of teasing Barbara. If she hoped to keep her secrets, she'd do best never to mention kisses again no matter the temptation.

Georgie gave her oldest sister an innocent smile and asked Jane to hand over the scissors.

"Have a care you don't snip too close to your knot," Charlotte told her. "I had to redo a seam from your last sewing that should have held much longer."

"Yes, Mother," Georgie teased her sister. Still, she left a good tail beyond the knot just in case. At least Charlotte seemed to have dropped her pointed attention, or perhaps guilt made Georgie think of secrets when her sister only questioned her sewing.

Just then, their father came in the door.

She joined her sisters to welcome him though they'd seen him in the morning. He never minded the attention. What had begun to distract him from his grief and them from theirs so long ago now had become tradition.

Georgie wondered how he would fare once they'd all gone off to get married. The idle thought renewed her blush enough to send her scurrying back to her seat and the mask of her sewing.

"So, girls, Charlotte tells me you've had no work at all to do this afternoon. How did you spend your time?"

Georgie let the others answer, and when it came to her turn offered only a shrug.

"There's no need to ask further from you," he said with a chuckle. "I've always known where you can be found."

Remembering Freddie's concerns, for the first time in her life, she had to force a laugh. Still, he spoke nothing but the truth. She had been in the forest.

Georgie shifted so she could thrust a foot forward. "You'll find no mud on my toes."

Their father shook his head. "I should be grateful you've learned to wear shoes at least. You never were one to suffer convention, and I'm afraid your upbringing did little to change your natural tendencies."

Charlotte gave a little cough, but when Georgie expected her to protest, instead she caught hold of their father's arm and pulled him free of the remaining sisters. Her voice, when she spoke, was too soft to reach Georgie's ears, but she had little doubt as to the meaning when their father looked her way.

Georgie suspected he was no more reassured by her innocent look than it appeared Charlotte had been earlier. Her weaknesses in sewing could not have been the cause.

"You can all go riding tomorrow. I'll leave word with the stable boys as to which horse for each of you."

Before she could relax at her father's pronouncement, he added, "You are to stay together. No wandering off and getting into trouble." The last came with a glare directed solely at Georgie.

She felt her face heat, denying any attempt to appear innocent whatever she might have planned.

He shook his head when she moved to protest, and Georgie settled back, knowing he would not listen, and unsure what she could say in any case. At least Charlotte's suspicions could not be too strong or their father would have Georgie locked in her room rather than counseling her to stay with the others.

She couldn't tell if her guilty conscience made her self-conscious, or if all too many times her older sister and father glanced her way through the rest of the evening.

For years, Freddie had been her very own secret, something she could claim when everything else was shared. Since he brought her flowers from his mother's garden, though, things had changed. Even before he'd kissed her, their secret felt more like a strong blow against her father's trust and a cause for her sister's concern than simple innocence.

When they'd tucked away the last of the dishes and went to scatter to their rooms, Georgie caught Charlotte's arm and held her back.

"You needn't worry so," she said once the others vanished up the stairs. "I swear to you, my virtue is not at risk."

Charlotte twisted until she could grab hold of both of Georgie's hands. "That you feel the need to say such a thing only makes me worry more."

Just as with her teasing about the kisses, Georgie wished she'd kept her own counsel now too late to call back her words. "It's not what you think."

Her sister shook her head. "You are much too innocent to understand the ways of men. What you think harmless could so easily destroy you."

Georgie met her sister's gaze, half expecting the dark look Charlotte wore when she thought on her London season, but only concern showed there. She'd never meant to cause worry. She might question Charlotte's right to act the mother, but in her heart she knew just how much her sister had sacrificed for all of them.

More than anything, she wanted to confess the truth, to explain Freddie was honorable and had nothing but honorable intentions despite how they'd come to know each other. If he'd wanted to take advantage of her, he'd had many opportunities, a fact that, no doubt, would relieve Charlotte not at all.

"You know you can tell me anything," Charlotte said. "Better to speak now and let me help than let this go any further."

The urge to speak vanished with Charlotte's words. What help would she offer except to tell their father. And if she did so, he would go straight to the Brookway Manor.

There'd be no question of waiting for Freddie to prove his worth, no chance of convincing his mother Georgie was anything less than the wild creature she resembled. What did it matter if she could move prettily on the ballroom floor when her father would be sure to explain just how Freddie had undone all convention? He'd never stop to consider how those very same accusations would paint her in a light ensuring she would never find peace with Lady Brookway.

"I spoke the truth. There is no need to worry. Nothing to say. You can be at ease."

Georgie kept her gaze steady under her sister's searching look. She would not risk everything to soothe her conscience, not when they'd been careful for so long.

Her sister might not believe Georgie, but she knew Freddie, and she knew his intentions. When he could declare his inclination would be soon enough for her family to know.

Charlotte shook her head one more time. "Georgiana, I can never be at ease with you. You have been getting into trouble almost from the moment you sprang free of our mother's womb. Just promise me you'll do yourself no harm."

A grin broke out across Georgie's face, relieved she could offer her sister something filled with truth and not the half lies she'd been spinning. "I promise you I will come to no harm."

She bit her tongue to keep from adding anything further, giving only a nod as she turned to follow the others up the flight of stairs leading to the room she shared with Jane.

Chapter Ten

reddie felt the urgency ever more heavily with his mother hinting and Georgie too busy to catch him on the few times he could slip away. They'd exchanged messages just once. Only three days had passed, but it was three days too many.

He'd promised Georgie he would figure something out. His promise weighed heavily, and he'd found no answer.

As he pulled his boots on by himself, much to the annoyance of his valet, Freddie realized he had no choice. Either he spoke to his father now and chanced the very support he so desperately needed, or his mother would have banns posted and him standing in front of the minister before he could say a word.

He let Peter help him into a jacket for the midday meal, too lost in thought to do more than nod his thanks. At least he'd be presentable at his mother's table. He would have to cast it off again before working in the fields.

The men spoke well of him, and he had a good plan for the land now in his care. It would have to be enough.

Decided, Freddie made his way to his father's study. If he could convince his father to give him the right to choose a bride, he could, at minimum, prevent his mother from making any promises he'd be obligated to meet.

He gave a light rap on the door and pushed it open. Though his father had said they would work together tonight after dinner, from the sounds within, Lord Brookway had already begun.

But when he stepped through the door, the person who glanced up from the desk was not his father.

"Oh, Frederick, were you looking for me? I have many letters to write. My mother was very helpful, as I might have mentioned, and I think I found the perfect match for you. I'm writing her parents now."

Freddie could not come up with any response as he stared at his mother, hoping only the horror he felt did not show on his expression.

She waited for him to take a seat. "She won't bring in a title any more than I did, but her father is a marquess. She's the third daughter, and he has two sons, but she will offer connections to a higher level of the peerage. Your options are limited what with your father's few properties and not so impressive income, but her dowry, if used properly, could improve your state, and more importantly, the state of your children."

He stared down at his hands, but they offered no answers. His thoughts shifted to Georgie, as they always did when the question of marriage was raised. He remembered how she'd been willing to run to Gretna Green with him rather than suffer a lifetime apart. And yet he quailed from telling his mother to leave off her matchmaking.

"Mother, I appreciate your wish to see me well married, but it is far too soon."

Lady Brookway laughed. "Which just goes to show how little you understand about this. The season is more than half over for this year. You must act quickly."

He pushed to his feet. "Or what? I'll have to wait another year? I'll have time to consider my choices? I'm just turned eighteen. I know enough about the marriage mart to know that's young for a man. And Father is not so old that I'll be coming into my title soon. Why do you feel you must rush this?"

Her brows pinched together as she stared up at him. "While what you say shows more knowledge than I would have expected, you cannot believe every season will have a female matching your needs and who is willing to see your value. It is a bit early for you perhaps, but better early then have you go looking and gain the reputation of being unworthy. Trust me when I say your focus on all things farming, while it might gain your father's approval, has little to lend itself to a young lady of position."

Freddie wanted nothing more than to tell her right then about his promise to Georgie. He had yet to speak to her father, but he'd made his intentions known and had no plan to do anything else.

He stared back at her for a long while in silence, debating what he had to lose or gain.

"Frederick, you're my son, and I love you dearly. But while my influence is broader than might be expected from your father's wife, even I cannot secure you a better title. I must do what I can for your children."

He stifled a groan at her words. All that mattered to her, all she saw as having any importance, had to do with titles. Even if Georgie's father were wealthy enough to overcome what Lady Brookway would see as a deplorable lack of social standing, it seemed the simple fact of Georgie's status as merely a landholder's daughter would make her unacceptable.

"When I marry, it will be for my own purposes," he ground out, unwilling to suffer her maneuverings any longer. "What titles my children may or may not aspire to will not be part of the consideration. I plan to marry for love."

His mother looked as though she couldn't decide whether to laugh or scowl. "You young people and your ridiculous ideas. My marriage was arranged, and while I'd hoped for a better match, as the fourth daughter of a viscount with only a modest dowry, I did rather well. Your father and I suit nicely. Had I the choosing, I'd most likely have ended up with a common soldier, entranced as I was with the sight of men in uniform like most young women. What then would be left to you? You certainly wouldn't have had the chance to learn land management. My dowry wouldn't have offered much presuming my parents did not disown me. Perhaps it might have bought you a commission in the military. Is that the life you'd prefer? I can tell you had it been so your choice in bride would have been even more limited."

Her words put an end to his argument, though not for the reasons she'd intended.

Freddie had never considered the possibility of being disowned. He'd focused on seeking harmony in his household.

More than ever he needed his father's agreement. He had little doubt his mother would hold the barony over his head should he tell her now just whom he planned for his love match, and his future title was all he had to recommend him to Georgie's father.

"Do what you wish, Mother, but do not commit me where I am not."

Her expression eased, though he knew she'd heard only what she chose to. "Of course, Frederick. I would not think to commit so blindly. You will have your chance to meet your intended before any contracts are made. You will see. The young women I choose for you will be fair of face and quite accomplished. You needn't fear your bride."

Her words only emphasized that which made him worry, but she had promised he would be given the chance to meet the potential brides before anything became final. While he'd have preferred to win her approval of his choice, for the time being, this gave him the space to carry out his own plans.

Freddie bent his head in a stiff bow and quit the room.

Nothing he could say would improve or change what she was already determined to do. Better he focused his attention on securing his father's consideration, something much less likely should he anger his lady mother.

With that in mind, Freddie popped into the kitchen to request a sack meal before returning to his room to shed the coat. He didn't think he could offer civilized conversation at the table, and his place was in the fields. He'd only returned to speak with his father, an opportunity lost at this hour.

GEORGIE WAS DELIGHTED TO SEE Lord Aubrey riding across the field where they gathered wild strawberries as the morning grew long. Barbara had been quite glum ever since she rose, a situation with much in common to Sarah's decision to stay back most likely. Her cousin offered little distraction for Georgie's sisters up to this point when opportunities to slip away and spend some hours in

Freddie's company had been scarce this summer. Her only consolation had been in watching the love blossom between her cousin and Lord Aubrey, a difficult task with him absent through much of the morning.

Marian teased him for his preoccupation, but Georgie could only laugh when he caught sight of Barbara and strode toward her without another word. Though always the gentleman, love had made him rude.

Charlotte watched the two of them with a pinched brow.

"Don't," Georgie said, putting a hand on her sister's arm. "What harm can they come to here in the field? Neither her virtue nor health are at risk, and she's been so unhappy this day. Let them enjoy the company."

That brought a laugh to Charlotte's lips, if not for the same reason. "And I should take counsel from you who teases her sisters about kisses stolen behind the hay? Really, Georgie, you're not the best judge of good behavior."

"Oh, let her be. Let them both be," Marian said as she walked past them to another part of the field. "Our little Georgie knows how to find happiness, something others might do well to study."

The flush that tinted Charlotte's cheek showed the comment found its mark, and Georgie regretted the dimming of her oldest sister's eyes.

Then Charlotte shook her head and allowed a smile. "There's little enough harm with all of us in evidence."

The words seemed spoken more to herself than Georgie as her sister set out to find the elusive white flowers offering hope for succulent berries as well.

Georgie watched Barbara and Lord Aubrey for a moment longer, wondering if she would ever have the chance to do the same with Freddie before they were wed. Would they court openly once the truth came out? Or would the truth cause her father to rush the event as Freddie believed he would despite their reassurances that she remained whole?

A sigh came from the depths of her being. Georgie placed her basket down to free both hands for brushing apart the weeds, but her mind remained focused on courtship. The road to love seemed such a complicated one no matter where she looked, and patience did not come to her easily. Still, Freddie was worth being patient for.

Her own melancholy washed away as she considered just how they'd been waiting of late and her lips curved in a knowing smile.

She spun in a circle, her memory locked to the last time they'd been together when they'd danced under the sheltering leaves as if in a formal ballroom. He wouldn't have bent to lay a kiss on her willing lips had they been surrounded by the lords and ladies of London.

"You'd do best to practice the dance steps elsewhere, little sister," Jane called. "You're more likely to crush the berries we seek than find them going through those moves."

Georgie offered her sister the formal curtsy Lady Pendleton had taught them all and turned her attention back to the task at hand. She wandered some distance in her quest for the rare treats, especially when she found a trail of the plants most likely the result of some small animal.

When next she glanced around, Georgie found her sisters easily enough, but Barbara and Lord Aubrey appeared to have fallen out of sight. Though no haystacks stood in this field, the haying unlikely to leave any strawberries unharmed, many rock piles stood at the edges that would provide shelter enough for an enterprising couple.

Perhaps they had decided to explore the delights of kisses after all. With Barbara hidden beneath her appearance as a simple country maid and Lord Aubrey too much the gentleman to risk more than those innocent pleasures, they deserved this happiness. Just as she deserved Freddie and he'd never do anything to compromise her.

The sound of Charlotte's scolding brought Georgie's head up a short while later, but she didn't turn to look until the scold became something much sharper.

At the sight of Barbara's disheveled appearance, Georgie dropped her basket and ran toward them. She arrived in time to hear her cousin beg Charlotte to tend Lord Aubrey before Barbara ran for his horse and left at a gallop to get help.

"I need to go find Lord Aubrey," Charlotte said, her voice tense with strain. "He's fallen off a ledge and lies injured in the forest. Marian, come with me. Jane, Georgie, mark the places and direct Father after us when he comes."

Charlotte gave the instructions in sharp, quick commands even as Georgie stood with her sisters, head spinning with the change in events from innocent joy to disaster.

"Georgie, are you listening?"

"Yes," she answered even before glancing to see her sisters halfway to the forest edge. "I'll wait on the side of the road. Go help him. We'll make sure Father finds you."

Crossing the field to reach the road took no time at all and yet seemed like forever as she castigated herself for not keeping better watch. While she'd been assuming a simple kiss, something had gone very wrong to leave Barbara with blood on her skirt and her lord seemingly with critical injury.

It helped not at all that her sisters had been equally inattentive. They most likely gave it no thought, assuming the two unfamiliar with these parts would stay within the field. She'd been the one to suspect they'd steal away, and she'd done nothing.

The stones marking the border offered only uncomfortable perches, but Georgie could not settle in any case.

She paced back and forth, her fingers twisted together hard enough to make them ache as she stared down the road for any sign of her father and the rescue party. She wished Charlotte had chosen her for an extra pair of hands in the woods. At least then she could have offered her woodcraft as an aid to Charlotte's healing skills.

Here, she had nothing to do beyond worry.

Barbara must be tortured by fear for Lord Aubrey. Georgie knew she would have been had her love been the one lying injured within the forest.

The thought twisted a knife in her gut as she realized Freddie wandered the same forest most days with only her simple training to protect him. She tried to remember he'd been years in the habit now. He knew as much, most likely, as she did about these parts, but the knowledge eased her fears not one bit.

What if he became injured when he came looking for her? Half the time they went on the hopes of crossing paths with no confidence that the other would be able to slip away. He could lie at the base of a rock fall or wild animals could gnaw on him for hours, days even, before she came. He could be doing so right now. More than a day had passed since they'd last exchanged messages even. No one beyond her would know where to look for him, nor would anyone know to ask her for the knowledge.

The cost of their secrecy ate at her as she waited for her father to come, growing ever more confident disaster waited only for the opportunity to attack. Their choices ensured even a simple injury could turn into much more when no one came to the rescue.

Chapter Eleven

he kitchen servants proved accommodating as usual, but once Freddie left them, the conversation with his mother returned full force and his anger with it. He marched up the stairs, his boots hitting the wood with more strength than necessary as he sought to divest himself of the jacket and every bit of his mother's pretensions.

She'd never resigned herself to the results of her marriage, at least not when his paternal grandfather's death meant her husband's new responsibilities kept them out here in the country. She'd been merry enough from what he could remember, living off her father's wealth even after marriage. He couldn't recall whether his father had felt the same.

He thrust the door open with perhaps more force than required, and it slammed into the wall, startling Peter who had been rearranging Freddie's clothing. When Freddie caught sight of his city suits, he scowled.

"Did my mother lead you to believe we were taking a trip up to London? If so, you, and she, are mistaken. I have duties here."

Peter moved away from the wardrobe. "I was merely checking no pests had breached the security of your chest. I was unaware of Lady Brookway's intentions. Do you wish me to confirm any plans with her?"

Proper as always, Peter reminded Freddie of the obligations he held in regards to his servants. Should he be disinherited, more than just Georgie and himself would suffer.

"No, Peter. Forgive me for taking my foul mood out on you. My mother can be…difficult…at times."

"If you say so. Will that be all then?"

Though his valet clearly would have welcomed an escape from his presence, Freddie felt a sudden urge to go to the forest. He was in no state to listen to the wisdom of the farm hands, and he had too much on his mind to watch over the flock.

Peter might have wanted to leave, but if Freddie changed without the man, he'd suffer many a pained look and muttered comment. He didn't think his composure could handle that and saw little hope for his mood in the near future.

"Help me change into a riding costume and send word down to the stables."

"My lord, didn't you say just this morning your intention was to spend the afternoon working the nearer fields?"

Freddie shrugged out of his jacket, forcing Peter to be quick on his feet to prevent the cloth from landing on the floor. "Plans change."

The words sounded ominous to his ears, and once spoken, he could no longer control his thoughts.

His mother threatened every plan he made.

First she took the steps he underwent to prove himself worthy of Georgie for an excuse to marry him off, then she let her own prejudice against the country and all who dwelled within it make anyone not of the peerage unsuitable.

Peter laid a hand on his shoulder, the touch startling in a man who worked hard to maintain lines drawn between classes that had never held much meaning for Freddie.

"Whatever put such a frown on your face cannot be as bad as you think it. Your mother does what mothers do and works to your best interest."

Freddie forced the hot words back down his throat, knowing as always, Peter shared his mother's opinions. The valet had been chosen for that very reason long before Freddie had grown enough to develop his own positions.

"I understand her intentions, Peter, but the two are not always the same when set against the facts. I know you seek to comfort as well, but please restrain from offering advice in that which you do not know."

He could see in the man's stunned expression Peter thought his rejection came from the same place as his mother's pride, but he did not care about the man's position in society. What made him reject the words had more to do with how Peter, like his mother, believed everything revolved around London, the country worth only a quick sojourn.

"As you wish, sir." Peter's bow was every bit as stiff as any Freddie had offered his mother of late, and performed with much more grace. "Do you wish me to help you change first or shall I call down to the stables to prepare your horse."

Unwilling to spend another moment under the man's disapproving stare, Freddie waved him toward the door. "I am capable of changing myself for this. Please see to my ride."

If anything, Peter's nose lifted higher, but without the valet's aid, Freddie could choose a more rough dress that would serve better in the forest where he intended to take his foul mood and expend it on the thick trunk of a solid oak for all he'd suffer bruises and scrapes. Were the lives of others as difficult as he found his own of late? If so, he wondered that any survived to marry much less propagate the race. Of course all that served was to ensure another generation trapped in rules as tight as ever a bridle fastened around a horse's head.

GEORGIE CAUGHT SIGHT OF THE farm boys on horseback first. Still, her father appeared with the wagon before the horses reached, and passed, her. Guilt made Georgie reluctant to meet her father's gaze, but he wasted little time on her, clearly aware of the urgency.

"We can find them from here, Georgie. Take yourself back to the house."

Her father didn't stay to see if she'd listened to his command, and in that moment, Georgie knew she could not. The vision of Lord Aubrey from Barbara's description became overlaid with one of Freddie similarly injured. She couldn't rest until she made sure he did not lie hurt in their special place when she hadn't seen him for three long days.

She followed the field a good bit before turning into the forest for she dared not cross her father's path. Once under those leaves, Georgie sped through the woods, her footsteps crunching small branches and sending woodland creatures scattering away from her. The very speed made her breath come faster, and with each stride, her concern grew for all it had started a simple fear.

She burst through the final barrier to see her beloved Freddie, a frown marring his forehead as he jerked to his feet.

"Georgie? Georgiana, what is it? What is wrong?"

She fell into his open arms with a relieved sob, the echo of her full name from his lips telling her just how distraught she appeared.

He swayed back and forth, rubbing both hands down her arms as he attempted to comfort her. His touch soon restored her calm, revealing her fears no more than the creations of her imagination.

"Just tell me. Whatever it is, we will face it together."

A broken laugh came from her. "It's nothing. I swear it is nothing. I only missed you."

How could she explain her fears when they made so little sense, and yet every time she spoke to him, it seemed their future grew dimmer. Whether disaster or his mother, she feared they'd be torn apart just as Barbara and Lord Aubrey had been.

When she'd expected him to tease, Freddie only held Georgie apart so he could search her features, his frown just as strong as when she'd first come upon him.

"I promise you, there is nothing wrong with me at least. Lord Aubrey had a serious accident. Charlotte and my father are seeing to him now, but the thought of you in the woods alone terrified me. What if it had been you who'd fallen down the drop and no one knew where to search?"

He brushed aside the strands of blond hair that had fallen loose around her face. "I cannot promise never to have a mishap, but neither will I seek one." His lips twisted up on one side in the semblance of a smile. "We have enough to stand between us without injury to add to it."

She froze as the tension in his last words sent the false concerns from her mind.

"What has your mother done now?" Georgie asked, her unreasoned fear replaced in an instant with well-founded annoyance.

He turned away and thrust fingers through his hair, a move that told her she'd found the right target.

"I had thought it would take her much longer, but she's already found a suitable bride. More than one. She plans to arrange introductions."

Georgie stamped one foot. "And you responded with the fact that you already had your bride chosen? That she need not waste her time and raise hopes where there are none?" Her tone said what her words did not, conveying her disbelief so he could not fail to mark it.

Freddie twisted to glare at her. "I told her I plan to choose my own bride, yes. She scoffed and all but patted me on the head for my delusions. If I were to have told her of you then, she'd have thought you a ruse, or worse, an attempt to combat her planning and therefore the object of her instant dislike."

Georgie planted her fists on each hip and returned his glare. "Does it matter so much what she thinks? You are a man full-grown. Can you not stand for your convictions?"

"You don't understand. If I force the issue now, my father will see me as a willful boy, not a man. That will not help our case. Persisting in this unprepared will only lead to me being disowned."

This time Georgie was the first to turn away, staring hard at the tree where she'd left many a sweet note as she blinked the tears from her eyes. "Is that what this is all about? You are as tied to your title as ever your mother has been. Or perhaps you are not the man you see yourself as. Maybe you just wanted to dally with a simple girl, our friendship having no meaning now that you think yourself beyond it. You never had any intention of holding to your promise."

Freddie put a hand on her shoulder, but she shook it off.

"It's not that, I swear. If my father disowns me, what will I have to offer you? Why would your father listen to my suit? And how would we live?"

She turned back then, uncaring of the liquid gathered on her lashes. "If those questions would deter you, then you don't love me as much as I love you. You might as well go back to your mother and accept whomever she chooses. I'm clearly not worth the risk."

Before he could attempt to convince her once again, to delay her so he could continue enjoying her kisses with no need for an honorable offering, she stormed off. Perhaps she should have gone straight to the farmhouse after all instead of coming here. Perhaps she should never come to the glade again, and perhaps she should never have come in the first place.

Charlotte's warnings rang sharp in her ears.

She'd been so sure, so confident in her understanding, but all Freddie brought her were pretty words wrapped around reasons for why they must stay secret. She'd never loved anyone as she loved Freddie, but she would not become his harlot and listen to the woes his sanctified wife offered him.

Chapter Twelve

Freddie stared after her, shaken by how quickly his frustrations had turned Georgie against him. He took a step in the same direction, the memory of her tears setting his chest to burn, but then he stopped. What could he tell her that he hadn't already said? She'd denied his reasons, and he had nothing more to offer.

The urge to slam his fist into a tree returned with full force, but much like his reasons, it would solve nothing. He was too much of a coward to speak with his father and stand up to his mother. Georgie, his sweet young farm girl, had been willing to risk everything for him. What had he risked to be with her?

He might not have intended any of the acts she accused him of, but the result had been the same. As long as they met in secret, he could enjoy her company without risk. And if they were discovered, his reputation would not be destroyed. Only hers.

A curse came from his lips loud enough to set nearby birds to flight.

He didn't know why she loved him. He could not imagine why she waited for him when he'd only proved himself worthless in her eyes. She'd expected better of him.

So had he.

Freddie sank back to the rock where he'd been sitting when she'd rushed up. Georgie had been in such a panic he'd heard her coming from far off and believed some large animal crashed through the forest.

He'd been contemplating his woes while she'd been worried harm had come to him. It did not seem a reasonable exchange.

He reviewed the events of the day, from his busy morning in the fields to the unsatisfying encounter with his mother. All of which led him here where he'd disappointed Georgie so soundly she wouldn't even give him a chance to explain.

He froze, his review absent of one critical aspect he might just have remembered to tell Georgie had she given him a moment to gather his thoughts.

He had been on his way to speak with his father when his mother intervened. He'd been about to place his future happiness and hers on the line to end this half-state they existed in, and who's to say he wouldn't have done so that very night?

Instead of the support and encouragement he needed to hold firm on his convictions as she'd claimed he could not, she'd cut the ground from beneath his feet and accused him of all manner of inappropriate designs.

His mother thought him a simpleton, not even capable of knowing what he wanted out of life.

Georgie saw him as weak-willed, clinging to his mother's apron strings—as if his mother would ever wear something so simple—and incapable of making his intentions known.

He glared at the tree across the brook for lack of a proper target. The female sort had brought him nothing but trouble. Their grief weighed much more heavily than any pleasure for this day at least. Give him a flock of sheep any day. He might not be the wisest shepherd, but at least he had a hope of becoming one.

Sheep had basic expectations. They wanted grass to chew, a sturdy fence to keep them well confined, and a shepherd ready to stand between them and any danger. He could count on them to behave as sheep did. Perhaps not the smartest of animals, but they had a consistency that females of the human sort could not offer.

He'd attempted to stand between Georgie and a sound condemnation from his mother. Instead of joy at his protection, he was kicked in the knee. He tried to prove his maturity to his mother, and she saw him as even more ignorant and innocent of the world than she ever had before.

He could not please them even should he twist himself in knots and bring on a thundercloud of a headache to pound against his temples. Whatever direction he went, like an unruly horse, the two women would pull the other. Just when he thought them settled, they reared up and dumped him in the mud.

Again, Freddie roundly cursed, but this time his frustration and anger had found the correct targets. He would no longer take all the guilt and disgrace upon himself when he'd done nothing but attempt to improve the situation. They could all go hang as far as he was concerned.

He had a section of farmland to manage and sheep to tend. His responsibilities extended far and wide beyond their machinations, and he'd wasted far too much time dancing to the female tune when he had work to see to.

GEORGIE SLOWED HER PACE ONCE she came within eyesight of home. She could allow her heartbreak to show no more than her previous joy. Whatever Charlotte might have suspected, to confirm something untoward had been going on would only bring more pain and unhappiness not just to her but to many in her family.

Even as her breathing steadied, though, the dust from the approaching wagon caught her attention. She rushed forward, knowing only she had to be home when her father returned. She had not realized how long she'd spent with Freddie, the time compressed to a few agonizing minutes, but clearly her father had gone to the manor and come back. The delivery of Barbara's lord must have been swift with the Pendletons far more concerned for his safety than courtesies just as she'd been more worried for Freddie than afraid of her father's anger.

Her feet dragged despite the need to hurry. What had she to look forward to now? Would her love for Frederick Hathwell disappear as quickly as their friendship had from his mind? Or would she quietly fade away as Charlotte seemed to have, never again to find one worthy of her heart?

In the rush to attend her father, no one paid Georgie much mind, and she drew on their energy to mask her own lack of same. She slipped into place behind Jane in time to hear Charlotte and Marian both beg Father to go gently.

One look at Barbara's face as she left the house gave Georgie all the information she needed as to what had gone on in her absence. Reddened eyes and tear-stained cheeks told the story not just of Barbara's grief but also why her sisters felt their cousin had suffered enough.

"I'm sorely disappointed in your behavior, Barbara. You had no business running about in the woods with an unattached man, ignoring how I'd specifically forbidden you to seek him out."

Her father spoke to her cousin, but he might as well have been looking Georgie's way. Freddie may have had his own reasons for not wanting to seek her father, but he'd been right in one aspect. Had Father known just what she sought in the forest lo these many years, he'd have been just as quick to forbid her own association, and wise to do so as she now knew.

Though lost in her own grief, Georgie was not unaware of her cousin's pain. As Barbara swore to set Lord Aubrey aside as she should have from the start, Georgie added her own promise beneath her breath, attracting a curious look from Marian.

When it seemed her father had finished scolding Barbara, and Georgie herself though he remained unaware of his success, Georgie stepped forward to curl a hand around Barbara's arm. "Come, let's get you inside. You've heard your fill."

None could know Georgie spoke of her own state and chose to assist her cousin as much to avoid the attention of her sisters, or worse, her father now with his purpose fulfilled.

Barbara leaned into the touch, clearly distraught, and Georgie felt a twinge of guilt at using her cousin's crisis for a distraction. But one look at Barbara's face and her own upset melted away.

"I'll ask Cook to put on a pot of tea, and I'm sure we have some biscuits. I can't imagine you feel much hunger now, but your body needs food if you're to be strong."

If anything, her focus brought more questions into her sisters' expressions, but when she felt sure they would examine her mercilessly, Charlotte stepped between Marian and Georgie to take Barbara's other arm.

"Georgie is correct. You haven't eaten since this morning, and it's been quite a distressing day. Lord Aubrey is getting the care he needs. You must look to yourself lest you require a doctor's care as well."

"Besides," Jane added, "we are not the only ones to have missed luncheon. Father will be getting hungry too."

If only all their troubles could be solved by a quick meal. Still, once again words meant for Barbara proved as sound in Georgie's case. She would have to choose her time of mourning when no other could see her, and to find some place to claim her own that was not tainted with thoughts of Freddie.

For now, she could offer Barbara comfort of a sort the others would not understand. Both of them had set sights on a gentleman ill-suited for one reason or another, and both had lost their hearts before recognizing the truth of the matter.

Chapter Thirteen

The somber evening turned into an equally dim day, the sun hiding behind clouds as they ate breakfast in silence. A long night's contemplation did no more for Georgie than it appeared to have done for her cousin.

Barbara's whole body seemed to hum with tension as they went about the morning chores, the cows caring little for the heartbreak their attendants might have suffered.

With all the focus on their cousin, Georgie's own mood went unnoticed, or her sisters dismissed it as fellow feeling.

As much as Georgie tried to convince herself she'd misunderstood Freddie's meaning, that he feared more for his holdings than he loved her had been as clear as the whey pulled from curds. She had as little hope of reworking the previous day's events as Barbara's wish for Lord Aubrey not to have followed her into the forest came to be.

The cow Georgie milked shifted with a grunt when she pulled a bit too hard in her preoccupation, the timing of its rejection seeming to chastise her for ignorance of Freddie's stance.

Georgie laid a soothing hand on the warm hide. "It's all right. I'll take better care."

Jane shook her head at how Georgie spoke to the cow, but then Georgie had always found animals made for good companions. The cow might kick her should she pinch its teat, but never would it pretend a love too shallow to last the first real challenge.

"Where do you think you're going?"

Marian's sharp tone brought Georgie's head up in time to see Barbara walking away from the house instead of toward it, a milk pail splashing at her side. Georgie pulled her pail to one side so, should the cow grow tired of standing still, it wouldn't be knocked over, but the slight delay meant the others had already vanished from view.

Georgie caught hold of her skirt and ran after them, wondering what could have set Barbara off this time.

She arrived just after Sarah, joining a small crowd gathering around her father who stood facing off with the young man from the manor.

Her father minced no words as he told the man Lord Aubrey was no concern of theirs. They'd done their duty.

Georgie ached for poor Barbara to have to stand quiet as her uncle cast aside the smallest of tidbits, and even worse to discover he'd done so when Lord Aubrey had been asking after her.

But when her cousin responded to a request for her presence with, "I cannot," Georgie turned to stare at Barbara in shock.

The fear, not even the reality, of an injury had set her to disobeying her father and running into the forest after Freddie. Even now, with what had come between them, if he cried out for her, all would be forgiven faster than she could blink.

Something didn't feel right as Barbara continued to protest. Georgie's eyes narrowed. She considered the possible causes for her cousin's behavior while her sisters chastised Barbara.

Sarah stepped between to say, "Can't you see she holds herself responsible for his accident?"

While the statement made the others quiet down, it broke Georgie of her preoccupation.

"All the more reason to go to him," Georgie said, having realized what held her cousin back. Charlotte had warned against false speaking, and Lord Aubrey still had no notion of Barbara's true place in the Ferrier household, much less in her own where her father, the Viscount Whitfeld, held command.

She meant to say more, driven by how her own falsehoods had reached out to strangle what love she'd claimed, but the manor servant broke in first and finally Barbara gave way.

Georgie moved forward to take the pail when her father directed, but none of their minds remained on the chores. While the others saw Barbara to the wagon and out the gate, Georgie brought the pail through the kitchen then continued to her father's study instead of returning to her own milking.

Her love burned all the stronger for the realization that even should Freddie forget their harsh words and cry out to her on his sickbed, no one would come for her. No one in the Brookway Manor knew of her existence nor would they from the shortened version of her name. Should she show up at his door, she'd be excluded from his side, a stranger come to intrude on a private moment.

She felt sick to her stomach for how she'd condemned him so easily. Would she be as eager to throw everything away if she didn't have firm confidence in her father's love? He would be angry, no doubt, and the consequences would be severe for both of them, but even if they had eloped, her father would not cast her out. Rather, he'd force Freddie to join their family, keeping his own close despite any disagreement between them.

From what Freddie described, his own family had none of that closeness to depend on.

She knew she had little time, but still her hand trembled as she tried to write some gentle word to leave for her love. The ink blotted on the page, making a mess of her least attempt until she knew no message would suffice.

Even as she stared at the wasted paper, her words illegible to any who might come to use the remaining blank surface, a calm reached out and took hold of her.

Freddie had known her accusations about his motives false. There was no way he could have been untrue to her in all the years they'd spent together under the cloak of secrecy, but she'd never given him the chance to explain.

She'd left him before he could when she knew he would have swayed her. Only then she'd thought he'd try with falsehood, but when had lies come between the two of them? She had to go to their secret place, and she'd find either her very own Freddie or a loving note chiding her for her foolishness and agreeing to her desire for an elopement if only to keep a smile on her face.

So strong did the conviction fill her, she felt as if she could see the message before her even now, but that only made her more eager to go seek it out and read the words from his own hand.

She rushed through the rest of her chores and slipped away at the first chance, her sisters too distracted by their own thoughts to pay her much mind.

The distance to their glade, a place she'd sworn never to breach just yesterday, passed unnoticed beneath her racing feet. Where she'd come the previous day full of fear and panic, today only hope lived in her breast. Hope, and the love that had never left it.

"Freddie? Are you here?"

The silence that met her words offered no discouragement.

She could not expect him to spend every moment waiting for her here, especially not when he'd been so long the previous day, having clearly arrived some time before she found him there.

They had much to prepare if they were to leave this very night. He would have left her something, a message, a token, some reminder of what they were to each other, so she would know his decision.

Georgie thrust her hand into the hollow, her eyes eager to focus on the paper that must be within.

Her fingers found the same response her call had.

Leaves rustled against her hand and a twig scraped her skin, the debris most likely brought in by an animal intending to make a home of this hollow, unaware it had a purpose already.

No paper. No token. Nothing.

She stared at the shadowed opening, unwilling to believe the truth, or rather not wanting to believe.

Her breath came out in a huff as she examined exactly what she'd founded her newly won confidence on.

Nothing more than misguided hopes.

She glanced around the glade, but discovered no sign anyone had been here since the previous day, dew still marking the ground from the mist-filled morning enough to show footprints had there been any to see.

Here she'd been building up fantasies of an end to all their secrets in elopement, and he'd come to the same position in a very different way.

She'd figured out his plan. He had no reason to pretend any longer. Nothing to gain. He'd clearly accepted her dismissal as if it were a mild inconvenience instead of the heartbreaking tear she felt in her own chest.

Georgie's shoulders slumped, and only force of will kept her upright else she would have collapsed to the damp soil to cry her heart out on its yielding surface.

Instead, she turned and started the long trek back to the farmhouse.

She had only herself to blame, for this disappointment and every one before it.

Charlotte had warned her many a time about her wild ways. Had warned her nothing good would come of it.

She'd thought herself so much smarter, smarter even because she kept a secret so delicate no one could know for fear of it collapsing around her.

She'd have been wiser to wonder at her fear than to hold to the secret for so long. Once it had been true. Of that she could be sure. But boy became man and she became as nothing, a trifle to while away the hours until his mother found him a suitable bride.

When she reached the house, Georgie slipped into her room, thankful only Jane had found somewhere else to spend her time. Now that she had no secret to treasure, the task of keeping her sisters from knowing the truth of her heartache seemed too weighty for her to undertake.

FREDDIE WOKE LATE THE NEXT morning with a dull headache. He'd spent the evening down at the tavern rather than trying to govern his expression in an attempt to be polite to his mother at the dinner table.

In the painful clarity of light streaming in his window, however, he could not maintain the sense of being ill-used quite so firmly.

His mother did only as she'd been raised while Georgie had little reason to trust when he offered nothing but excuses. Everything weighed, as it always had, on his father's position in this. His mother's plans and Georgie's concerns would come to an end as soon as he proved himself to his father.

A groan issued from his lips as the thought offered not as much consolation as he'd hoped.

His father's judgment rested on Freddie's ability to prove himself responsible, and yet he'd let anger at his mother and then at Georgie keep him from the very tasks with which he hoped to set that proof.

Peter came to attention in the doorway before Freddie noticed it was open.

"What are we planning to do today?"

The sideways nature of the question made Freddie tense, wondering just what state he'd been in when he'd cast up on the manor entryway, but he had no choice. However his head might feel, however much he'd prefer the blinds were closed and he'd adopted hours more common in his mother's beloved London, he'd already failed in his efforts to secure his future for one day. He would not compound the error.

"I will be examining the soil this afternoon, so will be in need of some sturdy walking boots."

The men might have mentioned such the previous night, but if not, whatever they had planned, walking was more than likely to be involved. Somehow, he didn't think any of the manor workers would be lying abed nursing the consequences of their night's revels.

When he came down to breakfast, his father gave him a tight look but said nothing, perhaps believing the cold eggs punishment enough.

Freddie broke in with his plans for the day, nervously eager to prove himself ready, and Lord Brookway made no comment beyond a nod of what Freddie hoped could be read as approval despite his tardy arrival.

"We still have those grain orders to review," Lord Brookway commented as he looked down at the paper.

A hot flush raced up Freddie's neck as he remembered the plans his father had set for the day before.

"I am sorry," he murmured, unsure how to explain without revealing his secret. It must not come out today of all days when he'd made such a poor attempt at showing himself ready for a man's responsibilities.

His father raised an eyebrow as he glanced up. "I am to understand you spent the noontime with your mother instead." His gaze shifted to Lady Brookway, who was busy readying the tea, and back to Freddie. "It's enough to put any young man out of kilter."

Stunned at sympathy where he'd expected condemnation, Freddie managed a weak smile. "I'll try not to let it happen again."

Lord Brookway nodded and turned back to his paper, saying only, "See that you do."

Breakfast continued as if it were any other day from then on, much to Freddie's surprise. His mother made no mention of her efforts, nor did his father do anything to call attention to his faults.

Still, guilt kept him tense and eager to escape their presence in favor of the fields. The men welcomed him with enthusiasm bought, perhaps, by one round too many at the tavern, but then he rarely used his allowance, having few needs the manor servants did not already meet.

Georgie might not understand what drove him, but she'd never gone without any more than he had. It might seem all romantic and wonderful to run off together in a fit of passion, but the consequences would weigh much more heavily on her than on him if he were not disowned, and quite heavily on both of them if he were.

The day's labor, stopping only for a field luncheon with the men, gave him a lot of time to think.

It was not the thing to pay attention to the beggar children in the streets of London, but everyone of means knew there were places to avoid where one's station in life did nothing to protect and much to draw the worst possible element. The fate of the destitute might be less obvious out here in the country where, between hunting and a small plot of land to till, at least starvation could be held at bay, but Freddie had heard the sermon often enough to have turned over some of his allowance to help feed the poor even here.

Georgie would not suit such a life any more than she'd blend easily into the strictures of London society.

He had the perfect situation to offer her here at the Brookway Manor where she would be kept in the manner to which she'd become accustomed, or rather one a good bit better, and yet still could take advantage of the ease found in the country where her behavior would not be scorned. She might think his concerns foolish now, but she'd come to understand them in time. Though her anger might burn hot, it always cooled, and when it did, she'd realize he had only her best interests at heart.

The idea surprised a laugh out of him.

His mother would say the same, but the difference lay in what drove the interest. He knew Georgie's heart as well as he knew his own. His mother knew him not at all.

"Coming down to the tavern again?"

The question pulled him from his thoughts to realize the farm workers had already collected their tools. The sun hung low along the horizon, time for haying done for the day.

The light made his decision for him, filtered as it was through Georgie's forest.

"Not today," he told the men to their disappointment. "I have something to see to."

The men shrugged and one came to take his rake from him.

He waved them on their way with a cheerful smile as he strode toward the forest, more grateful than he'd expected to be for his walking boots and the easing of his headache.

Though it would be too late to catch her there, Freddie hoped she too would have come to this day with a better understanding of how wrong everything had gone in the previous one. As with other times when they'd argued, she could have left him a sweet note, one full of contrition, yes, but mainly of confidence in him and in his love.

He reached the glade just as the sun sank low enough that it could not filter through the branches, leaving only a hint of light to guide him. Normally he would have left the forest undisturbed in the patterns of its night life, but even with Georgie's warnings echoing through his mind, he wanted to check the tree.

No dangerous beasts held command of the glade when he reached it, and another of Georgie's teachings came to him in the whisper and squeak of small animals and birds settling to their rest. The forest would be silent if danger lurked.

He turned his back on it to thrust a hand into the trunk and search blindly for any hint of paper.

He found none.

Disappointment swept over him for just a moment before he stepped back and shook his head.

She'd been very upset. It might take some time for her anger to fade, but he could be patient. After all, he planned to have a lifetime with her. What did he care about a few short days?

It wasn't as though she would be roaming beyond the forest. If ever he found her absence trying, he could always go and visit her at the farm. He'd heard the quality of the man's cattle far exceeded what would be expected of a farmer's horse breeding. A viewing would offer an excuse, and the opportunity to introduce himself to the man who would someday be bound to Freddie by his daughter's marriage.

Chapter Fourteen

eorgie heard a commotion outside her door and forced herself to stir from contemplation of her bleak future. She could not imagine finding another to give her heart to, not knowing the pain it caused when that person played her false as surely every man did. But her sisters would come after her if she did not appear, and their scrutiny would only make this harder to bear.

Already Charlotte and her father had grown suspicious. She must not do anything to prove their fears true. A greater humiliation she could not imagine than her father trying to force Freddie to marry where he had no intention of doing so. Worse, would his parents seek to pay off her father for a virtue she'd never risked?

The thought terrified her, not of the payment, but of her father's reaction. She could not face the idea so moved to the doorway to seek a distraction.

With dull eyes, she watched her cousin throw clothing into a trunk with little care to its state. It seemed she would lose her beloved cousin's company as well when Barbara would be the only one able to understand her pain should she reveal it.

"Tell us," Marian demanded, blocking Barbara's path when she attempted to leave the room. "What happened?"

"I need to talk to your father. He'd been right from the start. I should never have spoken with Aubrey and should never have gone to the manor. I can stay here no longer."

A flicker of curiosity died as quickly as it had risen, much like her anger could find no hold in the emptiness that surrounded Georgie. It seemed as if winter had come early to her. All the leaves had fallen and only skeletal tree limbs reaching toward the sky remained, leaving her exposed to censorious gazes.

When Charlotte urged her sisters downstairs to pack food for Barbara's journey, Georgie slipped away to her room once again. She'd bear a later scolding better than trying to hide how her life had ended from them in the bright kitchen. She couldn't even find the strength to cry. Her grief, so deep and overwhelming, festered rather than bursting forth in a form from which she had any hope of recovery.

The door opened behind her where she lay face down on her bed with her arms folded over her pillow. She ignored this intrusion as well. It would only be Jane come to gossip. Better she think her sister asleep than that she disturb Georgie's misery.

Large hands seized both her shoulders and lifted her onto her feet.

Georgie stared up into her father's furious expression, barely aware of Charlotte going through the chest of drawers Georgie shared with Jane.

"You are a willful child," he said, boring into her with his gaze. "You think you can carry on behind our backs, make a mockery of every restraint, and not a soul will notice? I sent you straight home."

She opened her mouth to answer, though she no idea as to what words would suffice, and her gaze shifted to Charlotte, the one who must have informed him of her absence.

Her father's hold tightened until Georgie's voice became an unintelligible squeak, drawing her attention back to him in time to see his eyes narrowed in an alarming manner.

"I might not have a title as some do, but I am a respected farmer. I have a reputation in this area, a reputation shared by all my daughters except one. We are a respectable family, Georgiana. We have always held to high standards. Your whole life you've been taught what is proper for all we did not enforce it as strongly with you."

The strength seemed to drain out of him, and he released her to sit on the edge of her bed, head in his hands. "You can't go running about the countryside with some farm hand as you have been. You'll lose all chance of a good marriage if you throw your virtue away behind a haystack. I thought I'd raised you better than that. I should never have put so much of the burden on your sister's shoulders when your mother died. I should have paid more attention to your schooling."

He raised his head then to stare at her with such desperation the tears she'd thought beyond her pricked her eyes.

"How did I go so wrong? You are much like your mother, and I missed her so much. I fear I indulged you more than any young girl could handle, letting you continue running off to the forest as she had done when I knew the dangers, and not just those from the wild beasts. I just couldn't bring myself to quash that in you."

Georgie stretched out a hand to comfort him, but before her eyes he gained control of his emotions and thrust to his feet.

"You won't get out of this with a pretty smile and soft words, Georgiana. From what your sister has told me, it has gone well beyond such neat repairs. Your cousin Barbara leaves for London this very hour. You will be going with her. No more running wild. You'll learn propriety in the greater strictures of London society. May my sister have better luck controlling you for should she fail, you will destroy not just your reputation but that of each and every one of your sisters, ensuring none of them has the chance to find the happiness they deserve."

"But Father—" She didn't know what she'd meant to say, but he only caught her arm again and strode from the room, tugging her along despite her protests.

She sent a pleading glance to Charlotte who trailed after with a small bundle of what must have been clothing for London.

Her sister gave a head shake. Rather than helping, she seemed in full agreement with the harshness of this punishment. Surely they could not believe she'd done something worthy of exile?

Georgie started to struggle in earnest.

Whatever slim chance there was of Freddie coming with an apology rested on her being here. Or at the very least, she would not have him think her so distraught she needed to leave the area to avoid him.

"I won't go. You can't make me. Father, don't do this."

Neither her words nor her attempts to break free of his hold made any impression as her father marched her out to the yard where both farm hands, and her cousin and sisters waited.

Barbara said something, but Georgie didn't hear her father's reply as she cried out.

Ignoring her protests as though she said nothing, her father swung Georgie up into the air only to let her land on cloth sacks padding the wagon bed.

She pushed to her knees and grabbed the side of the wagon so she could rise, but her father's glare made her limbs too weak to support Georgie. She sank onto the rough cushions and crossed her arms, her own narrowed gaze telling him exactly what she thought of this.

He showed no sign of weakening, no regret at all in his decision to cast his youngest daughter from the bosom of her family when she needed them the most. Even worse, he turned away with no comment, seemingly able to dismiss her from his mind as thoroughly as he had his life.

Marian and Jane avoided her gaze, but Charlotte stood there watching, lips pinched together on a frown, until Barbara said her farewells, and she and Sarah joined Georgie in the wagon.

Georgie expected Charlotte to repent, to convince Father not to banish her, right up until Thomas clicked his tongue and set the horses moving.

She twisted to stare blindly over the backs of the horses rather than let her sisters see any sign of the grief she felt in being taken from the only home she knew. First Freddie betrayed their friendship and destroyed their love then her father saw fit to send her from the very home she'd believed he would forgive anything to keep her in. She hadn't done what they'd accused her of, but what did it matter? Had he the depth of love she'd believed of him, he would never have done something like this. Her father proved no better than Freddie's family, and Charlotte much the same.

STARING AT THE TAILS OF the horses as they swished almost in unison soon grew more tiring than the journey itself, the longest Georgie had ever taken. Even when she'd accompanied her father to a horse market once when just seven year old, it hadn't seemed so long.

"Can you at least tell me what happened?"

The soft-voiced question startled Georgie into twisting around, but of course, it had not been meant for her.

Sarah leaned toward Barbara, one hand on her mistress's knee as she urged Georgie's cousin to reveal what had happened at the manor.

Barbara shifted so the hand fell away and said nothing.

How Georgie longed for someone to ask her the same question.

She turned back to her contemplation of the horses, isolated by more than her exile.

Where she'd always had Freddie, now she had no one to talk to, to share those confidences too raw for general conversation and yet which burned when held within. She might love her sisters, but she'd never had the kind of bond Sarah shared with Barbara though duties and station separated them.

When Charlotte sought her secrets, she pried as a mother would to find the errors and correct them before harm could come of them. Only Georgie had been able to tell her mother almost everything.

Homesickness swept over her not for the farmhouse, not for her sisters, but for the time before her mother died.

She wished with all the power of her heart she'd told her mother of her secret friend, shared that confidence the way they would talk about the woods when no one else could hear. Georgie believed she would have told her mother had she been given the chance, even if her mother would have scolded her just as Charlotte would.

Georgie could have asked her mother about him. She could have shared the confusion he sparked just as she'd shared the way the woods called to her when her father would have preferred she acted more like her sisters and learned decorum.

Sure, he'd laughed and called her wild child with the rest, but she'd seen it in his eyes even then. He'd tamed her mother, leaving her to seek the wild through Georgie, and he'd wanted nothing more than to pull his daughter from the wild as well. That his stance had softened with her mother's death could only be as he'd said. He'd seen in her what had drawn him to her mother and could not chance cutting out this last memory of the woman he loved from their lives, from his life.

"You know you love him," Sarah said, again cutting through the silence. "And if my eyes did not deceive me, he feels the same."

"Leave off, Sarah." Though the words could have held anger, Barbara's tone had more of exhaustion than bite. "It was poorly done. I should never have kept the truth from him, and now I shall suffer for that choice. But at least let me suffer in silence."

Georgie shook her head to see the stricken look on Sarah's features.

If she'd had so close a friend, she would have treated her much better. How many times had talking things out with Freddie made the worst burden lighter?

An icy chill raced through her despite the heat of day.

She had no cause to chastise Barbara, spoken or not. She sat here bemoaning her lack of a bosom friend when she'd cast hers aside without waiting to hear what drove him. She knew well enough from her own experience how misunderstanding could cut deep without an intention of doing so. Was the lack of a note the very next day such clear evidence?

A tiny hope rose now, too late to follow her instinct to stay at the farmhouse. She should have known Freddie would come for her. Only bruised pride had rejected the possibility.

She'd acted as poorly as Barbara did now, running away instead of confronting the man she loved to get her answers.

Georgie moved restlessly in the wagon, but what choice did she have? She could have sought him out rather than taking an untouched glade as proof. Instead, she'd returned home to sulk and to be sent off to London for the polish she never sought and desired even less now.

She didn't need a season. She didn't need fancy dresses and balls. She needed Freddie, the one person she'd left behind without a word or message of her own to tell him why she no longer came to meet him.

The sharp image of Freddie waiting for her as the days passed cut into her hard enough she considered leaping from the wagon and walking all the way home. Only knowing she had no chance of doing so when she'd paid little attention to their route kept her seated. That and the consternation she'd cause poor Thomas when he returned home without either her or the ability to state she'd been safely delivered.

She stared back the way they'd come with as much focus as she'd looked forward, but neither point offered any comfort.

"He'll come after you."

Georgie stifled a laugh as once again Sarah's words seemed designed for her ears even as Barbara said, "He cannot. He doesn't know who I am."

The look that passed between the two other women held so much private history, Georgie felt compelled to keep her silence even as she wanted to jump up and spin through one of the dances Lady Pendleton had taught them.

Freddie might not know where she went, but he'd be sure to find out one way or another just as Barbara's Lord Aubrey would. Her father might think everything settled with both of them, but just as likely his doorstep would become crowded as first one and then the other sought knowledge of their whereabouts.

She'd been a fool to accuse Freddie of wanting her for nothing but her kisses as though they hadn't shared both fears and delights since they were just children, but he'd forgiven her foolishness before as many times as she had accepted his own faults. If he truly worried over being disowned, his reasons had little to do with craving a title. She felt sure of it now, too late to call back her hurtful words.

She shook off the glum thought. No matter what she'd said, how much her words had hurt him, her Freddie would see clear to the pain beneath them. He'd know she wanted nothing more than to be with him and only fear of losing their future made her see him as less than he was. Freddie would be on the road to London at her heels, ready to sweep her off her feet like some wild highwayman and carry her off before he'd let her turn aside the love they shared.

Georgie squinted down the road behind them, a fanciful thought turning a distant dust cloud into her love charging after the wagon even then.

When the vehicle producing the cloud turned aside, she didn't care.

If not now, then soon. He would be coming.

He would always come after her, even if her father sent her to the ends of the earth. She need only remember to have faith in his love despite all the troubles life placed between them. She would stay true to him this time, and when he did come for her, she'd beg his forgiveness for what she'd said, what she'd thought about him, until all their differences washed away much like the leaves rode the brook past where they met and vanished into the distance, no longer of any significance.

Chapter Fifteen

reddie lingered in his room as the sun rose into the sky, not because of another night of heavy drinking but because he wanted to pen a note for Georgie.

He needed to stay focused on the farm management. He'd promised his father, and more rested on this than Lord Brookway had any way of knowing.

Still, memory of the empty tree had haunted his sleep for two nights until he woke this morning with the realization he'd left the hollow just as empty as he'd found it.

Georgie could have come hoping for some sign from him with their quarrel more than two days old only to walk away disappointed. He knew his love well enough to recognize finding no evidence he'd returned would only add to the marks against him if the edge of her anger still remained.

Freddie pressed a finger to his temple without realizing the ink would stain his skin until too late.

He rubbed with a cloth hard enough to turn his forehead bright red before he managed to remove the dark shadow, but what explanation could he have given his parents at breakfast? He'd grown a little old for the excuse of practicing his sums, though his tutors never seemed to benefit from his efforts considering how often he so described the cause of frequent ink stains to his parents.

What excuses had Georgie used if questioned about evidence of her many messages to him?

He wished now he'd thought to keep the notes, but secrecy didn't lend to the preservation of such gifts, and the forest made an unhappy storage spot, something he'd discovered when his first cache became the nest for a field mouse.

Georgie had laughed long and hard at his disgruntled expression before explaining nature was ever diligent about making use of what lay discarded. She talked of worms and beetles, tree rot, and fires until his head spun and he could only gape at her, amazed at the depth of knowledge trapped beneath her blond strands.

How he wished she were here now to tell him everything would be fine.

She'd won his heart with her enthusiasm and kind spirit long before he'd reached an age to consider marriage. He'd been happy enough just to bask in her cheer and to learn at her feet. A version of worship it had been, though not of any hero such as society would recognize.

Great naval officers, politicians, or solicitors would have been his mother's wish for capturing his attention, not a wild, uncontrolled forest sprite with little consideration for station or wealth.

Just the memory of Georgie's smile brought warmth to his chest and made him long for this time of distance to be over already.

A cough from the doorway brought the passage of some small moments to his notice at least.

"Your parents are seated at the table."

Peter's dry tone offered little sympathy, his loyalties firmly with the lord and lady as they'd always been.

"Please inform them I'll be down shortly." He suppressed a laugh as the perfect excuse came to him, one he could use in the coming months though he'd do well to make it as often a truth. "I'm recording some of what the men have been showing me so I do not forget anything."

"As you say."

The valet turned sharply and headed off before Freddie could question the man's tone, but it led him to wonder whether Peter had been as taken in by his studious nature as Freddie had always assumed. At the very least, Freddie knew the man had never shared any suspicions with Lady Brookway, or Freddie would have heard about it long before now.

He dismissed the issue from his mind and concentrated on the still blank page in front of him. With his parents waiting, he could not waste another minute. His small bit of freedom had been used up in thoughts of Georgie as often occurred.

When Freddie headed down to join the meal, he had a hastily jotted note tucked in his pocket so it would be with him whenever he found a chance to slip away to the tree. He'd have preferred a well-written, poetic missive, but better a simple note than that she came only to find him absent and all indications she'd been gone from his heart as well.

GEORGIE GLANCED AROUND HER AT the cream of London society and barely managed to suppress a grin.

Lady Whitfeld had been everything Barbara spoke of and more. Her aunt accepted Georgie's unexpected presence with delight and immediately set about putting together what she called a small gathering for the next evening. It would serve as an informal introduction until Georgie could be presented, she'd announced.

Her aunt had more in common with a powerful thunderstorm than the refined lady of society Georgie had been expecting. What memories she had of the Whitfeld household's visit to the farm when she was younger offered little hint of the woman Lady Whitfeld became in her own environment.

How Freddie would laugh to see Georgie now with her hair all up in curls, powder hiding her freckles, and wearing such a pretty dress without a single tear or smear of dirt.

She smoothed a hand down the fine muslin gown they'd settled on for this event. It hung looser on her form in some ways, but the undergarments pinched, and the board thrust in her bodice kept her from leaning forward to enjoy the poetry being read on a small raised area at one end of the ballroom.

More people than the whole farm could boast filled the space beyond the reader. Most of the men and women were only a handful of years older than her though there were some matrons in attendance other than Lady Whitfeld. Georgie wondered at first if they came to enjoy the reading or to chaperone the many white-clad debutantes here.

Soon, she realized few if any of the guests came to listen as she watched one group after another engaging in quiet conversations around her. Or not so quiet as one of the lords seated near Barbara made a keen observation that set those surrounding to laugh.

The other, the marquess if she recalled correctly, responded with a witty comment of his own, pitched to be heard over the laughter and so drowning out the reading all together.

Georgie held back another smile to hear them bickering over her cousin like dogs with a bone. She couldn't wait to tell Freddie all about this. Ever since she realized how she'd misjudged him, the trip to London, though meant as a punishment, had become a romp. She'd have such grand tales to tell when he came for her, and she'd be able to show him just how nicely his wild love could behave in company when given the need. His mother would have little reason to complain.

Her lips pressed together at the thought of his mother and all the trouble Lady Brookway had caused. Why couldn't she be more like Georgie's aunt? Would it be so hard to open her heart and her home to a country cousin?

By some good chance, her laughter at the idea of his mother having common cousins coincided with another humorous comment from the dueling lords, leaving her without the need for an explanation she couldn't give.

Of course her aunt was welcoming. Though she seemed the titled lady now, she'd grown up right alongside Georgie's very own father, a merchant's daughter with strong country ties. It would speak poorly of her aunt if she grew to scorn those who shared her own upbringing.

As the group nearby quieted, Georgie caught a line of poetry that transported her back to the glade and Freddie. She'd been on her rock with him sprawled on a blanket below. He'd quoted some of the poetry assigned by his tutor, including the one now being read.

She'd expected to mock Freddie then, to compare the worthless lines with something more important like the fishing she'd taught him. Instead, the images drawn in his voice captivated her, bringing forth a reverent silence.

A visceral longing for her Freddie hit with the strength of a blow, but she could tell no one of her sorrow. She couldn't even share the memory.

Such was the cost of their secrecy.

As the reader stumbled, Georgie wondered if Freddie had stood in front of a group like this one on any of his trips to London. Had his mother nudged him forward to prove his breeding despite growing up in the country?

Even as the question wandered through her mind, Georgie saw him for once as he suspected all others saw him, not a mature, thinking person, but barely a boy on the cusp of becoming an adult at best.

A mere eighteen, he'd be younger than those who had read so far by at least two years if she had any way of judging. He would be unlikely to be considered grown enough to participate, not in this, nor the search for a match.

No wonder his mother thought him incapable of choosing a bride.

Understanding at a deeper level than before filled her. She'd believed he exaggerated when claiming his father would see him as a child demanding the pretense of adult responsibilities, but Lord Brookway could have seen his interest in her as no greater than for one of his childhood toys.

Surrounded by the very height of London society, the men elegant and well dressed whether or not they had the form to carry it off, she couldn't miss how the Freddie she knew would be scorned for his country styles and practices. These gentlemen didn't toss out lines of poetry for her entertainment between catching fish and sharing picnic lunches. Each one established a presence, adopting a posture and voice that neared commanding. This reading had less to do with enjoying the words and more with a performance designed to introduce potential suitors as much as the balls would allow men to assess the available debutantes.

Her aunt had tried to explain all this, to make it clear how every minute spent in the presence of society meant being assessed and judged, but Georgie had not understood the whole of it until just now. How easy it would be to think she and Freddie just played at being adults in their plans for a future. They'd never sought the company of others or any situation where their care for each other could be tested.

She stumbled on the last, her sharply indrawn breath attracting attention for a moment before some other pulled the focus away again.

They had been so shielded in their isolation, too protected as she could see now.

Though neither she nor Freddie sought the test, as soon as they let real world concerns intrude on their idyll, like some poem brought under the harsh light of reality, their perfect joy had fallen to pieces.

It hurt all the more to know she had been the one to bring about their downfall.

Freddie had started the process by seeking his parents' validation, the act which raised his mother's interest, but Georgie should have expected such a reaction. She might have been raised in the country, but her father had read many a letter from his sister over the years. Talk in London involved little else but marriage and the seeking of same.

While Father's paper had contained other news, that her aunt, even before Cousin Barbara grew of age, would think to share such a thing only pointed to it being a driving force of society. Its powers remained whether here in the city or in the outer reaches where those with titles still maintained the standards of nobility.

Such thoughts soured her mood and made even the most talented of the readers an annoying babble in her ears.

She'd gone through life unhindered by propriety and expectation, her wild nature met with smiling indulgence and no thought to tightening her bridle so she'd learn a better way. Perhaps her father considered it a kindness, or more likely he suspected she had the intelligence to see her own foolishness when given time. If only she'd seen it earlier. If she'd told her father of Freddie, introduced them properly, questions of age and suitability might never have come to be.

Not that those questions had regardless.

Supposition, both Charlotte's and her father's, governed his opinion, and not to her benefit. Where she should have sought his wisdom, instead she earned exile through withholding the truth and tempting fate with her teasing.

It seemed so clear now, here, where she could do nothing but pray Freddie would see beyond her anger to the ignorance beneath and seek to correct her mistake no matter how far she'd fled.

A spattering of applause jerked Georgie from her thoughts to discover the evening's entertainments complete. She had no memory of the last few readers, nor even of the efforts made by Barbara's suitors, efforts which fell on deaf ears if she were any judge.

Once again, her cousin's foolishness informed her own.

Barbara clearly remained besotted, and Georgie could not imagine Lord Aubrey any less so. Like him, her Freddie would not be so quick to cast her aside. What confidence she lacked in her own wisdom she knew he contained fourfold.

He'd been the one to move toward securing their future, and whatever the consequences of his decision, it had been the right one. Had he no care for her, he would not have put forth the effort to prove his maturity.

In considering the two of them, if any had been wanton, on her head the label found firmer seating. She'd been willing to give her kisses without consideration to anything beyond, exactly what her father and sister had feared even though they were confused about her companion.

Barbara touched her arm to indicate they should rise and move to where a table of delicacies had been set for the guests to sup.

Finally, Georgie understood her role in all this. She would put on a good face and keep Barbara too distracted to settle on any one suitor. Surely entertaining her country cousin would prove important enough to delay any decision on Barbara's part.

In this, she would earn some good will as she kept Barbara unencumbered until such time as Lord Aubrey appeared to state his claim. If it served a distraction for her own cares as well, all the better. Freddie needed time to discover where she'd gone and to decide how best to announce his suit.

Cheered, she let a broad smile pull at her lips, but not so broad as to be mistaken for a grin.

"Of course," she said, answering the unspoken question. "I'm positively famished after such a grand event. I cannot imagine a whole season of the same, and certainly not with such attentive admirers as you've collected. Our home must have seemed so dull in comparison."

Chapter Sixteen

When dawn broke on the second day, despite the poetry reading running well into the early hours of the morning, Georgie came awake with the habits of a lifetime. The first thought to leap into her mind was of Freddie.

How could she leave him to wonder at her absence?

Georgie pushed aside the covers and crossed to where a desk and writing supplies stood. The words came as easily as milking a cow. She poured her new understanding out to Freddie along with her regrets about their argument, a burden she hadn't recognized lifting from her shoulders.

Once she'd finished, though, Georgie realized she couldn't very well post the letter addressed to him. What if he received it in front of his mother? Would he be expected to read the message aloud as was the tradition in her home? Nor did she have any confidant who could be trusted to deliver it privately for her. Their secrecy punished them in yet another way.

She stared morosely at the paper, but soon her hope-filled nature reasserted itself and she tucked the letter into the drawer containing her country clothes. No one would disturb it there.

Freddie knew her far too well to think she'd dismissed him so easily from her mind. He would find a way to discover her whereabouts, and he would come for her, letter or no letter.

Georgie realized she'd begun to pace back and forth, the linen nightdress billowing about her. She'd never been good at waiting, patience not listed among her virtues, and yet she found herself in the untenable position of having to wait for everything.

She could not go down again until an appropriate hour to be seen as awake.

Mr. Simmons had carefully ushered Georgie back to her room the previous morning, the butler horrified to find her in the kitchen though the other Whitfeld servants had been welcoming. Despite his stern exterior and strong sense of propriety, she could tell he was only trying his best to help her fit in. Everyone had been so patient with her country ways.

In the case of Barbara, she must keep her cousin busy until Lord Aubrey appeared and put an end to her cousin's miseries. And of course, she waited until Freddie came up from the country to claim her as his own.

The thought provoked a bout of delighted laughter she stifled too late, but in the dying echoes of the sound, she finally heard the noise she'd been waiting for, that of Barbara's door opening and footsteps heading toward the stairs.

Sarah must have entered without Georgie noticing because surely she'd stay to see Barbara prepared for the morning and perhaps even come help Georgie next.

That thought kept her gaze on the door for a while before she decided Sarah must be under the mistaken belief she had yet to rise and didn't want to disturb her.

Rather than wait for however long the maids decided was appropriate, Georgie set about pulling on one of the dresses Barbara had shifted from her own wardrobe to the one in this room. Georgie had to choose a simple design with ties both in the front and in the back low enough for her to reach on her own. Somehow, she doubted such needs drove Barbara to select this dress in the first place, but she was grateful at whatever had led to this purchase. It seemed the act of adornment required more decisions here in London than dressing for a week would require back home.

Still, she only went down to breakfast. As yesterday had shown, she'd be expected to change no less than two other times, and with this choice likely to be an incorrect one, Lady Whitfeld would be sure to send someone to help her.

When Georgie moved to follow the sounds she'd heard once reaching the bottom of the stairs, Mr. Simmons appeared as if out of thin air. His expression held restrained disapproval, something Georgie felt sure she'd soon become accustomed to.

"The breakfast room is this way, Miss Georgiana. If you would follow me."

Georgie narrowed her gaze as she studied the man, seeing a glimmer of humor hidden beneath his refinement.

"What is it? Did I choose the wrong dress after all?"

Even as the question came out, she wished it unspoken. Had she learned nothing from his response to her visit to the kitchens?

His eyebrows rose, and he looked her over, apparently believing her question a command.

"You are properly dressed for a morning in," he said in a level tone.

She frowned at him, but waved for the butler to lead her to the correct room, unable to deduce what had provoked his entertainment if not her appearance.

He opened a door in the opposite direction from where she'd been headed, the town house much more complicated than her home, and with stairs she wasn't supposed to use.

She half expected to find the room empty what with the noise coming from the back of the house, but Lady Whitfeld sat at her place with hands folded in her lap.

Though a vision of peace, Georgie's eyes narrowed again as she took in the tension in her aunt's shoulders. She'd have been concerned if not for the smile twitching at the corners of Lady Whitfeld's mouth.

"Ah, there you are, Georgiana. Take a seat. The tea will be steeped shortly. I've sent Lord Whitfeld to fetch them."

The pieces fell together with her aunt's odd phrasing, and Georgie laughed aloud. "He's arrived then?"

Lady Whitfeld gave her a tight look. "Just whom were you expecting?"

The attempt at a severe tone failed due to a twinkle in her aunt's eyes.

"Lord Aubrey, of course. He was persistent enough before, and Barbara's a fool to think a simple wagon ride enough to keep him from her. More likely any delays came of his injuries."

Lady Whitfeld shook her head, a frown pinching her brows, but she did not ask what Georgie meant, instead saying only, "Have the courtesy to pretend surprise when they come to the table, my dear. Indulge me in this."

Georgie slipped into her place with a smile. "Of course."

Her aunt had no way of knowing her relief. She no longer had to pretend she expected Barbara to bring her about everywhere as she had been to prevent her cousin's acceptance of an ill-considered alliance to any one of her other suitors. And now Georgie had only one more event to wait on. She suspected her love might have a harder time of it what with Lord Aubrey having already been known to her father and Freddie a stranger.

She hoped it didn't take him too long, though.

"Frederick."

He froze at the sound of his name, only one foot in the breakfast room and his mind on what the men had shown him the previous day. A quick glance revealed Lord Brookway had yet to make an appearance, or perhaps he'd eaten even earlier as he'd mentioned some business in the village.

"Good morning, Mother."

Though he'd attempted to keep his tone neutral, from the tightening of his mother's features, some of his strain must have been apparent.

Lady Brookway placed both hands on the table, fingers spread wide. "Your father says I have been putting too much pressure on you. He thinks the first signs of maturity something to celebrate rather than plan against."

He could tell the words required some effort, but could think of no way to distract his mother from this uncomfortable conversation. To his mind, the so-called first signs held exactly the meaning she had conferred on them. Her problem came in not knowing the target of his intentions.

One of the servants entered the room, a fact he learned because his mother made an irritated gestured that was followed by a quiet, "Yes, my lady," from behind him.

"Sit down. I can't think with you looming above me."

Her sharp tone reminded him of how he'd stood through most of their previous encounters on this subject. Freddie took his seat, hoping compliance would shorten the confrontation and bring back the servant with food.

She gave him a tight smile as if able to read his thoughts.

"I have yet to send the invitations, so bowing to your father's wishes, I'll delay until winter. It means only we won't be able to send you men off on a hunt if you get too restless, not if we don't want the whole manor damp and muddy."

Freddie stared at her in confusion. "What invitations?"

He could have cursed his quick tongue a moment later when he realized she could take the question as a sign of interest.

"I had the grand idea of a country party. With you being so busy here on the farm and your father unable to spare the time for a trip to London regardless, I thought I could invite a select company including, of course, some of your potential brides. They'd come for a week visit to show off the property, enjoy some entertainment, and give you the chance to get to know one another."

The confusion might have lifted, but his stare did not. "You want to bring people here?"

In all the time they'd been in the country, his mother had shown no interest in such activities.

Lady Brookway gave a delicate shrug. "It has come to my attention you intend to make your life out here despite my hopes. If that's to be the case, it seems I have little choice but to help improve the society in this far-flung corner."

"It's hardly so far, Mother. London is less than a day's journey by horseback."

The comment drew a sour smile. "And yet it seems too much of an effort for your father, and now you, to make the trip."

She made a dismissive wave of one hand and Freddie wondered if another servant had made the attempt to provide sustenance when she continued, "The physical distance is less of an issue than the lack of society. I'd thought perhaps the Pendletons might make overtures now with the young baron taking up residence. His position is much stronger than ours as you know. But they've shown no such inclination, having been all but recluses since their arrival."

Freddie smiled as memory of dancing with Georgie rose in his mind. "The Lady Pendleton has taken to offering dancing lessons to the local females. Perhaps she intends a ball?"

His mother's gaze grew sharp. "Just how did you come by this information?"

Recognizing the trap too late, Freddie attempted a wave much like her earlier one. "I can't recall. Perhaps down at the tavern. It seems she's used some of her manservants to stand in for gentlemen in the lessons."

Lady Brookway sank back into her chair with a sigh. "Then she's teaching commoners. More likely something to entertain her in the dull country than any true hope." She straightened again. "And I'm not comfortable with all the time you spend down at the tavern, Frederick. You need to exercise more of an effort to meet with those of your own station."

A chuckle came from his lips at her statement. "Father spends time there as well. Do you chastise him? And just whom would you have me speak with beyond yourself and Father? As you said, the Pendletons are only recently come and have been secluded since they arrived last year."

She put a hand to her forehead as if the need to come up with appropriate companions proved exhausting. "Then you should have no objection to me inviting suitable persons down from London. Perhaps even the Pendletons would deign to leave their wedding hermitage for the occasion."

The idea had some merit after all if she planned to invite those already here.

Freddie smiled at the thought of pretending an instant interest in Miss Georgiana Ferrier to mask their secret friendship. "You could invite the local landholders as well, giving us more contact with those nearby than visits to the tavern you seem to abhor."

Lady Brookway released a laugh she would normally condemn, her derision obvious without speaking. She did not, however, choose to hold back her words as she said, "Few of the landholders, as you so kindly name them, are people of significance. Sure, they may possess some small property, but it is filled with smelly animals while those same landholders must perform work best left to the servants."

Freddie let go of any reality in which his mother welcomed Georgie into her home with the slightest acceptance. On the heels of his realization came the understanding that her opinion mattered less than he would have thought when compared to having Georgie at his side.

He released a short laugh of his own.

"Just what is it you think my father and I have been about? It's not all papers and commands. Why, Lord Pendleton is well known as somewhat of an innovative genius in matters of farmland management. Think you he came by this skill merely sitting in his study?"

She had no answer beyond a scowl, but he shouldn't have expected one. He might love her for being his mother, but he had few illusions about her opinions. Hadn't he spent his childhood bound by those very restrictions and hating every moment of it?

"It's just as well I hadn't made arrangements for you to meet one of the young ladies I'd selected. The way you talk, she'd run back to London on her own two feet rather than chance being sequestered out here with nothing to discuss but the oil extracted from wool."

If she'd meant to provoke contrition, her arrow went far from the mark as Freddie stared at her with his mouth hanging open. He'd never thought she knew even so much as that they produced wool on their lands, much less the value of the oil.

"What? You think I'm deaf to all you've been discussing with your father at times when a more refined topic would be much welcomed? I know exactly what I'd be sentencing some poor young girl to. It's why I tried my best to see you equipped for a position in London where you could mingle with your own class as you do when we visit my family."

A cough from behind him brought her head up with an irritated look.

"Yes. Come ahead," she told the servant before returning her attention to Freddie. "We might as well eat since there's nothing else to be done about you. You're well past the age of refinement. I have half a mind to track down those tutors of yours and give them a talking to. They've clearly failed in the intent of their task, though from what your father has said, you picked up the lessons well enough. Mathematics, philosophy, and law are worth so much more in London than out here where you have only sheep to listen to your pondering."

"Ah, but they make such good listeners."

His comment startled Lady Brookway at first then drew a reluctant smile across her features.

"I suppose I should be grateful you haven't forgotten how to think, though I'd had a much different audience in mind for you."

Accepting the hidden apology in her words, Freddie shrugged. "I suspect I have turned out other than your expectations in many aspects, but I am still your son."

"You are at that. There are other mothers who would be hard pressed to claim a moment of their children's time between the wild behaviors. You at least plan to sow your wild oats into the rich soil and will leave neither debts nor illegitimate children in your wake."

Freddie chose to devote his attention to the steaming porridge placed before him rather than attempt a reply. His thoughts, however, were not so easily turned aside as they raced to the one woman he'd be happy to sow children with. Had she found the note he'd slipped into the tree at the midday break for a meal yesterday? Surely she would not be clinging to her anger still.

LORD WHITFELD RETURNED FIRST, A cheerful smile on his face. His hands rubbed together much like Georgie had seen her father do when coming back from a particularly successful purchase.

Georgie laughed at the sight of it then had to explain, half expecting her uncle to be upset by the comparison.

He only chuckled. "If God has the odd notion to give you daughters, Georgiana, you will understand this moment as only a parent having successfully disposed of a daughter can.

"Disposing of me? Are you as desperate as all that to have me gone?"

Georgie looked beyond her uncle to see Barbara on Lord Aubrey's arm, both wearing smiles embarrassing to observe.

"Now, Barbara, you know full well your father was just making fun. We hope to see you quite often even once you marry. Don't we, dear?"

Lord Whitfeld aimed a wink at Georgie before turning to face his daughter. "Of course we do. Life would be ever so dull without you to stir things up. But you're not married yet, and you have some work to do before your wedding comes about."

Barbara tugged Lord Aubrey around the table and they both sat. Only then did she answer her father with, "Yes. Yes. I have said I will speak with each and every one of the suitors who plied for my hand. I'm just grateful I held firm against them."

Her mother gave a sharp laugh. "Held firm? Is that what it's called when you could barely show any interest?" She turned to Lord Aubrey, pressing a hand to his arm. "We had no idea she was pining for another in all her running about or we'd have better understood her refusal to choose just one."

"I had no idea either," Lord Aubrey replied. "Less of an idea than you might suppose. But fate saw its way to ensure we found each other despite a rocky beginning, and I, for one, have little intention of letting her out of my sight."

Barbara tapped his arm with the handle of her knife. "Except you will. You're taking Georgie off to meet Isabella, remember?"

Georgie had been enjoying the banter even though it made her long for Freddie's company, but she had to speak up at the last. "I'm fine with staying here, Barbara. I'm not some child who needs a nanny. I can help Sarah with her duties."

"You will not, Georgiana Ferrier. A guest of my house and a member of my family? You will not be working with the servants." Her aunt glanced toward Lord Aubrey as though expecting him to spread unsightly gossip, or so it seemed.

Lord Aubrey laughed, clearly reading the same into the look. "You forget I've seen both of these young women barefoot in the field. This is nothing new to me."

"Barefoot?" Lady Whitfeld's voice grew faint on the word, and she seemed to pale.

"It's only so I can begin the arduous task of informing my other suitors," Barbara broke in before her mother fainted from distress. "I think it shall be tedious here with all the comings and goings and long waits between. I couldn't imagine forcing such a thing on you, nor can my dear Aubrey be present. You'll like Isabella. The two of you should suit nicely."

Georgie read the entreaty in Barbara's gaze though whether to prevent her aunt from succumbing to hysterics or to remove Lord Aubrey from the situation, Georgie couldn't tell.

Swallowing back a sigh, she said only, "If your sister is half as entertaining as you have proved to be, Lord Aubrey, I'm sure I'll be delighted to meet her."

The grateful look Barbara sent her way more than made up for the annoyance of being shunted off as though she could not be counted upon to make herself scarce. Or maybe there she'd found the heart of the problem. Her aunt worried as to just what she'd discover for entertainment.

"But there's no need to rush away," Barbara added. "We have time enough for a leisurely breakfast. While my cousin might know you quite well, Aubrey, my parents have only just become acquainted with the man who seeks to marry their daughter."

"Not seeks. Will."

He softened the correction with a smile of such affection Georgie glanced down at her plate rather than intrude. She allowed a slight smile to curl her own lips at the proof of their connection. Now if only her Freddie would appear and make the claim for her hand. No matter what distractions her aunt and cousin proposed, he was never far from her thoughts, and she'd be sorely tried if she must wait for the chance to speak with Freddie and clear their disagreement until her father decided she had absorbed enough culturing to return home.

Chapter Seventeen

hen they finally climbed into Aubrey's well-sprung carriage, much of the day had passed.

Even in Georgie's thoughts, his name sounded bare, but he'd asked her as part of the family to call him by no more than his given name. She'd never expected to spend her time with anyone owning to such a title beyond Barbara. Even her aunt seemed more Lady Whitfeld than a sister to Georgie's father with the way she presented herself.

The coachman cracked a whip over the heads of two magnificent beasts her father would envy. Off they went, sending her into the heart of the titled class without even the friendly face of her cousin to comfort her. She'd much rather have scrubbed pots with Sarah, if the lady's maid even performed such tasks in London.

Aubrey leaned forward to catch hold of one of her hands, his familiarity reminding her of all the time he'd spent in her company over the summer and making a mockery of her isolation.

"You might think this a ploy to keep you separate from Lady Whitfeld after her response this morning, or perhaps to keep me separate." He laughed once but then his face took on a serious cast. "While I can't but think the goal part of Barbara's planning, the truth of the matter is my eagerness is not altogether unselfish."

Georgie shrugged. "You can't be planning to pry loose all of Barbara's secrets. You've spent almost as much time in her presence as I have. Her last visit before this one, I was only a child."

Her comment brought a smile to his lips even as he shook his head. "As much as the thought attracts, I'm afraid I must learn to seek what knowledge I desire from the source. And I suspect she'll be informative at last."

"I expect you're right. She did nothing but bemoan your loss until now."

Georgie slapped a hand across her betraying mouth too late to hold back what she hadn't realized she'd known.

"It seems you have some secrets after all, but not the sort I have any need of. She left me with little doubt of her affections." As much as his words possessed a level tone, the splash of red on his cheeks gave him away.

Georgie only grinned, keeping her answer confined even as she appreciated the confirmation they had indeed explored kisses as she'd proposed. His look she'd caught a time or two on Freddie's face.

The view outside the carriage window had sudden allure, and she stared at the many houses, all so close together, slipping by. Surely he would excuse her lack of city experience and not look close enough to see water gathering in her eyes that had nothing to do with the wind of their passage, certainly not at this sedate pace.

Once or twice a year, Freddie had come up here with his parents. He'd gone to poetry readings most likely even if he'd be too young to read at one, and he'd told her of theatrical performances, elegant shows of illusion, and all sorts of fancy things the like of which they didn't have in the country. How could she suppose kisses would be enough to keep him at her side?

The question struck hard, but not in the manner she'd expected.

Hadn't she impressed many a gentleman and lady at the reading? Lady Whitfeld told her so before they all retired for the night. Dress her up in one of Barbara's gowns and she could be as much a member of society for all anyone knew.

Freddie should be proud to have caught her attention so strongly. He'd have nothing to be embarrassed about should he wish to come to London on occasion. She wouldn't like to live here, but to visit seemed a reasonable plan.

After all, she didn't intend to have Freddie cast off his own life when they bound theirs together. It would no more be fair to him than for him to expect her to move to London and live always in one of these houses pressed together where, no matter how fancy the carriage, at this speed they'd hardly cross any distance at all.

Aubrey coughed once, drawing her attention back to him.

"We haven't much time before we reach my parents' town house. I need to explain why it's so important you meet Isabella."

"Your sister? Is she ill? If so, I'm afraid you have collected the wrong Ferrier. What little I know of herbs and such I learned from Charlotte, and only a small part of her teachings found root." She frowned, putting a hand on his knee to comfort. "I wish I could offer you more."

He waved both hands to stop her, a smile all too close to a grin on his features. "No, nothing like that. Isabella is quite healthy. Always has been as far back as I remember."

"Then what is it?" If anything, her frown deepened and gave the warning twinge of a headache. Everything seemed so complicated here.

He fell silent, staring out the same window she'd contemplated not so long ago.

Speaking to the outdoors, he said, "She could serve to have a nice, outgoing friend like you. She's good-hearted and quite engaging when she puts down her guard, but I fear she'll never find happiness. Her nature is shy outside of the family, especially when in the presence of gentlemen. Since your father sent you up here to finish out the season, I wondered if you would help me with her. I suspect we will be attending all the same events in any case."

Georgie felt a twinge of gratitude that he hadn't chosen to look at her while making his pronouncement. The expression on her face felt unlikely to inspire confidence. She had little interest in a season, or even a partial one, and no need for traditional success what with Freddie sure to come and claim her hand any day now.

"I know this is a huge responsibility to put on your young shoulders. I don't expect a miracle, mind you. Just if you could spread one measure of your cheerful nature in my sister's direction, I feel sure she'd find the confidence to make her own way."

Whether from the hint of desperation in his tone or the memory of how he'd treated all of them as equals despite their different stations, Georgie could feel herself weakening. What harm could it do if all he wanted was a companion for his little sister? He'd been honest from the start so why would he bend words to mask his sister's true nature now.

"I'll do it," she exclaimed, a bit too loudly for the semi-enclosed space. "Do my best to help your sister, that is," Georgie added in a softer tone.

After all, she needed something to keep her busy until Freddie discovered what happened and came to collect her. She couldn't very well expect Barbara to devote every minute to her entertainment, nor would she scorn her aunt's hospitality by finding work among the servants as she would have at home.

Georgie released a light laugh at the thought, and she could see Aubrey taking it as a sign she warmed to the idea.

At home, should she find herself with an idle moment, she'd be off into the woods to drop a note for Freddie or to check for one from him, and of course, for the chance they'd arrive at the same time all unbidden to steal an hour or two at each other's side.

A flash of guilt went through her at the memory. When she should have left a message, she'd stumbled over the words and given up. Yet she'd condemned him for being no more eloquent than she was.

If Georgie took the bare hollow for a sign of his disaffection when she still believed him false, how much worse must it have been when he arrived to find it similarly vacant? His understanding of her anger had no falsehood about it. How her silence on the matter must have increased the harm, especially as days went by with no word.

She lifted a hand to the curtain framing the carriage window and stared at the sights much like how Barbara had sought comfort in the window fabric of her room when she'd all but given up on Aubrey.

Georgie saw nothing of the streets beyond. Instead, her vision had turned inward, tormenting her with images of Freddie and how each time he went to their special place to find no sign of her his loss would burn all the hotter. She prayed he'd seek word even should her father learn the truth. Better to face her father's anger than to have Freddie think her so enraged she cut every communication between them for all of time.

AᴜBREY SWEPT PAST THE BUTLER with Georgie's hand wrapped around his arm. She tried to take in the house despite the speed of their passage.

Barbara's residence had been elegant enough, but Georgie didn't need to be told the artwork presented here had a much longer history. Nor did she miss the glimpse of one of the newest pianofortes as they passed a room set aside solely for musical events from what she could tell.

Head spinning, Georgie wondered what she could possibly do to make a young woman who grew up among such finery comfortable in the presence of society. She'd been so proud of how she'd carried off the poetry reading, but what if her success had been either reflected glory from Barbara or simple kindness when the truth would show her a bumbling fool?

Laughter escaped the room at the end, bright light streaming out the door. The scent of blooming flowers teased her nose.

At least here she'd feel more comfortable, though she doubted the flowers on display were the same as those she'd collected in the forest, or even, perhaps, the like of those Freddie had once stolen from his mother's garden to give to her.

The memory eased her discomfort enough so when they stepped through the door, Georgie was able to smile.

"Aubrey, there you are. We've been waiting to hear of your adventures in the country. Imagine our surprise to learn you'd begged an early breakfast and escaped while we were still abed."

"Isabella—"

Georgie pulled her hand free as she took in the smiling young woman clearly at ease with her company in this intimate sitting room. She opened her mouth to cry foul at Aubrey's description of his sister, her estimation of his honesty dropping, when the sister in question caught sight of Georgie where previously Aubrey must have blocked the view.

All animation drained from Isabella's expression, and her gaze dropped to the embroidery in her lap.

Georgie felt as much as heard the soft sigh from Aubrey, so close were they standing, before he straightened his shoulders.

"Georgiana, let me introduce to you my family. Here are my sisters Adelaide and Susan with their husbands Charles and Philip. And finally, Isabella."

Even before he turned back to his youngest sister, ignoring the surprise on his sisters' faces at the familiarity in the introduction, Georgie understood what had happened. Isabella had been safely ensconced with her family and so enjoying herself, as animated as Aubrey had claimed her, when Georgie had intruded and taken all her comfort away.

A wash of sympathy raced through Georgie. She'd felt much the same when introduced to this house with all its finery, self-consciousness stealing her normal confidence.

"And this is Miss Georgiana Ferrier, lately from the country."

"Really, Aubrey," Susan said, but Adelaide hushed her before she could say anything more.

In the awkward silence that followed, Aubrey gestured for Georgie to take the chair on Isabella's open side.

"I'll call for more tea," he said.

With that, Aubrey strode from the room, leaving the six of them to seek some topic of conversation they might all enjoy.

Georgie had no idea what might entertain these strangers, but it had been clear her position in life had been discovered with the aborted protest. She didn't think they'd take kindly to her directing the conversation no matter how much the silence seemed to press.

She glanced at the first woman Aubrey introduced, assuming her the oldest from the order he'd used, but Adelaide's brow furrowed as their gazes crossed. Georgie realized even if she'd wanted to speak with the woman, she had no idea of the proper address. At least they knew from her introduction, but Aubrey had neglected the courtesy either because he was too accustomed to his family or with some grander purpose in mind she could not fathom.

Again, the sense of being out of place pressed down on Georgie, and like Isabella, she dropped her gaze to her lap where her fingers had twisted together to form a complicated knot.

When would Aubrey return? He seemed to be taking forever, further indicating this a plan, but how could he hope to win anything from her grand success in turning a laughing company into one of awkward silence?

Georgie looked toward the door, hoping she'd been mistaken and he would return right then. No one appeared, neither the one person in the household she knew nor a servant with more tea. At least the act of serving would have offered something to break the tension.

About to suggest she see what was taking so long, Georgie swallowed the comment, suddenly sure it would be seen as a criticism rather than the desperate move of an awkward guest. She settled back into her chair with a sigh, and as she did so, the intricate design on the embroidery in Isabella's lap caught her attention.

"What beautiful work," she said without thinking. "I could never do something so fine. Why, my sister Charlotte is always demanding I redo half my stitches when I set to repairing the latest tears I've made in my clothing."

Georgie felt the weight of attention too late to call back her words. All three women now stared at her with a mixture of curiosity and concern. The men had moved off to one side to discuss something in quiet voices that rumbled beneath the return to silence.

It took a moment for the meaning they'd found in her comment to catch up to Georgie.

How much worse could it be to discuss simple sewing than to work amongst the servants? She remembered her aunt's censure when Barbara spoke of repairing the perfectly good dress Lady Whitfeld had destroyed rather than chance it tainting anything in the house.

Or perhaps the need for such repairs caught their attention.

She shrank into the chair, wishing she'd never let first Barbara then Aubrey talk her into this, but even as her spine pressed against the cushioned back, Georgie pushed herself straight.

She'd never been embarrassed of her family before, and she had no intention of starting now.

"I'm sorry if my manners seem a bit rude. I'm just up from the country, as Aubrey said, where I live on my father's farm. My cousin, Lady Barbara Whitfeld, asked Aubrey to introduce us with the hopes we would get along famously."

Georgie stopped before she said anything to condemn Aubrey's behavior, but where she'd half expected the three sisters to up and leave rather than spend another minute in her presence, Susan caught her gaze with the first smile she'd been offered since arriving.

"Lady Barbara? She seemed so nice, but there were all sorts of things said when she disappeared so abruptly. Isabella, here, is her staunchest defendant."

A tentative hand brushed the top of Georgie's arm. "So he found her after all?"

From the creak of chairs, both of the older sisters leaned in to hear Georgie's answer.

"Yes. She'd come to spend some time with her uncle, and me and my sisters of course. He met her there in the field."

She caught the edge of a shocked look on Adelaide's face, but her focus remained on Isabella.

The young woman seemed transformed, her eyes alight with secret knowledge and a blush making a becoming splash of color on her cheeks.

"I knew he would," Isabella said, her hands clasped over her embroidery. "Ever since she cut him in the park, he'd been obsessed. Though he said he wasn't searching for her still, I could tell he wanted to do nothing but."

"And I wasn't searching for her," Aubrey said as he returned to the room having caught the last. "I'd given her up for a sorry wager only to be captivated by a farm girl in a field."

"Really, Aubrey."

This time Adelaide spoke the scold, but he only laughed.

"Fate drove my horse, placing me where Georgie and her sisters had taken Lady Barbara berry picking. How was I to know it was the same fine lady my little sister thought so highly of?"

Though it was apparent Isabella knew more about his attachment than any of her sisters, Georgie listened with as much interest as the rest. She'd pieced together some of the story from offhand comments Sarah and Barbara both had made, but it still seemed a fantastical tale, and one he had apparently not seen fit to share with his relatives before approaching Georgie's uncle to set his claim.

From such a poor start, the sisters soon warmed to Georgie, welcoming her into the family in place of Barbara, whose activities Aubrey only hinted at and Georgie added nothing that might fuel rumors. From what Susan had mentioned, her cousin had already been a subject of the gossips a little too much for Georgie's liking. Besides, they had no limit to topics now that they had begun speaking from Aubrey's adventures in love to the two older sisters sharing their own trials, much to the consternation of their respective spouses. Even so, Georgie detected an indulgence beneath the glares of each of the other men.

They returned to the subject of Isabella's embroidery, then, something she had quite a talent for. Georgie answered curious questions about her own home life as well, it being as exotic to these ladies as their home seemed to her.

A laugh came forth at Susan's expression when Georgie described feeding the pigs. It echoed around the room much like the laughter she'd heard spilling out the door when first approaching. Georgie reflected on how the joyful event had been fully restored despite her intrusion, happy Aubrey's prediction had become truth. If she could help Isabella the slightest amount, at least her time of waiting would not be wasted.

Chapter Eighteen

You worked hard today, Mr. Hathwell. You deserve to stand us a round at the tavern."

Freddie laughed with the others on the phrasing, but the idea had merit. He'd left his mother at breakfast and gone to work, taking only a short break midday to slip off and check the tree. The note lay where he'd set it, undisturbed except for the signs of nibbles from some small animal. Better he work his frustrations off in the fields each day than spend it arguing with his parents.

Four full days had passed since he'd last spoken with Georgie, not so many by most measures, but with a disagreement standing between them, she'd be sure to seek him out once her anger cooled. Her cousin's visit must have kept her to the farm as it had before, preventing her from coming to look for him, and even from taking a moment to check the tree.

He told himself to be patient when he wanted nothing more than to ride up to her farmhouse and demand she speak to him. A smile teased his cheek at the thought of her father's response were he to attempt such a forward approach.

She'd kept their friendship secret from her family much as he had his. He'd have to explain how they'd come to know each other even before revealing his intentions.

For a minute, that seemed the best way to overcome their situation. But only for a minute.

His mother would be just as likely to offer to buy him off should Georgie's father come banging on the manor door demanding recompense, and in no way would such an introduction ease the difficulties they already faced.

"Looks to have deeper things on his mind, boys. We'll be seeing you in the morning, my lord."

Freddie focused on the faces around him, realizing his thoughts had wandered to Georgie much as they had throughout the day. He missed her, but he could do nothing until she found a free moment to retrieve his note and leave one of her own.

"I think a trip to the village is just what I'm needing tonight to wipe the cobwebs from my mind."

"Cobwebs is it?" the youngest of the men said with a wink. "That's not what we would call our girls, but you titled folks have a language all of your own."

The curse Freddie voiced as he felt a flush rise to color his cheeks did little to deflect the charge. "If I had a lady waiting, why would I spend so much time with the likes of you?"

They could have taken offense, but he'd proved himself enough of late they only shook their heads and laughed.

"Come along then," one of them said, waving an arm in encouragement. "If your lady isn't waiting, better you stay out of her reach until her anger cools."

The advice seemed much more reasonable than his half plan to storm the Ferrier property in search of news, and he wouldn't have to change his clothing to get some food in his rumbling belly either.

They laughed and joked all the way down to the village, making a significant walk into no time at all, though perhaps some of the physical exercise Freddie had been undergoing also had an impact.

He felt at home among this rough company. His mother might condemn it, and had, but these men understood how to work hard for a living unlike many of those titled folks he'd met in London. When they played, they did so with equal focus and attention.

He knew all was not lightness and joy in their lives, but then neither was the life of a man of property and position. None of the Brookway workers showed up after services for a bag of grain or loaf of bread to keep their bellies from touching their spines, and he swore to be part of the cause for that comfort. He would learn the ways of the land, and he would manage the properties so they remained prosperous and became more so.

One of the men knocked him on his shoulder. "Hear, hear," the man said with a wide grin.

Again, heat flooded Freddie's face as he realized he'd spoken the last aloud.

"It's a good man to think not just on his own wealth but on those who make that wealth happen," one of the others said, an older man with enough lines in his face to show times had not always been good.

Freddie glanced up to see the tavern nearby, a grateful happenstance as he didn't know whether he should protest the man's statement or confirm it. He'd seen himself how much work went into ensuring the land produced and the sheep grew thick coats. He'd earned the men's approval by sloughing off his jacket and working alongside them so knew only too well the labor involved.

At the same time, he sought a broader meaning to his studies, not the day-to-day labors but the choices to make that would keep the whole of the manor lands productive. Had he the words, he might have said as how the two formed a balance of labors, one where both those who worked the land and those who managed it were necessary for success.

Even that much would be met by scorn from some of the nobility who saw no value in commoners. Those believed the farm workers possessed such small wisdom that without a guiding hand, they'd starve to death in a grain-filled field.

He shook his head, his mind bringing forth country situations most who held such opinions would understand no better than they did the way of the farm worker.

"Fair enough," the man closest said. "I don't suppose we can expect you to stand every round just because you came with us from the field."

Freddie blinked in confusion, realizing his motion had been taken as an answer for a question he hadn't heard. Still, he wouldn't have much in his purse if he did stand every round, and he had need of funds what with his upcoming nuptials.

Well, if Georgie would ever get the chance to speak with him again.

On such a morose thought, he dropped onto a bench that had seen better days but which proved sturdy.

A tankard of bitter beer thudded down in front of him, the pale liquid splashing over the sides and into the woodgrain of the table.

He glanced at the tavern maid, and she shrugged a shoulder toward the bar. "He stood you for this one, my lord."

Freddie raised the tankard in thanks, smiling at the oldest worker who most likely offered it in gratitude for his silence on the matter of who produced the Brookway income.

They'd grown comfortable in his presence, but such a comment before the wrong ears could cause trouble. He supposed he should be happy they considered trouble a bad thing. It offered a further sign that, though not wealthy in comparison to some, their holdings were firm.

"Oh, aye. And off they went to London, that Ferrier cousin. Heard she come in some fancy carriage with a coat of arms, but she returned back in Thomas's wagon, bumping and rattling the whole way. You should have heard him tell all about the butler who almost tripped on the stairs as he rushed down to tell Thomas to move along with his nose stuck so high in the air the hair of his nostrils quivered."

Raising his tankard to mask the move, Freddie glanced toward the nearby table. Her cousin had left already from what he'd just heard, gone back to London.

They didn't look like Ferrier servants, but then he'd never met any of them so how could he tell? It didn't matter. They'd have no reason to tell tales, not when this Thomas seemed to have better ones.

He wondered how her cousin had come to arrive in a crested carriage in the first place. Maybe she had a titled friend who lent her the equipage or perhaps dropped her at the farm on the way to some other event like the week his mother had been talking about.

Freddie almost laughed at the thought of some London butler faced with a vehicle used to transport grain and farm animals to market more often than trips up to the city. Even then, such a wagon would be unlikely to seek those parts where the residents were wealthy enough to have butlers. It would seem Georgie's cousin came from wealthy merchant stock, though he half-remembered Georgie mentioning a London merchant grandfather, so of course she would have.

Contemplation of the unknown cousin entertained Freddie right up to the moment he realized this meant Georgie no longer had anything but the standard chores to distract her from finding him.

He half rose right then only to sink back down with a rueful chuckle.

Dark had fallen outside, the day's labor taking most of the sunlight. She would be no more likely to be at the forest now with her cousin gone than she would have with her obligations to her guest still in full force. The men hadn't said when all this occurred, though to have heard the story from this Thomas, it had to have been a day at least.

The other men returned from the bar with their drinks and plunked down at the same table, ensuring he'd have to stay even if there were any chance of her being there. He'd get enough teasing now they suspected he had a girl without adding to it. At least his mother had no reason to come near them long enough to hear a word of this and his father stayed busy with the ledger.

Somehow, he didn't think having his parents learn of Georgie through gossip among the farm workers would prove any better a path than her father beating down the manor door.

He tried to turn his thoughts from Georgie and listen to what the men discussed. Freddie succeeded enough to realize when the time had come for his promised round of the bitter ale that little resembled his father's porter. Even as he exchanged joking comments, though, in the back of his mind he wondered why, if her cousin had been gone a full day, Georgie had not found the time to spare to collect his note this morning. Surely four days had been long enough to settle her concerns and give her the perspective to realize she'd accused him falsely. So where was she?

Aubrey pushed to his feet long after the tea and biscuits had given way to sandwiches that were soon consumed as well.

"I'd best return Georgie to the Whitfelds before Barbara and her family send out the dogs to hunt me down."

"Really Aubrey," Adelaide said over the chuckles of the others. "This isn't the country. No one keeps a full pack of hunting dogs in the city."

"Lord Whitfeld would have them sent up specially, I'm sure."

With the cheerful bantering all around her, Georgie hadn't noticed how late it had become. Most of the sunlight she'd noticed upon her arrival had vanished and servants had slipped in to light the space with oil lamps.

"Aubrey is correct." Georgie rose as well. "We've stayed away much longer than was intended. I can't neglect my cousin's company as much as I've enjoyed yours."

"As have we." This from Susan, the middle sister. "You've given us a view into a much different version of our beloved brother. I would never have imagined him relaxing in the country before." She shot a teasing glance at the brother in question, provoking a laugh.

"I can say only love drove me to it." Aubrey gave each of his sisters a kiss on the cheek and swept a bow in the direction of the husbands. "Charles. Philip."

Isabella caught Georgie's hand before she could follow Aubrey into the hall where he went to request the carriage.

"I am so glad to have met you." His sister's gaze fell on the last word, the first sign of her shy nature in some hours.

"And I you," Georgie answered, giving Isabella's hand a squeeze. Then she remembered Aubrey's request and added, "I know so few people in London beyond my family. It would be ever so nice to see you at the events Lady Whitfeld has planned for me to attend."

That brought Isabella's gaze back, though the expression contained in her lovely gray eyes held more fear than joy.

"It will be fun," Georgie persisted. "I'll have a friend at my side instead of being surrounded by strangers."

Isabella ducked her head but not for long as she peeped at Georgie. "I can't imagine strangers offer much fear to someone like you."

"The carriage has arrived," a servant called from the doorway, a clear sign Georgie was delaying their departure.

"It's always better with a friend," she said even as she walked toward the door.

Isabella gave a slight smile and nod, as close to an acceptance of Georgie's thought as she would get.

Susan and Adelaide rose as well, following Georgie out so they could say their farewells to their brother, or so Georgie thought.

"No one is falling for your masquerade, brother." Susan sent a fierce scowl his direction.

"You only steal our guest away so you can spend more time with your lady." Adelaide added her own teasing and brought heat to Georgie's cheeks.

Georgie had been so worried when she first entered that uncomfortable room, but she'd warmed to Aubrey's sisters as much as it seemed they'd enjoyed her company.

Aubrey laughed. "You wouldn't want her pining after me, would you?"

A momentary confusion struck Georgie and his sisters as well, if their expressions were any hint as to their thoughts, but then she realized he'd meant Barbara.

"Regardless, I promise to collect Georgie and Barbara both for a visit tomorrow. Is that enough to satisfy you?"

The chorus of agreement certainly satisfied Georgie, who felt her cheeks grow even hotter.

"Very well, then. That's settled. We shouldn't keep the horses waiting."

Once in the carriage, Georgie leaned out the window to wave goodbye as all three sisters had come to the door to see them off. She chuckled to herself when she compared her melancholy mood on the way to the St. Vincent town house with her regret at leaving.

Aubrey lifted an eyebrow at her, but she merely shook her head, unwilling to explain.

Chapter Nineteen

reddie woke to the memory of what he'd learned in the tavern the night before. Georgie's normal life had been restored a full day ago or more with no sign of her presence.

"Peter," he called, expecting his valet to be nearby as he always seemed to be, but no one answered.

He swung out of bed and thrust the curtains open to see only a bare hint of sunlight, the night still laying claim to most of the sky.

Peter would hardly be expecting him to rise so early, but the morning brought with it the realization it would not be unthinkable for her to delay long enough to set the Ferrier house to rights after their cousin's visit. She would never have abandoned her sisters to that labor, and even if she might have, the questions provoked by such an action would have dissuaded her.

Georgie could have left him a note late yesterday as the first time she'd been able to slip away. Her message would surely show how, when her anger passed, she knew he wouldn't have behaved as she'd accused. It had to.

Taking the suggestion of his father's absence the previous morning, Freddie went straight to the kitchen where Mrs. Baker worked hard to prepare their breakfast.

"Could I trouble you for a napkin of bread and cheese?"

All motion froze at the sound of his voice then restarted just as suddenly when they recognized just whom of the family had come to their domain.

Mrs. Baker wiped flour-coated hands on her apron and came over to him. "You're not eating breakfast?"

The way her brow furrowed in concern made him grin. "Oh, I'll be eating if you'll make me up a serving, just not at the table. I have an errand to run before I get started on my other tasks for the day."

His reply eased her expression, but the twinkle in her eyes made him suspect the teasing from the farm workers had a source a little closer to the manor. "I can make you up a basket full of delicious treats if you'll just wait a moment."

Though tempted by the thought of whatever Mrs. Baker had in mind, still Freddie shook his head. "Just a napkin's worth. I'm not going far and intend to be back for a full luncheon with the men. Bread and cheese will be quick and suit me fine."

She shrugged, disappointment marking her heat-reddened face.

"I'll be happy to see some of your treats at luncheon, though, and the men would not argue a share."

That brought her smile back into place as she bustled about collecting him the meal he'd requested.

This early, there was no way Georgie would be waiting for him. She'd told him often enough she milked the cows and had a hand in feeding the farm birds as well. She'd be awake already, but much too busy to slip away.

The afternoons often found her with an hour or two to spare. Long enough, surely, to slip off to their place and leave him some sign his torment had come to an end. It wouldn't be like her to drag the punishment out, especially not once she realized it hadn't been deserved, or at least that she hadn't given him the chance to explain.

"There you go, young lord. You make sure to eat it all up. From what the men have been saying, you've been pulling your share of the labor so need your sustenance."

Freddie gave her a half bow in thanks and turned to the door, remembering at the last moment to ask, "Can you send word to my parents of my plan? I wouldn't want them delaying their own breakfast in expectation of my arrival."

"Surely we will. Porridge is meant to be served hot, don't you know?"

She laughed at her own joke, and he laughed with her before heading to the stables to borrow a horse.

He supposed this maturity meant he should purchase a beast for his own use rather than always taking one of his father's. There was room enough in the stables, and he had funds for a decent if not fancy horse.

Freddie swung the bundle of food-filled napkin from his hand as he contemplated selecting a horse of his own. He had a good seat, but like the beast his coin could afford, no one would commend him for the skill.

"Off for a morning ride, my lord?" one of the stable boys called.

"And in need of a horse if you could pull one out?"

Though it sounded like a question, the boy recognized the command underneath and vanished into the stables, leaving Freddie to consider a world in which he called out for his own horse to be brought forth rather than whichever might need to stretch its legs.

He almost gave in to the urge to whistle as the sun crested the horizon and sent color across the sky. Everything seemed just about perfect.

He'd done good work with the men and had a much better understanding of the goings on at the farm. His father seemed to appreciate his efforts, and even his mother had eased away from rushing him to the altar with some suitable stranger.

The boy brought a tall bay stallion out, one Freddie knew had an even temper and solid gait. It might not be the fastest in the Brookway stables, but would surely get him to the forest and back.

"My thanks," he told the boy as he mounted in a smooth motion.

After taking a moment to secure his breakfast, he set off for the forest and soon found himself at a familiar point. The sunlight shone through the trees to dapple a path he'd never have seen if not for Georgie's training. It wasn't wide enough for his horse, though.

Freddie tied the reins to a sturdy tree branch, and breakfast in hand, he strode into the forest. His legs ate up the distance between him and his love's sweet note. If she should somehow exceed his expectation and appear there herself, they could share the simple meal. If not, he'd be satisfied with a message telling him all was forgiven and forgotten. The offense had been sorely felt whether he'd meant to deal the blow or not, but Georgie wouldn't hold fast to her hurt.

The realization slowed his pace until he reached the glade with measured steps, his approach to the tree almost solemn. What he found within would signal the beginning of their next stage, the one in which they worked together to bring their families to the point of acceptance. He, for one, would not suffer any other result no matter what it took to achieve.

A smile teased his lips as he stuck a hand into the still-shadowed hollow and it grew to full stretch when his questing fingers found paper.

He pulled out the message and froze.

What lay between his fingertips was a mere scrap of paper, a fragment instead of the message he'd expected. Even worse, when he turned it over, the small amount of script it contained bore the design of his hand, not hers.

Freddie stared at the paper, his perfect day clouding over though no hint of rain showed in the cheerful sunlight filtering through the branches.

She had torn his message to pieces without, he had to assume, even reading it to find his explanation within.

He stumbled back to sink against the stone she used as her favorite perch and stared at the hollow, a sense of betrayal pressing down on him until he lacked the strength to rise.

Here he'd been planning their future together while, more than not forgiving him, she refused to consider such a forgiveness earned—no—deserved.

His fingers stroked the paper as though to soothe the hurt she'd inflicted on it, but he could no more mend his message than the pain in his chest.

Again he froze, this time to raise the piece of paper up so the light could shine on it clearly.

A relief as strong as his sense of betrayal only moments before washed over him when his eyes confirmed what his fingers had discerned.

The edge had not been torn apart by human hands. Rather some field mouse, perhaps the same one as before, saw fit to nibble his message into pieces small enough to carry off to line a nest, the laid paper softer than any fragment of wood pulp a woodland creature could obtain on its own.

He laughed aloud at how Georgie had driven him to such a mercurial nature, so happy, so sad, and then again cheered in a few quick minutes. She might have been his love, but she offered neither peace nor quiet. Rather, life with Georgie would be an endless round of delights and frustrations, enough to keep a man nimble and hale through as many years as he'd be blessed to see.

A quick shove against the rock drove him to his feet so he could replace the scrap. He had no use for it now, nor could Georgie read his message any longer. The mouse might as well have what enjoyment it could attain.

Freddie wished he'd taken a minute in his early waking to write a new message, but he'd wanted to see her response before penning his own.

For a third time since coming to their glade, he paused, his mind catching up with his thoughts in a not so pleasant manner.

Her cousin had been gone a full day or longer and yet she had not come to the tree to leave a message of her own.

Had she done so, she would have seen his message and buried the paper scrap to return it to the earth rather than chance it being found. She'd never have left his message to become bedding for the mice.

He needed to know why she hadn't come. If her anger still lingered, he needed to speak with her and turn it aside. He didn't want to consider the other explanation, though once thought it would not leave.

Her cousin had left somewhat abruptly or else her father would have arranged a seat on the stagecoach rather than send a young woman of means all the way to London in a farm vehicle. He could see little reason unless another dangerous illness had come to the Ferrier farm.

As much as he would have expected the men at the tavern to have mentioned such, perhaps the family hoped to keep it quiet rather than cause a panic as had happened with the scarlet fever that stole Georgie's mother.

Again his chest ached, but this time fear drove the response. He couldn't lose her, not now when he came so close to claiming Georgie for his own. He had to be wrong. He had to be.

Finding his breathing disordered, Freddie held the air in, forcing his body to listen to his command and regain control once again. He had no reason to suspect she'd come to harm. His Georgie had been nothing but healthy since he'd met her that long ago day. She held no resemblance to a sickly child then nor did she now.

He would just make good on the idea of a horse for his own purposes and find out how things fared at the Ferrier farm at the same time rather than let worry drive him to distraction. He would soon discover nothing more pressing than chores ignored to entertain their cousin kept his Georgie from him, and she'd laugh to hear how he built nightmares from her simple absence.

The image fixed firmly in his mind, Freddie returned to his horse and the manor. Despite his confidence in the logical explanation, he had no stomach for even the simple meal Mrs. Baker had prepared for him, nor would he until he had confirmed Georgie's health with his very own eyes.

Chapter Twenty

Though his sisters' charges about Aubrey's hope to spend more time with Barbara were likely true, Lady Whitfeld made it clear the late hour allowed only a short visit the previous evening. Before he left, Aubrey announced his sisters had secured a box at the theater for the upcoming night and he'd be honored if both young ladies would join him there, spending the afternoon with his sisters first, of course.

Poor Barbara had no idea why such a simple statement made Georgie dissolve into giggles until she recounted just how they'd left the St. Vincent residence. The two of them chuckled all through the preparation for bed, but Georgie dropped off quickly with the thought of seeing her first London theatrical event.

Heeding Aubrey's warning, Barbara and Georgie were properly dressed in visiting gowns when he came to collect them early the next afternoon. In what seemed no time at all, Georgie was once again on the steps of the St. Vincent town house, only this time with her cousin at her side.

"Just what have you told them about me?" Barbara asked as Aubrey gave both of them an arm.

Georgie heard a tinge of nervousness in her cousin's voice and remembered her own less than welcoming introduction the previous day. "He said little enough to make them intrigued, at least until yesterday when he told all."

A blush splashed across Barbara's cheeks, but Aubrey drew her close before she could speak.

"I told them nothing that wouldn't fit in the lines of a love poem for there is nothing else to tell. Georgiana showed a similar restraint."

Barbara glanced to Georgie, accepting a nod of agreement.

"You need not worry. They'll love you. My sister Isabella is already quite enamored of you and was before I'd awoken to my own interest."

Georgie laughed as she reached across to brush Barbara's arm. "He is not just saying so. You should have heard even her sisters when they learned I was a relation of yours. Isabella has been an advocate when you were not here to speak for yourself."

She could have kicked herself in saying the last as Barbara's color drained.

"I didn't mean anything. There was gossip, as you must know, but Aubrey's sisters are most kind. They would neither repeat nor believe it without evidence of which there is none."

Georgie forgave herself the hint of untruth about his sisters at first, but then Barbara would come properly introduced, and she doubted Aubrey would leave her alone with them as he had Georgie. If nothing else, he planned to make the most of every minute he had at her side.

"Well, then, I guess we'd best get this over with."

Aubrey chuckled. "They're my family, and soon to be yours, not some illness to recover from."

Barbara raised one eyebrow in an imitation of her mother Georgie could now recognize. "That remains to be seen, does it not?"

He refused to rise to the challenge, only tucking Barbara's arm a little tighter through his own as he drew all three of them up the steps.

If ever Barbara sought to break with him, Georgie could tell she'd have as little chance of success as of the Thames drying up in its banks.

When they arrived at the front parlor, however, only Isabella sat in attendance. She rose to greet them, and much to Georgie's delight, began the welcome with her.

"How wonderful you were able to return, Georgiana."

Her gaze dropped at the last moment, but Georgie considered it a remarkable change in any case. "Please, call me Georgie. It's what I prefer as my mother used to do so."

Isabella glanced up again to smile before she turned to the woman she'd only seen at a distance.

Georgie stepped forward, looping her arm through Isabella's. "And this is my cousin, Lady Barbara Whitfeld, though I suppose it seems the height of foolishness to stand on such ceremony."

Isabella's cheeks reddened just a touch as she reached out a hand in greeting, her head bowed. "I did so want to meet you."

Before Barbara could counter the statement, a difficult task considering she'd barely known of Isabella's existence until Aubrey suggested Georgie could help, Aubrey stepped in. "And so here she is. Am I not the most indulgent brother?"

Isabella moved back, silently urging them all in to take seats, but when Georgie thought her struck once again by shyness, she caught sight of the barely suppressed humor in the young woman's expression.

"I'm sure it is for my indulgence you brought her here, and none of your own."

Aubrey endeavored to look offended, but soon gave up to say, "I brought Georgie here to keep you company. Is that not sufficient for reward?"

They all laughed then, settling around the room with Georgie at Isabella's side while Aubrey took up a firm position next to the fireplace where Barbara chose to sit.

"My sisters had other duties to attend to? After their response the previous day, I felt sure they'd be eagerly waiting to bombard my lady with their questions."

Isabella paused to pick up yet another piece of beautiful needlework before she said, "I sent them off. They'll have enough of a chance tonight at the theater, and I didn't want to scare Lady Barbara from the start. You've had such a time catching her."

Barbara sent a glare to Aubrey and Georgie both, but though he lifted his hands in surrender, Isabella slapped a palm across her lips.

"I am so sorry. I didn't mean... Really, I know almost nothing of his courtship, only that he sought you after the park with such little success. And my sisters are quite nice. You'll be sure to like them. It's more I didn't want you overwhelmed when Georgie told me you have no brothers or sisters of your own. You can't be used to how it is in bigger families."

Georgie brushed Isabella's arm and shook her head. "Don't worry so. She's spent enough time with me and my sisters to have all too strong of an understanding while she's well able to hold her own with your brother."

"And you must call me Barbara. After all, we're almost family."

The smug look on Aubrey's face almost undid Georgie's composure, but Isabella's clear discomfort drew her attention away.

"Why don't you tell us how you managed a brook that shimmers almost as prettily as the one by my home?"

She'd meant only to ease Isabella's fears, but the thought of home and the brook made it hard to concentrate as Isabella explained about the silk threads and described the colors she used, her animation returning. Luckily, Barbara was quick to ask her own questions, allowing Georgie's mind to wander.

Georgie wondered just what Freddie was doing at this exact moment, and whether he ever thought of her. Or had he counted his blessings in being quit with no sign of her attempting to seek him out.

As soon as he returned from the forest, Freddie spoke to his father about the possibility of purchasing a horse.

Lord Brookway thought it an excellent idea.

"You'd never know it, but we have a skilled horse breeder not far from here," Lord Brookway offered before Freddie could make the suggestion of Georgie's father. "I've heard talk of his results all the way in London though I knew him long before his efforts reached the attention of those in the city. More than one of my stable came first from his farm. Ferrier is the man's name."

When Freddie had been looking for some excuse to reject his father's recommendation, instead he stared at the man for a moment, stunned at the thought of their families interacting on another level.

Lord Brookway raised his eyebrows at Freddie's silence. "I can give you his direction if you'd like."

Freddie coughed as a belated excuse for his lack of response. "I've heard of Ferrier down at the tavern myself. I should have expected you knew of him."

His father tapped a finger to his temple. "I've learned a thing or two since returning to the country, my boy."

The tease served as a reminder Lord Brookway had not always been a resident of London for all he seemed to prefer it. No wonder Freddie's mother thought he would transfer his sense of belonging so easily at first.

"I'd best be about it, then," Freddie said, keeping the realization to himself.

His father waved him off with a cheerful smile and Freddie collected a different horse to start on a path he'd learned some years earlier when he started planning his courtship.

The farm came into view quickly, the distance between their homes smaller than the gulf between the families.

An older man worked a stallion of some beauty in the field just outside of it.

Freddie rode up to the fence and dismounted, watching the skill of both man and horse for some moments without drawing attention to himself.

His arrival, however, had not passed unnoticed, and the man soon released the lead rein and sent his stallion off before approaching the fence.

Whether because of his stride or the familiar blue eyes staring from his face, Freddie had no doubt in his mind he stood before none other than Georgie's father in the flesh. What seemed a simple plan now brought with it the daunting realization he'd be making an impression on the same man who would receive his request to court Georgie officially.

"How can I be of service, my lord?"

Though he'd worn rough clothing with the intention of working in the fields, Ferrier seemed well able to distinguish between him and any other of the workers.

Ferrier stuck out a hand in greeting. "No need to look so concerned. It's the horse as gave you away. Lord Brookway spoke with me once about breeding that one, and though I declined, preferring to own my stock, somehow I doubt he's letting just anyone ride him. I suppose you're the son all grown, then?"

The resemblance to Georgie only grew with how little weight this man put on Freddie's nobility, a strange contrast to the way things were at the manor. At least Ferrier did not seem to scorn him for his status, but it would be unlikely to add to his suit.

Ferrier stood patiently awaiting his response, a fact which drew a flush onto Freddie's cheeks.

"Yes, I am Mr. Hathwell. I've come to talk about a horse."

The farmer let out a burst of laughter at Freddie's awkward speech. "Somehow I doubted you'd come about my daughters."

If anything, Freddie's cheeks grew hotter, and he half wanted to confess right then and there before he did more to convince the man he had not a steady thought in his brain. Still, he couldn't let the opening pass. At least the man seemed much too jolly for there to be illness or injury in his home.

"How are your daughters? My mother did ask me to inquire after them."

Ferrier's eyebrows lowered, but when Freddie expected anger, the farmer shrugged. "I knew those dance lessons would stir things up, but the girls so wanted to go. Now the girls are brought to the attention of the local nobility when I'd thought the chance lost with my dear wife. I'm sure I'll never hear the end of it."

Freddie couldn't very well set his fears at rest by revealing he'd used his mother as an excuse. It would take much more than dance lessons to make any of Ferrier's daughters an equal in her eye for all Lady Pendleton had proved an apt teacher, as talented in her way as Ferrier had been in training the horse from Georgie's skill at dancing.

This time his silence worked to his benefit as Ferrier added in a grumble, "All my daughters are well."

"And the youngest? Is she still taking the lessons?" He wondered if she'd chosen to leave dancing in her past as she seemed to have him what with them all being healthy according to her very own father.

"My youngest? No, she is no longer."

Before Freddie could decide if the news proved good or bad, the farmer continued with, "She's off to London to visit with her cousin, my Georgie is."

Startled to hear someone else lay claim to her as Freddie always had despite this being her father, it took a moment for the information to sink in. The men at the tavern made no mention of others joining the cousin on the trip back to London, though why would they?

Everything made sense all of a sudden.

Why she'd been absent from the hollow. Why she'd never picked up his message nor left one of her own. She hadn't been holding a grudge. She'd been gone to London.

His relief died a quick death as he imagined her charming who knew how many strong young men with her vivacious nature and deep beauty. She'd have many more suitable choices there, and her cousin would be sure to introduce her to dozens.

"What kind of horse are you seeking?"

For the barest moment, the question made no sense to him at all.

Freddie worried his expression had been all too revealing so gave a laugh to cover up his confusion. "I'm looking for a riding horse, one I can trust to stay where I tether him and who won't balk at spending the day riding fences or out in the field. As much as I admire the stallion you were working just now, I'm merely a decent seat. I'll leave the spirited beasts to others who are more talented."

Something resembling approval showed in Ferrier's expression at his statement where Freddie had been expecting scorn.

"It's a wise man as knows his limits, but my stallion isn't up for sale as of yet and may never be. The thought of ending his bloodline cuts me to the bone." Ferrier brushed a hand through his hair, brow furrowed in thought. "I might have a couple to suit you. Catch ahold of your reins and follow me back to the stables. We'll get your beast some water while we talk."

He did as instructed and managed to hold up his end of the conversation, even arranging for the purchase of an older but spry riding horse, not the strongest or youngest of the man's cattle but one

Ferrier was willing to part with, and for a sum Freddie could provide. There were arrangements to be made in the manor stables, so Ferrier agreed to deliver the horse the following day in return for the opportunity to see what Lord Brookway had acquired since the last time he'd been to the Brookway Manor.

Freddie liked the farmer and hoped the feeling mutual. Though Ferrier thought this a limited encounter, someday this man would be his father-in-law.

Despite his confidence in that outcome, the news he'd just learned sent doubts whirling through his mind as he headed back to the manor. The dimming sun only echoed his mood as it hung low in the sky.

Georgie in London.

Wild as she was, she'd as likely be scorned as win hearts among the London merchants, Freddie realized, his doubts fading. And he did her a poor turn in thinking her so fickle. She'd been nothing but true to their love even when she had reason to believe he held it in less respect. He had the one message he'd saved as proof her love ran deep, but with her gone, he had no way to tell her just how wrong she'd been about his own.

Freddie didn't know which was the worst of the two. Her the sweetheart of the city folk or miserable there. He had little doubt the trip to London had not been at her prompting. As mad as she'd been, Georgie confronted her pains not ran from them, but then she'd been more than angry. She'd believed his love a lie.

The urge to dig his heels into the stallion's side and charge all the way up to London swept over him, but reason held him back. He had no idea where Georgie could be found. If she did flourish, he would not destroy the reputation she built there by banging on doors up and down the merchant residences seeking her. He could only pray she had no contact with true society.

If she did something to offend, his mother would never agree to a match between them and would do everything in her power to tear them apart forever. Though he refused to consider a future in which Lady Brookway succeeded at her aim, neither could he see one filled with pleasantries if such an event came about.

Chapter Twenty-One

reddie spent some time at the stables upon his return to make sure everything was prepared for his new horse. The stable boys, eager to prove they had as much to teach the young lord as any of the farm workers, showed him every aspect of care they provided the horses. They led him through the interior, discussing where to place his horse and learning all they could about its demeanor.

He listened carefully as they explained how important it was to choose a stall next to another horse of similar temperament, or at least one that wouldn't pose a problem. Freddie nodded at all the right places even when he already knew some of the information. As much as he felt in need of a wash and something to ease his stomach, he let them talk their fill.

It didn't serve to lack understanding in any portion of his estate, which it might become all the sooner in reality if not name. He suspected his parents would be happy to return to London as he'd planned should he prove a reasonable hand at managing the place. Freddie didn't overlook the chance for solving both their problems at once, fulfilling his parents' need to be in the city and avoiding the potential clashes between his well-bred mother and his wild love.

"We thought you might be having another meal down at the tavern," Lord Brookway said when Freddie stepped through the doorway of the dining room sometime later, his skin sparkling clean and no hint of horse about him.

Freddie shook his head, rounding the table to take his spot so the maids could finish serving the first course. "I knew you would be eager to hear of my visit to Ferrier. I wouldn't deprive you."

Lady Brookway seemed to tense, then she gave what in any other person would have been an unladylike snort.

"Is this what I have to look forward to?" she asked the room at large. "Always talking of farm duties and horses. I think I preferred the days of math tutors. At least then we'd have the hope of a poetry recitation as are often held by London society."

Horses fled Freddie's thoughts faster than the speeds he believed his new animal could attain. Memories of reading to Georgie under the dappling of the forest leaves were replaced swiftly with visions of her rapt attention directed to some London dandy holding court before an audience of the ton.

"My dear, you've scared the boy speechless with all your talk of society and performance. Better he keep his focus on farms and horses now so when he's ready to seek a bride, he'll have a solid fortune to offer her. Young men with small titles and small means offer little competition to those with an improvement in either state and so their choices are as small as what they have to bring to the table."

Lady Brookway gave her husband a glare. "Are you saying I was the scrapings at the bottom of the barrel?"

Arching one eyebrow, Lord Brookway answered with, "No more than you are claiming me small in the same measures, I'd hope."

Freddie ignored them both. They might not have the most passionate of marriages, but they were amicable and happy with each other if not with how their life turned out.

Then Lord Brookway shrugged. "Perhaps I was seeking to improve myself through your connections. Why your father accepted my request, I'll never know, especially since we lived on one of his properties when first married because I could not afford a suitable London address on my own."

"I may have given him to believe I had some affection for such a dashing young baron." The look she sent Lord Brookway this time had little ire and too much of the passion Freddie had believed they lacked.

"And besides, he had daughters a plenty to find suitors for."

She harrumphed, but the blush Lord Brookway had lit in her cheeks remained long enough to make Freddie decidedly uncomfortable.

Lord Brookway laughed aloud, waving his fork in Freddie's direction. "Would you look at him now? Most definitely too young for the marriage mart, and perhaps we've grown too familiar in his presence. That expression reveals nothing less than a fervent wish to be anywhere but here. No fear, Frederick. Your parents are done with their merriment, and we can turn the conversation back to horses and farming. I have a surprise for you, but first tell me about Ferrier."

With no small measure of relief, Freddie recounted his visit, including the recognition not of his person but of the beast he'd ridden.

Lord Brookway shook his head at that. "I told you the man had a way with horseflesh, did I not? You were most likely penned in by one tutor or another at the time of his visits, or perhaps too young to care in any case."

Freddie suspected there was a good chance he'd been sequestered off with the man's daughter while his father and hers discussed the breeding of their respective stock, but knew better than to make the comment. Instead, he continued his tale until he reached the end with their own stable boys.

"Seems to me you did quite well with both your negotiating and not letting the sight of finer stock turn your head. A good, solid horse will serve you better and longer than some fancy ride that has a taste for scraping you off at the least excuse. It's a well-known fact lives of the titled class are just as often cut short by way of horse or carriage than ever are lost in battle."

Lady Brookway chuckled as she raised her glass to sip. "You exaggerate, my dear, and it's mostly the males who are so stricken, but it is true enough risk themselves so wastefully. It's good to see our son does not share in those weaknesses for all he shows an unhealthy interest in laboring out in the field."

Freddie tensed for another lecture, but his father turned to him then as though she hadn't spoken.

"But with the question of your horse settled, perhaps you'd be interested in hearing what I've been about?"

"Yes, Father. Please tell me." Anything to turn the focus off himself before his mother recounted all of what she saw to be his failings.

"I took a ride out to the new mill Lord Pendleton had installed. I've heard interesting things about its innovation and wanted to see the sight myself. I would have asked you along, but you had your own business to see to."

The pride in his father's voice as he said the last made Freddie sit a little straighter. He'd been more interested in discovering what had happened with Georgie than the horse to be truthful, but if it aided in the effort to prove his maturity, he certainly would not contest the benefit. He had indeed purchased a horse.

Again, the urge to ride off to London as soon as his horse arrived swept over him, but he had yet to progress in the pursuit of obtaining her direction there. Perhaps he would have done better to eat at the tavern after all. He might have run across Ferrier's Thomas and ascertained her location with some discrete inquiries masked as a wish to hear the tale of his trials from the man direct.

"And just what do you think of that, my son?"

Freddie started, realizing his father had continued to speak while he pondered the problem of Georgie. "I'm sorry, Father. I'm afraid my thoughts wandered."

"Contemplating your new beast, I suppose. Well, listen up as this part is all for you."

"I will. What is it you have to tell me?"

Lord Brookway leaned back, a broad smile on his face. "When I was at the mill, who should come to see how the workings were holding up but the very same Lord Pendleton. We began talking, and as you know, he's quite well thought of for his land management. When he heard you'd shown a serious interest, he agreed to meet with you tomorrow early afternoon to share some of his experiences and take you around his own property to show what he's done there. How does that suit you?"

He looked first to Freddie, but his satisfied expression soon turned toward Lady Brookway as though to counter all her arguments against her son taking an interest in land management.

"It's such an honor, Frederick." His mother smiled as if the meeting had nothing to do with the farming she scorned. "He has a strong reputation for more than just his property management, and his mother is a known leader in the ton. Why, not being invited to one of Lady Pendleton's events is quite the dash to one's standing. Oh, I suppose it's the Dowager Lady Pendleton now. I don't see the current Lady Pendleton doing much to impact London society."

Lord Brookway shook his head. "Give her time. She's yet to settle into her new role and from how Lord Pendleton was quick to return to her side, I think she's quite happy to be the center of his attention for the time being."

Freddie let their exchange wash over him as he struggled to conform his expression to the anticipation his father expected of him. He wanted nothing more than to lock himself in his room so he could plan some way to find this Thomas and get the answers from him Freddie needed to seek the love of his life on the streets of London. Nowhere in that plan was there room for a lesson in land management no matter how well learned or connected this lord might be.

Life had been so much simpler when he had only paid tutors to slip free of and his Georgie would be waiting for him like as not in their glade.

Instead, he could not cry off without offending one of the few titled families in the area, something his mother would never allow. What excuse could he offer? They had no knowledge of his troubles, no way to know he'd won and lost, if only for the moment, the woman he intended to marry, and he could not inform them of his state either.

"Thank you, Father. I will endeavor to make the most of this opportunity."

That seemed to satisfy both of his parents, and he could finally focus on the delicious meal Mrs. Baker had provided. Of course, with his thoughts on just what Georgie had found to occupy herself in London and how he could possibly find her there without creating an uproar, he couldn't have described a single bite.

GEORGIE WATCHED THE ACTORS ON the stage below with utmost fascination. This had little in common with the plays she'd seen performed in the village. The passion and complexity made it hard to contain her excitement, but the dim lighting, and occasional "hsst"s when someone spoke, told her well enough how to behave. The steady rumble of low voices despite the repeated warnings showed not all shared her absorption.

The actors left the stage and the curtain came down, leaving her bewildered as Aubrey rose and left the chamber.

"Is that where they end it? Does the king even think the prince is mad?"

Isabella laughed, the beautiful sound carrying in the tight space. "It is only an interval. My brother will have gone for some refreshments."

She fell silent somewhat abruptly as two young gentlemen entered the box, first greeting the elder St. Vincents before moving further in. Isabella watched their approach from the corner of widened eyes, her discomfort obvious should any think to look.

"So do you believe the prince is out of his mind?" Georgie asked, hoping to engage her new friend as a distraction.

It worked so well Isabella gave up her watchful stance to roll her eyes. "Really, Georgie, he speaks to ghosts and sees conspiracies everywhere."

"So a regular sort of royalty then."

Isabella joined Georgie in new laughter before she even registered the comment as coming from one of the visitors.

"It seems to me the ghost tells him only what he has already observed," the second gentleman said in a quiet voice.

"Ingham is too much of a logical thinker for theatrical works. He'd have us believe the ghost a reflection of the prince's fears rather than a manifestation."

Susan leaned forward in her chair behind them. "For all you are friends of Philip, you are being exceedingly rude. You can't very well join a conversation with two young ladies you have yet to meet."

Georgie gritted her teeth at this interruption. Better Isabella find comfort to be herself than that the proprieties were seen to. It was not as if they could get into any trouble here with her whole family looking on.

Barbara stepped forward then, pulling away from a conversation with Adelaide. "She's right, you know. Introductions are in order. Georgie, I would have you meet Mr. Ingham and Lord Riverton. And this, gentlemen, is Miss Georgiana Ferrier. I believe you are acquainted with Lady Isabella already?"

"My pleasure," they both recited, bowing first over Georgie's hand then Isabella's.

Though Isabella looked away when Lord Riverton bowed, she glanced up at Mr. Ingham in a most interesting fashion. Georgie tucked this observation away for later consideration as she turned the discussion back to the play in hopes of regaining the companionship of moments before.

Susan, her sisterly duties satisfied, sank back into the shadows without a further comment.

The next interruption came with Aubrey's return and refreshments.

"You'll need to be quick about it though. The bell is sure to sound soon."

Georgie looked to Isabella for an explanation of Aubrey's comment, but Lord Riverton caught sight of her confusion first and said, "It sounds the end to the interval and the return of the play."

She nodded her thanks, aware she'd given away her ignorance, something she felt sure would have upset her had she any interest in the young gentleman at all.

As it was, upon learning his name, she'd been doing her best not to think of Freddie. A river was not so much different from the brook that marked his name and their special place.

How he would have enjoyed this play with its confusion of loyalty and purpose. Though his parents were not engaged in any treachery, they did work against his interests in wanting a future he had little inclination for.

Georgie wondered if he had seen a performance one of the times he'd been in London with his parents. She supposed he must have what with so many of the titled folk present here.

He rarely spoke of his visits beyond the time spent with his grandparents and cousins, though whether to avoid making her feel the country bumpkin or from a lack of interest, she could not tell. She'd have to ask him when he came for her.

"I fear our conversation is less alluring than her thoughts," Lord Riverton said, jolting Georgie out of her preoccupation. "Longing for the interval to end and the story to continue, I suppose?"

She scrambled for an answer that would not appear rude, and oddly her thoughts of Freddie offered one. "It's only I suspect you have seen this play before and know its story. I fear in your eagerness to discuss, you might tell me what I've yet to learn."

Lord Riverton threw back his head and laughed. "She has a clever tongue, Ingham. Perhaps you should consider her for your own lack in a mate."

Georgie felt the heat of a blush sweep her face, but worse, she saw her new friend pull back a little further into the shadows. Aubrey and Barbara had asked for her help in drawing Isabella out, and she suspected she'd found the very way to do it. Should Mr. Ingham choose to lean his attention in her direction, it would both be useless for him, bound as she was to her Freddie, and damaging to any hopes Isabella might hold.

"It is not particularly clever to state the obvious," Georgie said into the awkward silence to follow. "If that's your measure, I know many who would amaze you."

Her sharp tone drew the attention of even the Lady St. Vincent seated on the other side of the box. Georgie felt uncomfortable under the stares, but at least the question of Mr. Ingham's inclination remained unanswered.

Lord Riverton gave her a nod, though whether of dismissal or approval, she couldn't tell as just then the warning bell sounded.

"We'd best be off to our seats," Mr. Ingham said, rising to emphasize his words.

"Indeed." Lord Riverton followed without complaint when no effort was made to offer them any of the empty chairs in the St. Vincent box.

Isabella touched Georgie's arm, leaning close to whisper, "You really shouldn't speak so. It will gain you a reputation."

She shrugged. "He spoke first, though more prettily, and I wouldn't have you put on the spot."

A shocked glance showed she'd read the situation truthfully, then Isabella shook her head. "Why should I be concerned if you gain the interest of an intelligent man? It is, after all, what the season is about, or so they tell me."

The curtain rose, putting an end to the protest Georgie would have made, but the exchange only made her more eager to learn the truth about this Mr. Ingham. She had trouble focusing on the actors below despite how much she'd wanted to see how the play untangled its events into a satisfying conclusion. As it was, she heard barely half of what the actors said.

Chapter Twenty-Two

reddie had hoped to ride his new horse to the meeting, but Mr. Ferrier had not arrived by the time he had to leave for the Pendleton Manor. They had made no specific arrangements, so he could not complain, but somehow riding one of his father's stable made him feel more like a boy than a man ready to take on his future.

Lord Pendleton did not seem to notice in any case as he met Freddie at the stables, leading a beast of his own.

"I thought we'd begin with a tour of the nearest sections. I can tell you what I'm doing in each and you can describe your own plans."

"I can't imagine they are as significant as yours, Lord Pendleton."

The man laughed. "Call me Jasper and I'll call you Frederick if that's all right with you. Too many lords tossed around and people will think we're praying for more than a good bit of sun to finish off the later crops."

Freddie smiled for the first time since waking up this morning, thinking he could come to like Lord Pendleton, or rather Jasper. "I go by Freddie to my friends."

"Freddie, then. And don't think your plans any different than mine. There are only so many things you can stick in the ground and hope will sprout. Whether the plot is large or small, the process is much the same as long as you have enough property to rotate your harvests."

He continued describing his plans and what approaches he'd used on various crops as they rode. Freddie was happy to discover not just new things to consider but proof of how much he had picked up from the men already. When he described his own efforts, Jasper confirmed his assumptions with only a few suggestions that might show some improvement.

"Now tell me about your sheep. They are something I have little experience with despite my lands. When it comes to beasts, cows are more the Pendleton tradition."

Here again, Freddie discovered he'd learned more than he'd realized. Jasper still asked many a question Freddie could not answer, but he promised to query those with more knowledge than he could claim.

As they turned back to the Pendleton Manor, Freddie was surprised to realize how late it had grown. The hours had passed quickly in good company and with true purpose, but having noticed, his thoughts turned to what he knew of London ways and wondering what Georgie would be preparing for this very moment.

Freddie dismounted when Jasper did, and as they led their horses to the stables for tending, Jasper startled Freddie with a laugh.

"You haven't heard a word I've said since we arrived back here. Unless I miss my guess, that expression means a girl is involved. I've seen it all too recently on my friend Aubrey to mistake it."

He'd meant to turn the question aside as he had the farm workers' teasing, but when he met Jasper's gaze over the back of his father's horse, Freddie could hold it in no longer. Out poured the whole tale from their long ago beginnings to now with her somewhere in London doing who knew what.

"And I don't know whether to worry more that someone with better prospects will recognize the wonder Georgie is, or she'll do something to be shunned and make everything so much more difficult with my mother."

Freddie ran out of words as they handed off the horses and walked to the manor, his shoulders slumped for all he felt the burden lighter with someone, however unlikely, to share it.

"Only you must not tell any of this to my parents. If they learn the truth too soon, they'll do everything in their power to stand in my way."

Jasper waved off his butler and strode down the hall with Freddie trailing after. When they reached what was clearly his study, he entered and gestured for Freddie to take a chair.

As much as he'd wanted to cut this audience short, or not come at all so he could chase after Georgie, now Freddie found himself drained of the energy. His tale showed him just how hopeless it would be to pursue her to London for all that waiting on her return would be like to drive him insane.

Jasper sank behind the desk and rested his chin on steepled hands. "Would you let them?"

Freddie shook his head in confusion before he realized Jasper had returned to their conversation as though there'd been no interruption.

He firmed his shoulders. "No. No, I would not let them tear us apart, but I fear what it would mean to my relationship with my parents."

Jasper raised one eyebrow. "You fear for your inheritance?"

The glare he aimed at his new friend held more heat than he would have considered appropriate in any other setting, but he'd had too many question his motives of late.

"Yes, I fear for it. What would I have to offer a wife without my properties? I'm young, untried, and with all my skills and training geared to running an estate. Only a fool would take me on as more than an apprentice, which does not pay enough to keep a young woman raised to a certain level of property."

Taking no offense, Jasper leaned back in his chair with a smile. "That is sound reasoning, and no more than I would expect after having spent the afternoon with you. You're all set to establish yourself, but it would be many years before you'd be experienced enough to take on a whole property. You need to take care. I will say nothing, but word spreads here and in London both. Make sure you are the one to reveal this to your parents."

Even as he nodded, Freddie paused. "You're not surprised at my choice of a commoner?" He had wondered how many shared his mother's views, but it would seem Jasper was not one of them.

Jasper laughed as though reading his thoughts. "Someday I'll tell you the story of my own courtship, but no, I've learned the person is more important than the position. My lady wife was happy to encourage Aubrey in his pursuit of a Ferrier cousin. Why not a daughter? Though I fear the man may feel his house under siege."

"If only she'd stayed at home, I would have begun the siege yesterday for all the potential consequences. I'm tired of the secrets, and of the fear she'll decide on someone else while I try to balance my parents' needs against my own, but my state matters little with her hidden away in the city." He stared at his hands, trapped in the frustration of being unable to act.

The silence became uncomfortable, but when he glanced up, Jasper's measured stare offered no easing of the state. Freddie felt sure he'd failed somehow, and in this failure, he risked his future with Georgie.

"I just might be able to help you."

Whatever he'd expected to come from the other man's lips, an offer of assistance had never crossed Freddie's mind.

"How? I'm sure you know the Ferriers from what you said of their cousin, but you'll just raise suspicions if you inquire, especially so shortly after my own visit."

"I could use the excuse of Daphne's lessons."

Freddie gave a sour laugh. "I used that tact already, and surely the other sisters would have told your wife of Georgie's absence rather than leaving her to send you to inquire."

Jasper laughed as well, his a rich tone. "It will make her happy to learn word has spread of her efforts for all she won't appreciate the use you put it to. Though knowing my wife, perhaps she'd be all the more encouraging. It's a good thing, however, I was not proposing to storm the farmhouse in your stead. No, while I cannot tell you where her cousin keeps residence, I suspect your Georgie is housed there based on the contents of my latest message from Aubrey. He mentioned, in amongst telling of his own courting success, how his sister has a new friend fresh from the country. Who else could it be than Ferrier's daughter sent on with Barbara? The St. Vincents are only rarely in the country and so less likely than most to have other ties to it."

Leaning forward in his eagerness, Freddie demanded, "And where can your friend be found. I'll secure her direction from him if it takes everything I possess."

"I doubt it will take all of that." Jasper drew out a fresh piece of paper and a quill pen. "I'll write you a letter of introduction and explain your purpose. Aubrey is not the type to stand in the way of love. He's played both matchmaker and desperate suitor too recently to act in such a fashion. We can take up the question of your farming practices at a later date when you no longer need to race across the country in pursuit of your love."

He paused to laugh. "Perhaps we should do so before you're happily married. I can tell you from experience you'll have little interest in discussions of soil with your wife awaiting you as mine is sure to be now."

Jasper blotted the paper and folded it carefully in thirds before handing it over to Freddie.

"Thank you. You have no idea what this means to me."

Jasper waved off the thanks with a smile. "I know more than you might think. Don't wait a moment longer or you may just find your worst fears come true. Though if the lady in question returns your feelings, I doubt even the Dowager Lady Pendleton could persuade her to accept another in your place."

Freddie waited no longer but gave a quick bow before retracing his steps through the manor and down to the stables to reclaim his horse. A day that had begun in frustration and annoyance at having to play the student when Georgie's circumstances plagued him had turned more in his favor than he could have imagined. He would not waste another minute of it.

After what seemed like hours of preparation, and may very well have been considering how early they'd started, Georgie made her curtsy before the Prince Regent as required for full participation in what remained of the season, and more importantly, in the ball set for that very night. She didn't know what she'd expected, but the portly man in the chair little matched her image. He spent the whole time she stood before him talking to a handsome gentleman standing nearby, one of his attendants waving her on though the prince had yet to acknowledge her.

Barbara drew Georgie over to where her family stood with Aubrey and Isabella as well.

An afternoon engagement designed specifically for the prince to give his nod of approval to anyone hoping to become part of society, the whole thing seemed a little overdone to Georgie, but when she'd made such a comment earlier in the morning, she'd been sternly told to suggest nothing of the sort when they were where others could hear. A breach in convention of that magnitude could damage her standing to such a degree not even Lady Whitfeld could repair it.

"I'd expected it to be something more," she commented quietly as she joined them. "I doubt he would even recognize me should our path's cross."

Barbara shook her head, but smiled as though aware of how carefully Georgie crafted the statement. "It's not about him knowing you but about society knowing you're worthy to be known. It's part of the rituals that hold all of London together."

"Then I start to understand what was so attractive about our chores."

Barbara gave a startled laugh loud enough to draw a reproving glance from her mother, but Aubrey only slipped her arm through his and leaned in to murmur, "Careful, my love. While I'd not have you aspire to be society's darling, our lives could become quite complicated should your mother's efforts fail to quash the rumors."

Georgie blushed as much as her cousin, knowing the fault lay with her. No wonder Isabella shrank from all and sundry. One wrong word, one heartfelt laugh, and everything could come crashing to the ground.

"Who was the handsome gentleman next to the prince," she asked instead, turning to a more appropriate conversation.

Isabella stepped closer then. "That's none other than Beau Brummell. He is a darling of society for sure. Sets the fashion standards for men and women alike. He has excellent carriage."

Georgie turned to take another look, her interest more because the man had served as a distraction in her short time before the prince. "Do you like him?"

"Who? Beau Brummell? Why I don't know the man but by reputation. He's the prince's favorite and quite the wit from what I've heard. He cuts a dashing figure."

The dubious nature of Isabella's tone revealed much more than her words, and Georgie turned back to face her friend. "Who do you favor then? Surely there is someone here who has caught your eye?"

Isabella scanned the room as though taking Georgie's words to heart, but Georgie watched closely and she saw no sign of interest in her friend's expression regardless of where she cast her gaze.

"We might as well be off now," Lady Whitfeld said. "We have much to prepare for your first ball, and you've shown just how long it takes to choose a dress."

She waved away any protest Georgie might have made with, "No matter. This had to be done and so it has. Not just anyone could have procured you an audience in so short a time, you know."

"Thank you, Lady Whitfeld," Georgie murmured, feeling some sort of reply would be expected. She'd have been just as happy to stay home and write another letter to Freddie though she hadn't sent the first. But her aunt felt she'd grown too old to stay with a nursemaid and they could not possibly abandon her to attend the event. She suspected her father's hand in the decision as well, an attempt to find her a better match than the farm hand he supposed held her heart.

Georgie thought on her days at home.

Though the hours were very different, rising earlier and abed shortly after sunset, the constant activities seem much the same. She doubted her aunt would appreciate a ball or theatrical event being compared to milking cows or collecting wild herbs, but in neither case had Georgie the choice to go her own way while others carried out the assigned tasks.

As it was, Lady Whitfeld had declared this audience an outing for everyone to share in, Isabella as well since she and Aubrey had been with them when word came of the schedule. It seemed a little much at the time, and more so when the full extent of the audience took barely a blink, but Georgie could appreciate the comfort of her friends and family around her more than most.

She had not been raised to London society, and truth be told, she did not plan to cultivate much experience here either. No need then for her to make friends among the many members of the ton, and she wasn't the type to sit quietly on the wall as she'd seen some others do.

Whatever purpose she could serve Isabella, best she did so quickly. The moment Freddie came for her, she planned to quit this location and return to where every word would not be judged.

A twinge of nervousness struck her at the realization this had been Freddie's fear all along. Perhaps she'd do better to pay attention and learn what she could about how to behave in a proper manner for London society. She knew well enough her farm girl habits would not please his mother, but if she could mimic those here in London, his concern might be eased as could her way with the woman who would become her mother-in-law.

At least she would be able to wear more of Barbara's beautiful dresses. They had no place back on the farm, but here she could enjoy the swirling skirts and fancy embroidery to rival Isabella's stitches.

She tucked her arm through Isabella's as they neared the line of carriages. "You must come with us though I know you have your own preparations to make. Surely you can spend some time helping me decide what to wear."

Isabella's eyes sparkled with delight at the idea. "I could have Aubrey send for my dress as well if Barbara would lend me a maid for my hair. Then we could all go out at once."

"That sounds like a splendid idea," Lady Whitfeld said from behind them, having overheard the last. "Aubrey? You can see to it, can you not?"

Georgie caught the edge of a surprised look on Aubrey's face before he laughed, good natured as always. "Perhaps all my little sister needed was a companion of her own age," he said as though to himself.

She glanced toward Isabella, afraid the other girl had heard, but Isabella was half-way into the Whitfeld carriage. Georgie sent Aubrey a look every bit as reproving as the one her cousin received earlier. It would do his sister no good if he made her self-conscious.

Instead, Georgie planned to ensure the young men surrounding Isabella engaged her in conversation so she'd forget her cares and let herself enjoy the event. Why else had they gone to so much trouble if not to wring whatever pleasure there was to be had from this ball and every other social happening before Georgie returned to her father's home?

FREDDIE ARRIVED BACK AT THE Brookway Manor only to find the stables a minor chaos.

Ferrier had brought the horse.

"Ah, Mr. Hathwell. I had hoped to see you today and was disappointed when the stable boys said you weren't about."

Freddie dismounted and led the horse forward to greet the man whose daughter he planned to chase after all the way to London. He would have this very hour had Ferrier not been waiting.

"Is all well with my horse?"

"More than well. I'd guess he's itching for a ride. Thinking you'd want to acclimate him to his new master, I told my stable boys not to exercise him this morning. He's had only the time on a lead rein to arrive here."

A smile came unbidden as Freddie considered this act of providence. He would not have to strip his father's stables to seek Georgie. His own horse had need to stretch its legs as much as he had somewhere he desired to be.

"I'm of a mind to ride to London this very evening. Do you think he'll be up to such a journey?"

Ferrier lightly slapped the horse in question on the rump. "He can go that distance and more. He'll be happy for a longer journey than he's had for a while now. You'd best be careful riding at night though."

"I'm glad he has the stamina. Few highwaymen would consider a lone rider worthy of their interest, but I shall keep an eye out. With good horseflesh between my knees, I'm sure to outrun a thief. Follow me in and I'll pay you for the beast so you won't have to wait on my return. Henry, prepare this one for a trip and settle the other in for the night."

With a nod of appreciation, the farmer followed Freddie into the manor while the stable boys managed both horses.

He hadn't considered the impression his offer would make, but felt grateful he had the coin on hand to show he paid his debts, one more aspect in his favor once Ferrier learned of his true interests.

His father met him at the door, clearly having seen him ride up.

"How was the meeting with Lord Pendleton?" Lord Brookway asked before noticing Ferrier there. "Ferrier? My good man, have you come to see my breeding stock, or to add to it?"

The farmer raised his eyebrows, once again showing little deference. "I'd been given to understand the purchase to be Mr. Hathwell's."

His father laughed. "You are correct. It is my son making the purchase for all the beast will share the same stalls. I hear you gave him a solid horse from his telling."

"Solid enough for London and back, he is."

Lord Brookway turned an inquiring glance on Freddie who had been left out of the conversation until then.

"Are you planning such a trip?" his father asked.

Freddie gave a firm nod. "I'll be leaving for London this very night. As soon as I've had the chance to pack my things." He used a tone with little room for argument, remembering his adamant statement to Jasper that his parents and hers would not be allowed to stand in his way.

When he'd expected a protest, instead his father thumped him on the back. "I'd guess your appointment went very well then. Lord Pendleton sending you off to the city to explore some new avenue for profits? I knew you had a thing or two to learn from the man. I'll ask you to linger long enough for me to give you some arrangements of my own to make while you're there. No need to clutter our next visit with business if you're making a trip for that very purpose."

He turned to lead Freddie to the study, clearly having forgotten Ferrier's presence in his enthusiasm.

"I'll be with you in a moment, Father. First I have business to conduct with Mr. Ferrier."

Lord Brookway glanced back, looking from Freddie to the farmer. "I suppose you do at that."

He said nothing further, but Freddie could hear the pride in his voice.

Straightening his back, Freddie led Ferrier to the front parlor and asked him to wait while he went and fetched the payment. Just this simple act, taking responsibility for more than buying a round at the tavern, made Freddie feel more confident not only in this moment but in his pursuit of Georgie.

If both his father and hers saw him as a mature gentleman, they should have no argument against his wish to marry, and in respect for that maturity, should accept how he'd be firm in the choice of his wife.

The harder part might be to convince Georgie of the same. She'd had a very clear image of him when last they spoke. It had held little maturity and much less to attract. He knew well enough how many handsome young men London could lay claim to, and a good number of those with both property and titles.

Remembering Jasper's reassurance, he carried out the final steps of his preparation without letting morose thoughts cut through his hope. Both paying her father and collecting the information regarding his father's business proved his value. He had only to get to London and find her. His father might think he went on business and Ferrier that he tested his new horse, but whereas some might consider marriage a business proposition, he considered his Georgie nothing less than a pleasure. He did not plan to leave London without her at his side.

Chapter Twenty-Three

he carriage pulled up in front of a house more similar in size to the Pendleton Manor than any of the homes Georgie had been to since coming to London. She let the uniformed footman hand her down to a paved walk and stood there, gaping, as the others disembarked.

"You'll have to pretend better than that," Isabella whispered, lacing their arms together. "They can't suspect you've never been to a formal ball before despite most of them being aware you were presented just today. I swear the older women can smell fear."

Whether intended as a warning or not, her friend's words brought a smile to Georgie's lips and broke through the awe that threatened to cripple her. "Well, then, I'll have to treat everything like I would a curious squirrel and watch from the corners of my eyes."

Her comment drove all seriousness from Isabella's expression as her friend covered her mouth to smother a laugh. "I doubt any of them would appreciate being compared to a wild creature, Georgie. Be careful what you share over the dances you're sure to be offered. I'd hate for you to get a reputation as a cutting wit. It's a dangerous position without wealth and standing to back it up."

Aubrey came between them then, abandoning Barbara to her mother's care for once so he could escort the youngest women into the ball.

Georgie gave him a smile with more than a touch of gratitude for relieving her of the need to respond. Anything she came up with would be more likely to prove Isabella's fears than ease them. Still, as the man at the ballroom door announced them, his sonorous tones sending her name rolling through an elaborate company, she remembered the first warning about hiding her awe, joking or not.

Light showered down from the ceiling where candles, their flickering wicks encased in glass made to sparkle like gems, stood on many-armed structures. The music filled what was an immense space, a string quartet providing harmony to the sound of murmured voices. Even the greenery offered much to amaze with what could only be trees growing out of pots larger than the rain barrels set below the farmhouse eaves.

They made their way to where the host and hostess held court, Georgie giving another curtsy with a murmur of gratitude but letting the others speak. As promised, she kept her visual exploration to what she could see in her periphery, admiring ladies and gentlemen alike as much as the decorations.

A dance set formed on the floor, and Georgie turned to watch them, happy to see steps she knew performed with the same amount of grace she could manage.

A young man executed a flawless transition and for a moment, Georgie stood again beneath the gentle shadows of the branches, Freddie holding the tips of her fingers as they promenaded from one end of the glade to the other as though surrounded by other dancers. This had been what he'd most likely envisioned while she had at best seen a mostly empty ballroom with only men in work clothes to partner the few students.

Isabella caught her arm and pulled her further across the room after the rest of their group. Her friend looked as comfortable as any at this event, and more than some who clung to one wall or another. Georgie fought the sudden urge to find herself a spot beneath one of those over-sized plants where she could observe without being seen herself. Only thought of what the squirrels would make of such behavior kept her standing tall.

If she could not handle herself here among friends, just how did she expect to face Freddie's mother in the woman's own domain? She could become a squirrel in behavior, always clinging to a tree and ready to spring into flight at any moment, or she could enjoy herself here at what was likely to be a rare chance to see how those in London society lived. After all, her Freddie had showed his love for the country matched her own, and she doubted they'd spend much of their time here among the bejeweled and glamorous company. Hadn't he said the absence of time in London had been his mother's most common complaint, not his?

The memory brought a smile to her lips and eased the tension she'd been feeling.

If not even one who loved London could manage a reasonable amount of time here in these spaces, how much less would she have to come after her marriage. She had little inclination for this type of company. It had taken no special awareness to see judgment in the eyes of older women as they weighed each prospect, male or female, on a scale of wealth and property while she had even less interest in the true purpose of these gatherings with her heart already bound to another.

Barbara's complaints about the strict life served Georgie well now, reminding her how she must behave to weather the judgment without drawing attention to herself.

The thought no sooner passed through her head than she caught sight of a gentleman striding purposefully toward them.

Isabella followed her gaze and gave a smothered yelp, the color fading from her cheeks.

"Is he someone known to you?" Georgie asked, wondering if the young man had offended Isabella in some way.

Her friend gave a quick head shake and pressed her lips together firmly, leeching the color from them as well so she left only a ghostly appearance.

Georgie had been too focused on her own interests and needs. She'd forgotten the desperate request from Aubrey though she'd seen the edge of it herself at the theater.

Here, without the shelter of dim lighting or exacting rules governing who could approach and when, the extent of Isabella's retiring nature became evident to everyone, not just those close to her. An introduction Aubrey would be only too happy to provide offered slight protection when her friend looked ready to bolt.

"Come," Georgie said, tugging Isabella into the shadow of one of the trees she'd been eying for her own purposes.

Aubrey sent a frown in her direction even as the approaching man turned aside, but Georgie ignored them both.

Once they had found a place out of the view of all those judgmental eyes, Georgie turned Isabella to face her.

"Remember the squirrels? They chitter loudly and want nothing more than to steal the bread from your fingers, but they have no real command over anything."

The confusion in Isabella's expression made Georgie wonder if she'd ever seen a squirrel much less fought over a piece of bread with one, but then her friend blinked and a giggle escaped her lips.

"That's better. I want you to compare each of them, men and women alike, to squirrels, or perhaps rats depending." She drew her fingers up to her mouth to imitate the large teeth of a rat she'd once caught in the pantry, and Isabella laughed again.

Then Aubrey's sister sobered. "I don't know if I can. I see them, and all my mother's warnings and reminders about proper behavior and the dangers of unchaperoned men come racing up, turning the lot of them into monsters."

Georgie stared at her friend, wondering if Aubrey or any of the girl's family knew the root of her friend's shyness. She reached over and gave Isabella's cheeks a hard pinch to chase away the pallor.

"Well, now you know they are nothing but squirrels in the parlor. You can send them running with a quick sweep of your broom if need be. Come on. I've only danced in lessons or practice. I can't very well accept a turn on the dance floor while leaving you behind to suffer your brother's company. Or worse, your mother's. I suspect Aubrey wouldn't mind clasping hands with Barbara out there either. After all, they're not married yet and so are subject to the same limits any of us are."

Isabella looked dubious but put her shoulders back as though ready to do battle, the red from Georgie's pinch already fading.

No one would approach them with such a martial look in Isabella's eye. They'd be as terrified of her as she had been of them.

Georgie leaned in close just as she tugged Isabella from their shelter and whispered, "Besides, your mother is right to fear you letting one of the men in too close. Kisses can be quite delightful."

Her friend turned a startled gaze on her, but Georgie only lowered her head in a slow nod, ending the gesture with a wink.

As she'd hoped, red flooded her friend's face even as Isabella gave in to a guilty laugh that caught the attention of more than one nearby young gentleman.

"We'd best return to your brother's company before you're swept off without the shelter of a proper introduction," Georgie said with another wink.

Though Aubrey had frowned when they left, now he gave them a smile even as he turned to greet the first young gentleman to approach. Soon, despite their sorry beginning, both Isabella and Georgie were sweeping their way across the dance floor.

Whenever they met during a movement, Georgie did something to remind Isabella of her directive, and the admiring looks cast her friend's way were reward enough. Isabella managed to contain her laughter during the later sets, but the blush on her features remained. Satisfaction filled Georgie at having succeeded so well, though whether the animation would persist off the dance floor and on to other engagements, only time would tell.

The night wore on with no shortage of partners.

No sooner had they returned from one set than they were sent out on another until Georgie's head spun and not just with delight. She might have enjoyed her dance with Freddie in the forest a little more, but she could see she'd have to encourage Lady Pendleton to hold dances at the manor because the very activity was exhilarating...and exhausting.

"Aubrey, please," Isabella said upon their return. "Can we just sit along the wall and sip a cooling drink?" She cooled herself with the lace fan she wore strapped to her wrist.

Georgie agreed with the sentiment, but from the look of disappointment on the face of a young gentleman nearby, he'd hope to claim one of them for the next set.

"I'm sure Lord Simon would be happy to procure drinks for both the young ladies, would you not?" Aubrey asked.

"As you wish." The young lord in question gave them both a smile and went off in pursuit of refreshments.

"Oh," Isabella groaned, sinking into one of the provided chairs. "My feet ache and I feel quite overheated."

Georgie raised one eyebrow. "Are you trying to convince me you weren't enjoying yourself out there?"

Isabella ducked her head, a quiet giggle reaching Georgie's ears. "You have the oddest ideas, but how effective they proved to be. Squirrels, indeed."

"And rats. Don't forget the rats."

Aubrey and Barbara gave the two of them confused looks, but before either could attempt an explanation, Lady Whitfeld took the seat next to Georgie and caught her hand.

"Georgiana, I am not one bit surprised you've proved quite the favorite. Why you have had a refined collection of young men interested in making your acquaintance from well-placed merchants to lords. You're sure to come out of this season with a proposal or two to consider."

Georgie flushed, trying to stay still when she wanted to pull away with every fiber of her being.

"No need to be embarrassed. You are a beautiful young woman, and Barbara explained as how you've been preparing for this very event under the tutelage of the new Lady Pendleton. There's many who would sit at your side just for tidbits about that one, let me tell you."

She waved a hand to dismiss Lady Pendleton from the conversation. "That's neither here nor there beyond how talented she's proved to be in bringing out your grace. Why, when I remember the wild child you— No matter. You've grown into a lovely young woman who will have her choice of suitors, enough to make many with a much more elevated status envious."

Her aunt kept speaking on this topic, analyzing the suitability and value of each and every one of the young men Georgie had danced with, and some who had approached Lady Whitfeld or Aubrey with the request for an introduction while Georgie had been in a set.

After Lady Whitfeld dismissed the third because he lacked a title, with only a side mention of his other values, Georgie began to fume. She fervently wished her Freddie the farm hand her father and all the rest seemed to think him if only to prove her affections had nothing to do with a heavy purse or fancy titles.

Lord Simon's return could not have been better timed as his presence put an end to the detailed assessments.

He stood before them, talking of nothing of note for the remainder of the set, allowing both Isabella and Georgie to catch their breaths, but Georgie would have preferred staying on the dance floor until she collapsed in a faint to enduring another conversation like the last with Lady Whitfeld.

Her aunt was so determined to repeat her own elevation in rank she never considered whether Georgie would be happy in this place with all its restrictions. Could this have been what sent Charlotte home with sadness in her gaze?

Georgie's interests didn't matter a whit when compared to her ability to attract a title and a wealthy one at that. If only she could have told them the truth about Freddie. Though a baron's heir, and with only a small property, surely he had enough standing to be worthy in her aunt's eyes.

Some of her frustration eased into a chuckle as she realized this had been the same puzzle Freddie faced with his mother. How amusing for her to consider whether he'd be found acceptable when he'd been so concerned of her own ability to gain his mother's approval.

The musicians signaled the beginning of another set, and Georgie rose, much invigorated by her rest, or so it must have seemed to any onlooker. They could not know the heat in her cheeks came from how conceited even her blood became when adapted to the city environment.

"Come, Isabella, surely we've rested long enough and can obtain partners for this set."

That earned her a censorious look from her aunt, but Lord Simon stepped forward immediately to offer his hand to Georgie while another young man approached Isabella with a hopeful expression.

Before the music began, they'd taken their places once more, and Georgie did her best to wipe her aunt's words from her mind as she gave herself over to the steps and music. Conversations, when occasion allowed for them, she kept light and simple, determined to make the most of her first ball.

Chapter Twenty-Four

G eorgie enjoyed the evening, but her favorite part came when, while waiting for the St. Vincent and Whitfeld carriages to arrive, Isabella gave her an enthusiastic hug.

"Thank you so much, Georgie. I don't know when I've enjoyed myself as much in this season or before. I'd thought the theater outing a pleasant one, but you bring light and strength wherever you go. Your willingness to be blunt and honest no matter who stands before you…why it is contagious. Now if I could just borrow some of your confidence."

Georgie squeezed Isabella to her once before stepping back to say, "I'm glad you enjoyed this, though you misjudge me on all accounts. It wasn't the breeze from the outer door that had my skirt quivering when we arrived. If not for the lot of you, I would have turned tail and ran."

Isabella laughed her statement off, but it held more truth than the blunt honesty her friend thought she saw. Georgie had more secrets than the Prince Regent's spymaster. She'd considered whether she might be able to confess to Isabella because of her partiality to Mr. Ingham despite Lady St. Vincent's wish for a grander suitor, but tonight had revealed the partiality to be a matter of fear more than attraction. His retiring nature could hardly have reminded Isabella of Lady St. Vincent's warnings about men. With the stories having lost their sway, any number of titled and wealthy suitors were waiting to take his place if only Isabella held strong.

Aubrey caught her arm, startling Georgie out of her thoughts to discover he'd already handed his sister up into the carriage after their mother. He would join the two of them once the Whitfeld carriage pulled up for the rest of the company, Georgie included.

"My thanks as well. I have no idea what country magic you enacted, but my sister is a woman transformed. Where I'd despaired of her finding a suitable mate barring an arrangement made by our parents no matter how many seasons they gave her, now I suspect she won't reach the end of her first without an offer or two. You are a wonder."

Her cheeks flushed at the praise, this time containing no misconceptions. "I would do anything to see to my friend's happiness. She deserves to find someone who loves her for who she is, though from what we've learned of your own tale, I'd be surprised if any find that here."

Aubrey gave her fingers a light squeeze and released her as Barbara came up on her side.

"Don't worry, Georgie. With the combined efforts of your family and mine, we'll be sure to find someone suitable. You might never go home again."

He turned to face his love and so missed Georgie's shudder.

She'd do anything to ensure his kind wishes didn't come to be, though if Freddie asked it of her, she'd have no choice but to succumb. Not a single one of these elegant gentlemen, regardless of status, held a candle to the man she'd given her heart long before she even recognized the lending. Whatever the sacrifice, none would be too great to have Freddie for her own as long as she could do so without shaming her father.

She knew she'd been wrong to accuse Freddie of wanting to make her his mistress, but her rejection of such a role still stood. All the more reason he needed to rush here and collect her.

Georgie feared her aunt would encourage her brother to make Georgie stay through the season. If so, even should she manage to turn aside whatever offers came forward with her aunt's blessing if not her father's, she'd like as not find Freddie's mother had selected a suitable mate for him and brought her down to the Brookway Manor to press Freddie in the suit. Somehow, she didn't think her father or Freddie's parents would look kindly on her borrowing a horse from the Whitfeld stables and riding all the way back home, even if she knew the direction.

"And there's our carriage."

At first, Georgie thought her cousin had been speaking to her, but from the reluctance as Barbara pulled away from Aubrey, she realized they'd been holding up the line of carriages as others sought to leave for home or different pleasures.

A footman handed her up first and then Barbara before closing the door with a firm snap of the latch.

Her cousin settled onto the opposite bench with no sign of surprise.

"Your mother isn't coming?"

Barbara shook her head. "Mother decided to remain behind and make arrangements for some other event. She's lucky you returned with me. I've met the purpose of the season, and after all the trouble I got into when I fully participated, I'd have likely chosen to remain at home."

Georgie laughed. "Not from how you are all smiles on the dance floor, even with partners other than Aubrey. Besides, your mother would never have allowed you to retire if only to avoid the gossip regarding your state. It would have grown instead of fading once they found others to chatter on about."

Barbara put a limp hand to her forehead. "What you must think of us. All worry about gossip and appearance. It's a wonder you don't borrow my horse and set off for home."

Startled by how close her cousin came to her own thoughts, Georgie paused a moment too long before saying, "You've spent a good portion of the summer with my sisters. You might not have gone down to the tavern, but surely you don't think the country free of gossip for all Charlotte would like to pretend otherwise. Besides, I didn't seek to come here, but I would have missed the chance to befriend Isabella, and she's a delight."

"That she is, and it's good for you to have friends here beyond your family. After all, when you get offers, they're unlikely to be with an eye set to spending all their days out in the country."

Georgie stiffened at the implied criticism of her home, though why it should surprise her considering Barbara's thoughtless comments at the farm, she didn't know. "What if I already have a suitor who will not require me to move to London? You may prefer it here, though you seemed happy enough to enjoy the freedoms there, but I know where I belong and it's not in the city with its focus on entertainments, and confinement in both clothing and behavior."

Barbara leaned forward to put a hand on Georgie's knee. "Georgiana, no life a farm hand could offer you would compare to what you can aspire to. You've shown yourself capable of traveling in more august company. Why limit your future so? Life would be so much better if you won the interest of a wealthy, and titled, gentleman. Even if you cling to your farm hand, your father would never allow such an assignation in any case. If he thought you should set your sights low, he wouldn't have tossed you into the wagon at my side."

Shifting her leg so her cousin's hand fell away, Georgie scowled at Barbara. "Everyone thinks they know so much about me and what I want out of life. Perhaps my true desires would surprise every one of you. I rather think they would, except for one aspect. I'm eager to cheer on my new friend and make my aunt happy with the excuse to go to all the events planned for the season."

Her anger faltered then, and a smile crossed Georgie's lips. "Though from what I've seen, she'd be welcome without my presence or yours."

She frowned again as she continued, "But you will not change my mind. You will not find some gentleman better than my Freddie, or one who will wipe him from my heart. I thought you of all people would understand considering Aubrey offered for you when he thought you no more than I am in truth."

A dreamy look crossed Barbara's face at the mention of Aubrey, but she cast it aside in favor of catching hold of Georgie's hands and meeting her gaze.

Georgie narrowed her eyes in an attempt to show she was serious, but her best effort had little effect.

"Times are hard, Georgie. You think you have chores now. As a farm hand's wife, you'd have nothing but labors as you tried to earn enough to buy flour for bread. You might not have been brought up to the London life, but you were raised as a daughter of property. It's not so easy to cast that aside as you might think. Don't imagine love will fill your belly when the food runs out or warm your hands when there's nothing to burn in the fire."

A sharp laugh burst from Georgie then. "You think you know so much about country life. You've barely spent any time there since becoming a mature young woman but you're all quick to counsel me on the suffering to be found. You think the city free of poverty and hunger? I guess you were too tied up in thoughts of your fancy lord when we arrived to notice the beggars."

"I never said times were any less hard here in the city. In some ways, they are harder for those who lack, but you would not be among them. My mother will turn aside any suitor who cannot afford a wife easily enough, and you can be sure of a comfortable living at least if you don't end up with a gentleman who is very well off indeed. If your farm hand had such to offer, why wouldn't he have come to your father and ask for permission to court you instead of stealing you away and chancing your future?"

Barbara shook her head, pity marking her features. "You wouldn't be happy with such a life. You might think I know nothing, but unlike most of my gender, I read the paper and listen when the men discuss the ways of our world. If you think a hard plot of over-used soil is the same as the kitchen garden by your father's house, you couldn't be more wrong. At best you'd live on your father's charity, reminded every day of how you disappointed him. Worse would be Uncle Ferrier spurning you for your disobedience and leaving you with nothing."

Georgie had let Barbara carry on, seeing no good way to stop her without revealing the truth, but that she couldn't let stand. "My father would never."

A faint smile tugged Barbara's lips only to fade just as quickly. "No, I wouldn't believe it of him, but there have been others who chose Gretna Green to circumvent their parents and found the most loving turn hard when betrayed."

Something about how Barbara said the last word seemed to resonate in the small space of the carriage.

Betrayed.

She'd thought her secrets innocent because she never chanced her virtue whatever others might think. For her father to see it as a betrayal never crossed her mind. He'd be angry, even hurt, but she'd always believed he'd come to see as how they had little choice.

Georgie sank against the carriage wall and stared out beyond the curtain, the blackness broken by street lamps as a country lane never would be. Whether she stole a horse or did some unforgivable act to be sent home, the pain of her failure would fall on her father's shoulders. Already he blamed himself for her wild streak though it had come from her mother alone. Could she risk her father's love as well as his pride?

She knew the answer even before the question danced through her mind.

Whatever came of this season, she could not do anything to bring it to a close or risk breaking her father's heart. To draw harm down on her father was more than she could bear. She had only to cling to the hope of Freddie's love being as strong as her own.

He'd come for her or he'd wait for her, but they would keep their secrets no longer. Her father had the right to know, as did his parents. No good would come of hiding the truth, and already she suffered if only in hearing lecture after lecture of how she should cast aside a farm hand who had never existed.

Exhaustion swept over Georgie greater than the ball could account for.

She'd forgiven Freddie for protecting his inheritance as how could she not when he worked to preserve their future. She'd believed nothing could sunder her family and had flaunted that misguided faith before him rather than offering the gift of her own love in full measure.

By the time they reached the Whitfeld town house, she had sunken into a quiet state that could have been mistaken for sulking, but until she spoke to Freddie, she would not end the silence. Not with Barbara and not even with Isabella as much as she longed to have someone to share her fears with.

Georgie had gone into the secrecy willingly. Now she would pay the price for disregarding her father's wishes. She'd known from the start he would not approve. That he had not forbidden her visits with Freddie spoke poorly of her because she'd kept them from him and said nothing of his will in this matter.

Chapter Twenty-Five

The journey to London was tiring but uneventful. Freddie's new horse proved to have a steady, smooth gait, and the few travelers they'd come across were just as interested in getting to where they were going as he was. The glow of lanterns from a roadside inn almost convinced him to stop, his indecision clear enough to the horse it had tried to turn in, but until he reached London, he couldn't start planning his approach. On he went while the sun lit the sky and the world began to stir once again.

Merchants bringing goods into the city proper began to clog the road, and Freddie thought again of the inn where he could have secured a few hours rest before arriving on his grandparents' doorstep, travel stained and weary. He'd be lucky if their butler didn't turn him away before he could announce himself.

He'd planned to find lodgings and carry out his search without interference or obligations, but his mother had convinced him it would do irreparable harm to their family should he spurn the Lord and Lady Tamwood by arriving in London and failing to make his presence known to them. Business seemed too little an excuse when he couldn't give the true one, but he'd refused to linger another day while she sent word.

His horse stumbled as it tried to duck a mule's sidekick, tired as it was by the long journey.

Freddie swung down and led the horse through the gathering crowds, breathing out a sigh as he broke free of the edges and entered the wealthier areas where London hours held sway. In the peace and quiet, he had to admit the benefit of his mother's plan. Though he might joke to himself about being turned away, instead of searching London for suitable lodgings when he didn't know how short or long a visit he would be making, he would be welcomed, cared for, and offered food and a room without dipping any further into his savings.

By the time he reached their home, a measure of energy returned as he looked forward to seeing his grandparents and perhaps the cousins he remembered fondly.

The butler took one look at his face and gave a broad grin. "Mr. Hathwell. I didn't know we were expecting you, but Lady Tamwood will be delighted. Come in. I'll send one of the boys out to handle your beast."

Freddie shook his head in rueful amazement. It had been over a year since he'd come. He'd like to think he'd grown both taller and older in appearance, but nothing much slipped past a man who had been greeting him since he could not stand higher than the butler's knees without straining.

"Your parents are following after?"

"Not this time, Blake. I'm here on business."

Mr. Blake put a hand on each of Freddie shoulders and looked him over. "On business. You have grown up so quickly. Why, I remember when you would run through the house for the kitchens when you first arrived with no thought to anything but your stomach."

Freddie glanced down the corridor. "I could use something to fill me up right now if Mrs. Blake has anything prepared. I know it's early yet."

"My Martha would have my head if I dared suggest you wait until breakfast. Your grandmother has yet to rise, but we can get you settled in a room and with a tidy snack to hold you over."

Freddie smothered a yawn with a hand that held the strong stench of horse sweat. "And maybe a tub to wash in? I think she'd be happier to see me if I looked and smelled less like a stable boy."

The butler shook his head, but not in denial. "And the boy you were wouldn't think to proper presentation either. Come along, then. We'll get you set right now. The blue room, I think. That wasn't your favorite before, but it's a proper room to suit a young man of distinction as you have become."

Smothering a laugh at how easy it had been to convince Mr. Blake of his maturity, Freddie followed after the man's firm steps. If only his parents were as quickly accepting of his new state.

He shook off the thought as soon as it crossed his mind. Had his mother been truly convinced, he'd already be courting some London flower whatever he felt. He'd been in such a rush to prove himself worthy of Georgie, he'd failed to consider the impact of maturity in his mother's eyes.

"What's this, Blake? A visitor? Doesn't he know how rude such an hour is?"

Freddie glanced up the staircase to see his grandfather, the man looking all too spry for his age. "I apologize for the hour, Lord Tamwood, but I just arrived in from the country. Mr. Blake was setting me up with a room and a wash before I presented myself."

His grandfather peered down, only the faint lines at the corners of his eyes giving away his failing eyesight. He'd married Lady Tamwood late in his years, a match as much for love as position to hear him tell it. Freddie had uncles almost of an age with his grandmother from Lord Tamwood's first wife.

Lord Tamwood came down a few more steps then gave a startled laugh. "From the stench, I'd think you a simple messenger boy, but with that face, it's none other than little Freddie, is it not?"

Freddie gave him a smile as broad as the one Mr. Blake offered in greeting not so long ago. "It is. One and the same, though a little older and, I hope, wiser."

Mr. Blake straightened when Freddie wouldn't have thought the butler had any more to stretch. "He's here on business. All by himself as this isn't a pleasure visit."

Lord Tamwood gave Freddie an appraising look. "Well, I certainly hope you are not planning to go about like that, my boy."

"I'll leave you to find your own way to the blue room while I arrange your bath," the butler said, not waiting for an answer before he turned and left.

Freddie mounted the few steps remaining between him and his grandfather. "I'd hoped to stay with you while I am in town. There wasn't time to send a note ahead."

Lord Tamwood's bushy eyebrows rose. "Urgent business even. Why do I think it's my wife whose council you'll be seeking in these matters?"

His grandfather proved too astute by far as a flush heated Freddie's cheeks. He'd kept his parents ignorant with little effort, but it seemed he would have to provide more than a vague statement to explain his business to the older generation.

"My father, who sends his greetings as does my mother, of course, needs me to check on the farm equipment he requested, and I have a few things of my own to look into."

Lord Tamwood gave Freddie a gentle push up the stairs. "I'll be happy to help you with your father's requests in any way I can. Your own, I suspect, require a softer touch than I can provide. For the time being, though, you'd best make your way to the blue room and the bath. As much as your grandmother will be pleased to see you, she would prefer not to need a vinegar sponge to suffer your presence."

He said the last with a hearty laugh, but Freddie had no doubt as to the accuracy of the statement.

"I will go make myself presentable, Grandfather. I have much to accomplish while I'm here."

Lord Tamwood had resumed his journey down the stairs, but he turned back then to give Freddie a wink. "I'm sure you do, boy. I remember how it was when I had the heat of youth to drive me. My eyes may be dimming, but my memory, especially of those days, remains as sharp as ever."

Freddie offered no reply as he continued forward, wishing he could believe his grandfather's teasing a general statement about young men. He suspected, however, in his haste he'd laid clues to those willing to consider the possibility that were hard to dismiss.

As he set out his things in the blue room, Freddie realized his grandfather's ability to guess at least part of the truth opened opportunities he hadn't considered.

He had a letter of introduction to the one man who might know of Georgie's whereabouts, but he'd never been in charge of his doings while in London. Freddie had little idea of the expectations beyond that society kept much different hours. He had no idea how to go about proffering Jasper's letter without causing the same offense Lord Tamwood had suspected of him before he knew just who had intruded on his morning unannounced.

Freddie longed for the simplicity of his country life, but he could only find ease with Georgie at his side. As long as she'd been gone, he'd felt her absence as a hole in his heart, a gnawing emptiness that drew the joy from every moment and deepened each sorrow. This had to work. He had to find her and bring her back with him, his mother, tradition, and titles be damned.

GEORGIE SPENT A LONG NIGHT thinking on what Barbara had said, leaving her tired and out of sorts for the visit to the St. Vincents that afternoon.

She wasn't as blind to the straits of those in the country as her cousin thought, but then neither had she taken to kissing a farm hand behind the haystacks. Where Barbara's words struck hard was in how she'd pressed Freddie to cast everything aside. She'd told him to marry her without permission and without regard to her father's feelings any more than those of Freddie's family.

She saw Lady Brookway's actions as an attack on their love when the lady in question lacked knowledge crucial to understanding her son's heart. Whatever else, Georgie knew, with a firmness she'd have to convey to Freddie as soon as she had the chance, they must put an end to the secrecy.

"Did any of the young gentlemen you danced with last night make your heart flutter?"

She blinked, drawn back to the tea and Isabella's questions. "Not you, too? I had my fill of first Lady Whitfeld then Barbara listing their virtues." Georgie nodded toward where her cousin sat apart with Aubrey. "Can I not enjoy the event without pinning my future on it?"

Isabella gave her a sad smile. "The truth is you cannot. The event is designed to show off the young ladies and pair them up with suitable young gentlemen. There's little interest in simple enjoyment as to do so will transform you from a potential bride into a heartless scamp faster than you can blink."

"What about you?" Despite her annoyance, Georgie seized onto the topic to distract herself from the gravity of her own thoughts lest they take her over. "Did you enjoy the ball? You certainly danced with your share of partners."

A blush stained Isabella's cheeks. "I did. Much more so than any of the previous events thanks to you. Whenever I started getting nervous, I'd catch a glimpse of you puffing your cheeks or showing your teeth. I have to wonder what others thought of your antics, but I'm grateful for your help. And the times you made me burst into laughter, no one questioned it."

Georgie shook her head. "There's a reason to sorrow, not celebrate. If they couldn't see a cause and not a one questioned, it seems unprovoked laughter is a common event. Somehow I doubt it comes from delightful inner thoughts."

Peering at Georgie over the rim of her teacup, Isabella grinned. "I told you the purpose of these events. It is to catch a husband who is well positioned and wealthy to boot. If the young ladies must pretend to find their companions scintillating, so be it."

"That's more wrong than you know."

Her adamant exclamation drew the attention of not just her cousin but Isabella's sisters and their husbands as well.

Georgie sank back into her chair, heat flooding her features at the breach of propriety, but she stared at Isabella without flinching. "If they win their husbands by pretending," she said much more softly, "they'll spend the rest of their lives either in pretense or suffering for the lack of it."

Isabella's lips curled into a wry smile as she nodded. "But what other choice is there? You've seen as well as I have how little chance there is to delve into the heart of a person during the season. Every move is chaperoned, and sequestering yourself with any one gentleman will require the posting of banns even if all you ascertained is that you do not suit in the least."

"You seemed to enjoy Mr. Ingham's presence well enough. Are you saying you don't suit?"

Her friend glanced around the room as though checking on everyone's position before answering. "No. We don't suit at all. He has no standing, no title, and we have no need of his wealth, especially as it is a modest portion."

Georgie stared at Isabella, stunned. She'd heard Lady Whitfeld and Lady St. Vincent commenting on how lovely it was to see Isabella show interest in someone other than Mr. Ingham, but she would have sworn her friend had shown a marked fancy.

"Does his standing matter so much? Does a lack of title put him, and all others in the same state, beneath your notice?"

Isabella paled and put a hand on Georgie's arm. "Please don't think that way. I would hate to see you turn aside my friendship over some mistaken belief about my own opinions."

Staying still under the touch took more energy than she had expected, but Georgie had already drawn the disapproving attention once, and remembering her own thoughts, she could not chance offending without having it reflect back on her father.

"If my opinions are mistaken, why are you so quick to dismiss Mr. Ingham? Or is it fine to have one like me among your friends as long as you don't commit the error of joining your family to a gentleman of such low standing."

She regretted her scorn almost before it left her mouth as Isabella withdrew not just the hand Georgie had found so intrusive, but her whole self into the shy creature Georgie had only seen brief glimpses of since the first day.

"I have no real interest in Mr. Ingham," Isabella said in tones so soft Georgie had to lean close to hear them. "It was only how his quiet nature eased my fears. I did not feel the expectation of perfection because he lacks the attributes to command it. I would never dismiss you because of title or standing. You must know that. You have become a true friend despite the short time we've known each other."

Georgie reached out this time and caught both of Isabella's hands in her own. "I should never have thought it of you, but having had my fill of such talk last night, I remain too aware of the possibility." Her smile sank a bit as she continued, "But surely he does not deserve to be used so, and did not yesterday show your assessment of your own virtues to be quite poor and having little relation with the truth?"

Again, Isabella avoided her gaze to stare down at their linked hands.

"If you truly have no feelings for the man, you must leave him to find his own match," Georgie said when her friend did not speak. "It's only right."

"What have you two found so irresistible here in the corner?"

Susan came over to join them, putting an end to any further conversation about the man.

Georgie still felt unsettled, though whether for Mr. Ingham's sake or her own, she couldn't be sure. She had little experience with choosing friendships not for their own sake but out of a need to cling to the only bit of security one could find.

She'd never had a lack of self-confidence. Her sisters would lay the charge she could have done with less.

If only Isabella made the right decision in abandoning Mr. Ingham's company for that of other young men. Georgie feared Ingham already harbored some level of expectation when their pairing had been made note of enough for Barbara's mother to have made mention.

The world of London society seemed so caught up in the matter of titles, standing, and wealth until the people behind those aspects were forgotten, a tendency open to much abuse. If only Freddie would appear to pull her from this place before she erred as Isabella had done and brought hope where there could be none. Her aunt and cousin would be quick to encourage likely suitors with every good intention, and would continue to do so until she was able to reveal her connection to Freddie.

Georgie fought a twisted smile as she realized the very threat that sent her from him in anger, of his mother pairing him up with some lady of high standing, now threatened to take her from him again. Only this time it would be her bound to marry where her heart had not settled.

"You'll be coming to Lord Chesterburg's party tomorrow afternoon, Miss Georgiana, won't you?" Susan bestowed a gracious smile on Georgie, a vast change from their first meeting though she still seemed to emphasize Georgie's lack of a title a little too much. Or perhaps Georgie had grown too sensitive.

Georgie glanced to Isabella for confirmation and received a more trustworthy smile.

"If I've been invited, I would love to come." An afternoon party would have to mean a less constrained environment. If it were held outside as she'd heard Barbara mention could happen, she would even be able to stretch her legs. The dancing offered movements, but she'd spent too much time standing about between dances or sitting in the theater. Charlotte would laugh to know Georgie missed her chores when here in London, or perhaps she'd understand the urge all too well.

Susan laughed softly. "You are a guest of Lady Whitfeld. You are invited anywhere an event might be planned, I'm sure. Besides, you do so well for Isabella when we'd all but given up hope we'd take you in our own party if you were not going with your aunt."

Isabella colored at the description, but said nothing, so Georgie held her own tongue with effort. No wonder her friend had such difficulty. Isabella's family seemed to focus on her failures until there'd been no chance of anything else.

"I think an afternoon party would be delightful with Isabella. She makes such a good companion. I'll miss you horribly when I return home." Georgie said the last to Isabella and received a grateful smile.

"But you'll never have to return there, I'm sure," Isabella replied. "Well, other than for visits of course. You'll have your choice of suitors and all will be well."

Georgie laughed and shook her head. "Now here I thought our purpose to find you a match."

"There's gentlemen enough for the both of us," Isabella said with such confidence her sister gave her a surprised look, but for once Susan said nothing to belittle the thought.

Chapter Twenty-Six

reddie stretched out on the bed as he waited for the bath to be brought up only to wake some hours later to a cold tub and lengthening shadows visible through the open blinds.

He cursed the wasted time as he leapt up, ready to search all of London. When he reached out a hand to open the door, though, he caught sight of the dusty sleeve of his riding jacket.

Any hope for success depended on him impressing not just Georgie but her family, something he could not accomplish if forbidden entrance by the servants. Even more, he had to visit Jasper's friend first. Lord Aubrey St. Vincent would be unlikely to listen if Freddie hadn't taken the time to wash off his travel dirt.

The cold tub looked unwelcoming, but he could not very well make Lord Tamwood's servants empty the tub and then refill it with hot water a second time. Besides the lack of consideration, the minutes it would take ate at him when he'd wasted so many.

Mindful of the passing hours as much as the chilly water, Freddie washed quickly then tucked himself into clothing that wouldn't offend his grandmother as much as his stench might have. To run out without speaking with her would be all too rude, especially after sleeping through the day.

A servant caught his attention as he opened the door. "Her ladyship is waiting for you in the front parlor," he said in a clear imitation of Mr. Blake, broken when his voice cracked on the last word.

Freddie curbed the need to smile and gave the boy a serious nod. "Can you direct me?"

Though he knew the path well, Freddie felt it would give the boy a chance to recover from his embarrassment before reporting back to his other duties.

"There you are, my boy," Lady Tamwood cried as he entered the parlor. "Come and let me have a look at you. Lord Tamwood says you've grown mightily since we saw you last."

He stood still under her inspection, hoping he'd kept the flush from his cheeks as he considered what else his grandfather might have told her. The heat gathered there suggested failure.

"Enough. Sit and tell me what brought you racing up to London so swiftly you exhausted yourself and your horse from what Mr. Blake said. Your grandfather gave me a good idea, but I'd prefer to hear your version of events."

Freddie sank into the chair opposite her and groaned, knowing anything Lord Tamwood had conveyed would hold no more than supposition. "Whatever he said, I've told him nothing."

She laughed. "You said nothing with your tongue, but he didn't get to be such a ripe old age without learning to read the clues people give when they think to hold silent. But still, tell me the whole of it, and I will banish his theories entirely."

He stared at his twisting fingers, unsure whether he should attempt to prevaricate or if anything but the truth would be believed.

"Out with it, boy. Nothing you say could startle me, but you may be surprised at how much of a help I can be."

His shoulders slumped, but Freddie raised his head to meet his grandmother's amused gaze. "I need direction to the St. Vincent residence. You could help me with that."

She gave a slight smile. "And I will as soon as you explain your purpose there. Surely you wouldn't be doing something so foolish as to call the heir out over a girl, though he did come recently from your area."

"No, nothing like that, I swear. I have a letter of introduction from Lord Pendleton. He believes Lord Aubrey St. Vincent can assist me with some information."

She waved a hand, proving she would not be satisfied with any answer but the one she expected.

He would have fought the pressure had his grandfather misspoken, but he could not lie to her face, not and expect her to welcome his return after having secured Georgie's hand as well as his love's restored affections.

"You might as well be out with it, Frederick. I haven't the patience of a young girl hanging on your every word, and I've a good idea of what you'll say in any case."

She answered his thoughts too closely for him to stop another flush from coloring his cheeks.

He gave a rueful shake of his head and let go of any attempt to keep the secret. The whole of his history with Georgie spilled out. When he stopped to draw a breath before adding the latest events, he half expected her to interrupt with the suggestion he attempt a match with one of his own station as his mother had.

Lady Tamwood laughed. "Things weren't done such in my day, and somehow I doubt they are now even out in the country. You've made quite a mess of this, Freddie, and you're right to put an end to this disreputable business lest it shadow the both of you."

"You don't think I should set her aside?"

"Frederick!" Lady Tamwood thrust to her feet, waving the cane she'd adopted as an affectation long before she needed it. "I'd hope my daughter and the baron she married would have raised you better than that. You told me you've been having assignations with this girl since before either of you knew just how wrong it was to do so, and you persisted even after your feelings grew greater than simple friendship. You've spoken to her of marriage. Have you no honor that you would treat her so?"

Freddie rose as well, taking his grandmother's arm in a soothing gesture. "I did not say I would set her aside. I only asked if you thought I should. Her father is well respected, but he has neither a title nor the wealth to support one."

She lightly slapped his fingers where they curled around her arm. "And this fact changes exactly what?"

"Not a thing." Freddie made no attempt to suppress his grin. "It's only my mother is quite adamant on the subject."

Lady Tamwood pulled free only to regain her chair as she waved away his words. "From what you've told me, my daughter remains ignorant of the whole affair. She cannot expect you to break your promise simply because of station. The time to separate you passed long ago, and I'd think less of you if you would allow it to occur now."

"Which is why I came all in a rush. I mean to find my farm girl wherever she is hiding here in London and make it clear the time for secrets is long gone. I wish to claim her for my own, but I must do so before some London dandy catches her eye."

His grandmother's eyes narrowed as she said, "If that were a true possibility, best you let it happen now rather than after the marriage vows have been spoken. You cannot force a person to love where they do not."

"Oh, she loves truly. Better even than I did." He shook his head, unwilling to explain the whole of it. "We quarreled, and before our anger cooled, she'd gone off to London with her cousin. She thinks I meant to cast her aside and so believes no impediment to finding herself a husband. Perhaps she even thinks one in London would mean she wouldn't have to suffer to see me with another."

Lady Tamwood tsked under her breath. "You have made it even worse than I thought, and all the more reason to conduct yourself properly now. You must prove to her you want this marriage by engaging her affections in the traditional fashion from now on."

"I have to find her first," he said, unable to keep the glum from his tone.

"Which brings us to the St. Vincents. Still the son, I presume. Have you cards?"

Freddie shook his head, confused by the sudden change in topic.

"Of course not. You would have little need for them in the country, and you're barely old enough to require them now. I'll ring for Mr. Blake to bring you a stack of your grandfather's cards. Better the wrong ones than none at all. You'll have to say yours are currently being made. I'm of half a mind to order up some for you as now you're no longer a child."

Mr. Blake arrived then, and she explained both about the cards and the order for Freddie's own.

"Of course, my lady. I'll have an order sent out first thing tomorrow morning, though it will take some time to get them made, I fear."

"Which is why we need Lord Tamwood's cards. If Frederick has gone back to the country before they are printed, I will keep them until his return." She glanced at Freddie and winked. "I suspect we'll need to order a batch for his lady then as well."

The butler's eyebrows rose, but when he turned to face Freddie fully, his sober expression had returned. "Congratulations, Mr. Hathwell."

Freddie smiled back, but shook his head. "No congratulations as of yet, but I have hope."

"Very well then. Good hunting, my lord."

Freddie laughed at the thought of Georgie's expression upon hearing his suit compared to a hunt, but then hadn't he chased her down on horseback? "And with that, can you fetch the cards without delay? I have the need to get on with it."

Lady Tamwood used the silver handle of her cane to catch his arm when he rose. "Not this day, you will not. Cook is preparing a meal for you, and then you'll spend the rest of the evening playing cards with me. Had I known you were coming, I'd have made arrangements for your entertainment as surely Lord Aubrey St. Vincent has to his. You'll win no favors banging on his door with him gone, and even fewer if you burst in on whatever event he might be hosting."

When he would have protested, she only shook her head. "Remember, you have to do this well and proper, or it will lack conviction. I'll arrange for our carriage to take to you the St. Vincent residence during visiting hours. You can make your case then, and if they happen to be out for the afternoon, it will be an appropriate hour to leave your card."

She sighed. "If your business were less urgent, I'd have you leave one tomorrow in any case and wait for a response, but I can only expect you to rein in your enthusiasm for a short while. You've yet to reach the age of understanding such things, and I doubt your farm girl has either."

Freddie had no argument to the pronouncement so settled in for a quiet evening. He'd forgotten his grandmother's aggressive streak, however, and struggled to win a single hand no matter what game he proposed.

Chapter Twenty-Seven

Freddie arrived at the St. Vincent household at the earliest hour his grandmother would allow for visiting. He knew he should appreciate her counsel when he understood so little of London conventions, and yet, every minute wasted weighed on him. Both Georgie's success and her failure in society threatened their chance at a future together.

He'd meant what he'd said to Lady Tamwood. He would stand against his family, against society itself, if it meant having Georgie at his side, but there was no need to make it more difficult than it already was.

"Wait here with the carriage. I suspect I won't be long."

Armed with Jasper's letter and his grandfather's cards, Freddie mounted the steps. He need only get her direction from Lord Aubrey, and he'd be on his way.

The bell echoed through the door as though a vast space existed beyond, a further sign of the St. Vincents' wealth of position and pocket even if he hadn't noticed how well proportioned the town house was in comparison to others on this street.

Freddie forced himself to stand still and practice the patience his grandmother had emphasized so as not to be shifting from foot to foot in a child's eagerness when the butler answered the door.

A memory of Lady Tamwood's cautions sent him fumbling for his grandfather's cards even as the door swung open. Any chance he could appear calm and collected had been lost.

The man looked down a decidedly long nose at Freddie. "How may I assist you?" The polite question sounded anything but.

Relaxing his jaw with force of will, Freddie straightened, one of the cards in hand. "I have come to speak with Lord Aubrey."

The butler took the proffered card between two fingers and glanced at it. "I had understood the Lord Tamwood to be a much older gentleman."

Freddie scowled at the implication he'd lifted the cards without permission and answered as if unaware of the insult. "He is. My grandfather gave me some of his cards while mine are being made up. Please tell Lord Aubrey that Mr. Hathwell is awaiting his pleasure."

With a grudging nod, the man placed Freddie's card on a tray designed for this purpose from the three others already resting there. "I will inform his lordship."

Freddie thrust a foot forward when the man seemed likely to close the door as a dismissal. "My business is somewhat urgent. I'll wait for his response in your parlor."

A little nervous at how this man would respond to his insistence, Freddie still would not back down nor remove his foot despite the butler's pointed stare.

"I'm afraid that will not be possible."

"Of course it's possible. These are appropriate visiting hours and I am intent on visiting with Lord Aubrey. Please inform him I am here." Freddie spared a grateful thought for his grandmother's interference. No telling what this man would have done had Freddie come too early to be seen.

The man's face seemed to soften a little at that.

Freddie offered a slight smile to show his appreciation and understanding of the butler's attempt to do his job, but earned a head shake in return.

"You misunderstand me, Mr. Hathwell. It is not possible because Lord Aubrey is not presently at home."

Freddie gaped at him for a moment, his grandmother's wisdom having failed in this instance, but then he rallied. "His sister, then. The youngest. It's her I need to speak with after all. Lord Aubrey is to introduce me." He gave no more information, knowing the man would assume a promise where none existed and a wish to escort the girl instead of asking after her commoner friend.

The man's stiff posture softened even more at this, making Freddie regret the lie. He'd deliberately misled the butler though he'd not said a word.

"I'm afraid she has gone to the party as well. There's nothing to be done except to leave your card. I'm sure they'll send word as soon as they return."

Freddie's shoulders slumped, very little of it acting. "Dash it all, I'm too late. I was supposed to go to the party with them, but Lady Tamwood wanted a chit-chat this morning, and you must know it's not at all appropriate to disappoint a woman of her years. I'd never hear the end of it if I did."

He gave up any attempt at sticking to the truth and knew his grandmother would not chide him for maligning her in this very good cause. "It's a much different thing to show up with a lovely young lady on my arm than to come as I am. I'll be a laughing stock among my fellows and a target for all the unattached women. If only I could give it a miss, but my absence will be noted and not forgiven. As it is, I'm sure to be unfashionably late. I'll never live this one down."

The butler sent him a sympathetic glance. "I'm sure Lord Chesterburg will understand. After all, his mother is a contemporary of Lady Tamwood if I don't miss my guess."

Freddie suspected the man knew more about the peerage than most who could claim a title. He felt awful having tricked him into revealing the host, but he'd had no choice. If Lord Aubrey and his sister both were attending, perhaps he could get Georgie's address without delay.

He'd have to beg forgiveness for this later, presuming he ever set foot in the St. Vincent residence beyond the tip of his boot still resting across the threshold.

Freddie withdrew the offending boot and gave a slight bow. "I most certainly hope you are correct, but I'd best be on my way as late as I am. Thank you for your assistance."

The butler had a smile on his face when he closed the door at last, and though not for the sister's sake, Freddie did all this out of the pursuit of true happiness. Perhaps the man would forgive him after all.

"Take me to Lord Chesterburg's residence," he told the coachman as soon as he'd returned to the vehicle. The only saving grace lay in his having dressed reasonably for the visit, something that should prove satisfactory for an afternoon event as well.

The carriage ride left him all too much time to dwell on the company Georgie had found herself in. He'd never thought less of her for her status as a farmer's daughter, but he'd failed to consider how her cousin's engagement meant she now had higher connections. Freddie's title and bloodline might not be a match for the sister-in-law of an earl, but he measured his value, and Georgie's, on other scales.

Had London turned her head until she realized she'd have better opportunities than the son of a simple country baron? Georgie might think him beneath her now where she'd never have considered such a thing before. Even as a child, he'd seen how his mother changed when they came to town. He'd thought his Georgie different, but she'd never had the chance to test her partiality until now.

Freddie forced the thought from his mind. It would do no good and only served to undermine his determination when soon he would face a butler sure to be as efficient as the one at the St. Vincent residence. He refused to let anything stand in his way, but if he broke with convention, his own behavior would prevent him, and it would embarrass his grandparents at the same time.

If only he had an invitation to this party.

Where the last should have sent despair racing through him, instead, Freddie laughed aloud.

An afternoon party on such a lovely day. Where else could it be held than in the garden?

Memories of such events in his childhood rose, but rather than focus on the games they would play and scoldings when they'd upset some lady's glass, he saw again the garden walls. Hedges of iron fence short enough for him to climb or thick shrubbery on its own were by far the most common.

Thanks to Georgie's training, he felt sure he could make his way through the growth or clamber over even a fence close to his own height. Freddie thought such a plan held more merit than attempting to storm the butler, and much less chance of being discovered as long as he took care.

Decided, he faced his approaching destination with something close to eagerness.

Barbara and Lady Whitfeld spent the morning doing their best to destroy any hope Georgie might have had of a relaxing event. Their intent had been much different, though. They wanted her to make the best possible impression on society and they'd been too kind for her not to appreciate their misguided efforts.

"Don't go wandering in the garden without an escort," Barbara had counseled at one point.

"And don't ever go with only a young gentleman," Lady Whitfeld had added.

Georgie could recite their cautions all day without a break for air and still, it seemed, she'd never get to the end of them.

No strolls, not too much enthusiasm should there be a game of battledore and shuttlecock, be careful of any male under the age of sixty unless he came accompanied by a wife, and so on.

Her head had begun to ache long before they reached the Chesterburg Manor some two hours earlier, and despite the lovely hat Barbara lent her for the occasion, she feared the sun would burn right through her. Or maybe the fever came from an afternoon spent outdoors while doing little more than sit or stand in place while engaging in proper conversations.

She envied the very young children who ran around after a ball or on a hobby-horse, playing all manner of loud, uncontrolled games with no thought to propriety, reputation, or appearance. She'd have happily joined them.

Georgie dabbed at perspiration that threatened to stain the fichu Barbara had lent her to cover her chest. Which of the many rules would she break if she moved into the shade of the gazebo she could see tucked in the garden corner? With her luck, some young gentleman would think it an opportunity just as Isabella's mother had feared.

What Georgie would have given to be in the forest right now under the shelter of tree branches.

Her thoughts jumped to Freddie as they did at the least excuse.

Would he be confined to his father's study hard at work? Out in the fields with the men? Or did he sit near the shallows of their brook and wonder whatever had become of her?

"Then my brother turned on the cat and scolded it roundly for failing to fulfill its legal bargain of keeping the household free of mice in return for a warm hearth. We knew then he was destined for law or politics," Isabella said with a chuckle. "He thought it a just penalty for having let a mouse take up residence in the walls of his room, keeping him up at all hours with scrabbling and chewing sounds."

As she caught the end of another tale about Aubrey, Georgie felt gratified to see the two gentlemen who had come to pass the time with them listening in rapt attention to Isabella, though whether they gathered intelligence to torment Aubrey with or genuinely enjoyed Isabella's company, only time would tell. She suspected they most likely had both aims in mind, or would come to that point even had they been seeking the attentions of a beautiful young woman.

They could both enjoy the company and make use of her confidences. Of that, Georgie was sure.

The gentlemen certainly weren't standing there to engage with her, not with how her thoughts kept wandering. They must have thought her a simpleton or as shy as Isabella had appeared before Georgie took a hand in repairing her friend's unfortunate distress.

Georgie wondered if the choice of story had been an accident or a secret joke between the two of them, Isabella's thoughts on what had brought them together as well.

When she met Isabella's gaze, the twinkle in her friend's eyes implied the latter, and Georgie offered up a smile that stretched her lips wide and allowed her to tuck her upper teeth out in an imitation that caught Isabella with laughter.

The two men just gazed upon her more intently, the one nearest Georgie having the courtesy to offer Georgie a smile as well only to start when he saw her expression.

Georgie turned away to smother her laughter, letting him assume she'd been embarrassed or shy rather than amused by his stunned look.

Freddie would have enjoyed the secret language she shared with Isabella. He probably would have been just as amused by Georgie's expression. Like as not, he'd have set out to better her imitation, playing at being wild creatures the way they'd sometimes done with those that came through their glade when they sat quiet and still.

One of the men began a story of his own, and though Georgie knew she should listen, her thoughts and even her gaze continued to wander.

She tracked another child's game that sent the little scamps ducking and twisting between the guests, bringing forth gasps and cries of dismay. It would seem, at least to an outsider, half the purpose of the game could be found in the responses triggered among the adults.

One of the hedges shuddered, catching her attention as she tried to figure out what this game involved.

Had they been in the forest, such a great movement would be cause for alarm, but nothing worse than active children offered excitement despite the party being out of doors. After all the rules her aunt and cousin had imposed, Georgie had expected to bat a shuttlecock about in the air at the very least. She envied the children their hoops and sticks.

The idea of standing about in the hot sun for no other purpose but to say they were in a garden seemed the height of foolishness, or so she thought until she saw the branches part and none other than Freddie himself attempt to pull through.

A surprised laugh burst from her lips before she could control the response only to turn into a chuckle as she realized he must have chosen this path because he snuck in without an invitation. Her aunt and cousin had been so concerned lest she destroy her reputation and shame them in front of London society, yet the one to behave in a monstrously foolish manner held a position among the peerage by measure of blood. Perhaps she'd influenced him more than she'd thought.

Georgie realized Isabella was staring at her in concern, and the gentleman had cut his story short to do the same, though his expression held a raised eyebrow and what could almost be considered a sneer. Her behavior had clearly set her below this company in his estimation, though likely as much from how she'd ignored his interest as her ill-timed laughter.

Reminded of what had provoked her humor, Georgie glanced again to the hedge only to see Freddie had managed to free all but one foot at great cost to the shrubbery, not to mention his dignity.

She wanted to cheer him on, delighted to see him finally come to London. What other purpose could he have except to claim her as his own?

"I dare say. Did that fellow just come through the greenery?"

Georgie hadn't realized how the others would follow her gaze to discover Freddie before he could mask his method of entry. She scrambled for something to distract them, but could think of nothing except that nowhere in the long list of rules she'd been given had her aunt or cousin mentioned a restriction on breaching the hedge rather than coming in through the door.

Chapter Twenty-Eight

utting through the hedge had seemed a better plan to Freddie than blustering his way past another butler, especially considering his lack of success with the St. Vincent sentinel. He just hadn't expected the growth to be quite so dense. He and Georgie had crossed between bushes often enough in the forest, but the spacing offered wider gaps and the clothing he wore there had less bulk.

Freddie straightened his coat and tried to dust off any plant fragments, all the while keeping his gaze from the damage he'd done to the bush. There was nothing he could do about it now except regret his impulsive action, and too much interest in its state would only draw attention.

He strolled a few steps away from the broken branches to distance himself before turning to scan the gathering for any sign of Lord Aubrey St. Vincent.

Only then did he realize the other flaw in his plan. He had no idea how to identify Lord Aubrey.

Georgie drove him to wild acts he'd never have considered on his own. His mother would be horrified to learn of them, though he suspected his grandmother would laugh. All he could think of was finding Georgie no matter what stood in his way. He would make his intentions clear to her and both their families rather than chance circumstance breaking them apart.

The rules of society barely impinged on his consciousness, but he'd have done better to think through his approach before now. If he'd been announced, he could have inquired as to the whereabouts of Lord Aubrey St. Vincent and had a servant bring him to the other man. Now, he'd add blunder upon blunder by charging up to one group after another in his quest.

His gaze continued to assess the company even as a tightening in his chest confirmed his poor chances. Mired in this conclusion, he met the stare of a well-dressed young lady. She looked at him openly in a behavior as inappropriate as his own, her smile so broad as to make laugh lines crease around her eyes.

He frowned at her, wondering where her guardian had wandered off to, as one so forward clearly needed a shepherd more sensible than the two smartly dressed gentlemen at her side.

Under his pointed stare, her smile faded and her own eyes narrowed.

Freddie almost looked away, realizing he hardly found himself in a position to judge another's behavior, but her expression brought with it the shock of recognition.

He felt struck dumb. The fashionable gown and hair swept up into the latest style decorated none other than his very own Georgie.

The gentlemen beside her took on a different meaning, then, or at least held more personal importance with the knowledge of her identity. Georgie's transformation, until even he couldn't recognize the wild farm girl he loved, should have offered hope of his mother's acceptance. Instead, a new worry crept in.

He'd expected her to captivate them with her own brilliant, if unusual, nature. He'd never considered how she might become one of them for more than a moment, the idea too preposterous to be entertained.

And yet here she was, indistinguishable from any other young lady at first glance.

Memory of his mother's scorn for the country lanes he loved crashed down on him as he saw his Georgie become a member of London society.

Perhaps she did not share his love of the countryside after all. Perhaps she had only lacked the opportunity to discover city life before. Perhaps, like his mother, she would no longer find any value in their time in the forest when surrounded by those with more to offer.

Fear burned his heart until he sucked in a gasp of warm air that failed to cool his body any better than the jealousy now growing in him.

Here he'd been worried she would commit some act to destroy their chance at acceptance or that she'd be forced into an engagement by her aunt when she had given her heart to him. He'd failed to consider how his own offer might weaken in the face of those with a better title and stronger holdings. Others could present her with more than a brook he still didn't know for sure whose land it wound through. Her beauty and vivacious nature could not fail to captivate and enthrall. If his feelings for Georgie led him to act the fool, why would it be any less powerful in the London gentlemen?

It had not escaped his notice how her laughter faded when he'd appeared. His arrival had called forth little of the delight he'd hoped for—no, expected—based on their history despite the most recent quarrel. She seemed to find her current companions more entertaining than the thought of returning to him, and why should she not? He had little doubt they were already men in their own right with nothing to prove and with control over their choices.

Freddie's scowl deepened until his temples ached. He half wanted to slink back through the broken branches and let his mother have her way with lists of brides, none of whom would make his heart stumble the way Georgie could with a simple look.

The mere thought of another at his side firmed Freddie's spine. He, and no other, could match her wildness and love her for it. He refused to give her up no matter how grand the others might be. Freddie might not be the strongest suitor in this crowd, but he had something they lacked for all their quarrel seemed to have diminished its power for the moment.

He had both a prior arrangement and the benefit of having captured her heart. He need only remind her of that fact. If he could open her eyes, no matter how brilliant the sparkle of London might seem, its silver would tarnish when set against the deep greens of their forest.

This thought uppermost in his mind, Freddie shoved away both his jealousy and his shortcomings to march across the distance between them. The gentlemen courting his love so openly, even the other woman standing there, faded from his mind. None of them mattered as he kept his gaze locked to the woman he planned to claim.

She'd found it so easy to laugh for these strangers, but she needed more than laughter. She needed him.

One final step took Freddie within touching distance, but before he could plead his suit, the nearest of her suitors came back into view as he stepped between the two of them. Freddie scowled at the man and reached around to close his hand over Georgie's arm. He'd come much too far to let a stranger keep him from speaking with her. He'd just pull her aside so they could have a private moment.

GEORGIE LET OUT A GASP at the strength of Freddie's grip, as much from surprise as any pain he'd caused. He held her as fiercely as her father had when banishing her from the country, and from his scowl, Freddie thought he had as much reason to chastise.

She'd been waiting patiently for him to come all this time, and when he finally did, Freddie treated her like a misbehaving child. As if she'd chosen to come here. As if she'd run from him the way he used to escape his tutors.

Georgie jerked her arm to no avail, the last bit of delight at his arrival snuffed out.

"Let go of me, you bully. You are not my father." Her tone voiced all the bitterness caused by his mistreatment.

The gentleman who'd attempted a smile moments before only to be put off by her expression might have felt some guilt for his response because he stepped up to her side and glared at Freddie, now become her champion.

"Unhand the young lady, sir, or I'll have to make you do so," the gentleman who'd scorned her earlier said. "Miss Georgiana does not seem to welcome your familiarity."

Freddie looked at her with such bewilderment, her quick anger at his treatment all but faded. The emotion drained from Freddie's expression, leaving his features blank though tension hummed from his body through the connection on her arm.

When his hand fell away, contrarily, she wanted to grab his fingers and press them with hers, anything to break the sorrow that had deepened his frown and darkened his eyes.

In an exceptionally stiff voice she hardly recognized as his own, Freddie said, "My pardon. I thought she had a wish to speak with me, but it appears I am mistaken."

After a bow as sharp as his pinched features, he turned and headed back toward the abused hedge.

Georgie stared after him for a moment, stunned. She couldn't believe he would be so easily dissuaded, and by a man who meant nothing.

"Well, I am not so," she muttered under her breath. Georgie gripped her skirt and chased after him, breaking who knew how many of their precious rules.

Despite his head start and longer stride, she caught up with Freddie before he could step into the greenery once again and gripped his arm as firmly as he'd held hers earlier.

"All this time I've been waiting for you to come for me, and you give up at the first challenge? I'd thought you had stronger convictions than that."

He pulled away, bracing his fists on both hips so he could glower down at her. "It's clear you've found others with better circumstances than I will ever have. I have no interest in playing the fool for the entertainment of London society when I'll never measure up. I will not stand in your way."

A flush colored his cheeks as though aware of what he'd revealed with the last, but where he saw it as a failing, Georgie couldn't help but smile.

"I do not think a single one of the gentlemen here knows how to fish, or if they do, they'd never expect me to come along." She would have laughed at his stunned expression if not for the pain hidden beneath.

She leaned in close to add in a lower voice, "I've told you my heart is yours, but it seems you have little faith in the fact. There's not a one of these who could offer a fraction of what you already have."

Georgie pulled back, any enjoyment in his jealousy lost as she considered his willingness to step aside.

Her tone firmed though her words came out no louder. "I'll hold steady for you until you come to your senses or give in to your mother's ambitions, but I won't sit at home and mope while I'm waiting. You'll have to learn to accept I might have a civil conversation with a gentleman or two while I'm in London as much as you should know it would go no further. There is no other to suit me besides yourself."

Chapter Twenty-Nine

A touch of hurt in her expression froze Freddie, giving him time to think through his actions and what drove them. Whether jealous or retiring, he'd done little to earn her regard.

Why shouldn't she dress up and enjoy being in London? She'd always been on the look out for an adventure or two, whether searching for a wounded deer or tracking a rabbit to its burrow. He'd forgotten all the reasons he loved her in the first place or he would have known she had no danger of turning into his mother or of giving in to the pressures of these suitors.

A chuckle worked its way free of his chest, but he caught her hand in his in fear she would march away again, offended.

"You have made a fool of me, Georgie, through my own actions, not yours. I saw you there in elegant dress and proper manner, and I almost didn't recognize you at all. Then I saw the gentlemen watching your laughter as I love to do. I am not good enough for you, but I can't seem to let you go. Forgive me."

Her eyes stayed narrowed and his heart twisted, knowing he'd lost her not to London but to his own jealousy.

He went to release her, his gaze averted, but her fingers tightened around his, denying the gesture.

Freddie glanced at her, knowing he deserved whatever condemnation she had to offer him, but what he saw held more adoration than anger.

"Of course I forgive you, Freddie. I'll always forgive you, even when you're nothing more than a fool. You've been in my heart and on my mind every moment since my father tossed me into the confounded wagon."

It took a bit for her words to filter through the sudden burst of hope filling him. "Your father?"

"You didn't think I ran off to London with harsh words between us? When have I ever treated you so? My father forced me here for some culturing. They think you a farm boy and my virtue at risk."

His face heated at the last, but how could he have expected her to keep her family in full ignorance when his own behavior had the farm workers suspecting an assignation as would his family if they paid any attention to his comings and goings.

"I wrote you a letter to explain what had happened and to beg you to come for me, but then I couldn't send it. What would your mother think should you receive a letter from a woman, and from London as well?"

Freddie pulled her close, forgetting their audience as he gazed into her eyes, his full of all the love he held for her, the confusion and fears banished. "She would have thought I'd chosen a bride after all, and she'd be right. I have come for you. I've come to take you back right now and make it clear to both your family and mine. No more of this nonsense and secrecy. All it's done is brought harm to us and those we love."

Her lips curved in a smile that made him long to kiss her, but the sound of rapidly approaching footsteps reminded him just where they stood.

"I think the same," she said before they were interrupted. "Whatever the troubles, it's long past time to end the half-lies and evasions. We need to reveal the truth."

"Unhand her or there will be consequences." A hard grip closed on his shoulder before he could give her any reply, jerking him away from Georgie hard enough that their hands were torn apart.

Freddie turned to meet this new adversary, the second time he'd been charged with taking hold of Georgie against her will in as many minutes or so it seemed. Another of her admirers, he supposed, though this one came with not one but two young ladies. He suspected one of the latter being the same young woman who had been at Georgie's side when he arrived.

"Y our father would not be pleased by your behavior." Aubrey glowered at Georgie with an expression she'd never seen on his face.

"As though he'd have been pleased with yours?" Georgie snapped before considering how best to respond.

Barbara stood right beside Aubrey, her features flushed and her eyes narrowed. She'd clearly told him everything about Georgie's banishment—at least, everything she knew.

Freddie turned to face Aubrey as he had the gentlemen standing with her when he'd arrived. His time with the farmworkers had built new muscles on his lean frame, and he looked ready to use them.

Georgie's annoyance faded as she realized how poorly such an encounter would go. She stepped between the two men, her hand catching Freddie's arm even as she sent a pleading glance to her cousin to do the same with Aubrey.

"It's not what you think. I swear it's not." She appreciated their willingness to come to her defense, but if word got back to her father about how Freddie had brawled at a party, it would weigh against his suit.

They already had enough of a mark against them with the secrecy.

Barbara moved between as well, but her gaze didn't soften as she stared at Georgie. "So the gentleman isn't coercing you into this behavior?"

Despite the heat flooding her cheeks, Georgie shifted her hold to lace her arm through Freddie's. "This is no stranger, Cousin. It's Freddie."

Barbara gave him a quick looking over, her eyes widening as she took in his appearance. "This is your farm boy?" she asked in a dubious tone. Then she shook her head as she turned back to Georgie.

"He certainly can dress the part if not at the height of fashion, but no amount of borrowed clothing can change the truth. It takes more than appearance to make a good match."

Her glance dropped to Freddie's side, and Georgie followed the path to discover an errant piece of the hedge clinging there. With as much assurance as she could muster, she plucked the offending twig free and tossed it at the shrubbery.

"I love him." She hadn't meant to announce that to all and sundry, but once the words were out, she refused to pull them back. "You should understand better than most how the heart chooses. There is no chance at a finer match."

A flush darkened Barbara's features before Georgie could think of how her last words might be misunderstood.

Freddie straightened to his full, and impressive, height to give Barbara a short bow. "She did not mean her speech as it sounded, and I am not the farm boy you think me. I am, however, most definitely Georgie's."

Georgie released a quiet squeal sure to be on the list of forbidden behaviors and grinned up at him.

Though he'd said they would tell the truth from now on, and she'd believed him, to hear him state it so bluntly to those no more than strangers to him made her heart swell with love.

He glanced down at her, lips stretching in a matching grin before he turned back to the others with a serious mien.

"Mr. Hathwell of Brookway Manor at your service," he said, as formal as any of the gentlemen Georgie had been introduced to since coming to London.

She turned to look at him more completely, shock having kept her from realizing he stood as a match to any others here, as long as they didn't notice a hedge clipping he'd missed in his attempt to brush the evidence away. Barbara might have called out his fashion as old, but Georgie saw little difference between all but the most elegant in this company.

Barbara's eyes still held an echo of her surprise when Georgie glanced her way, but her cousin's head tipped to one side as she glanced between the two.

"I see this is a bit more complicated than it would have seemed," Barbara said, once again narrowing her gaze.

Aubrey stepped around her cousin to introduce himself. "Lord Aubrey St. Vincent."

Freddie turned a deep red at the introduction, but managed a bow all the same.

Then he reached into his coat pocket. "I came here looking for you, Lord Aubrey. I have a letter of introduction from Lord Pendleton."

Georgie turned to stare as, with an odd expression, Aubrey took the folded paper from Freddie's hand.

"I didn't know you knew the Pendletons," she said.

Freddie shrugged. "It's a small community, especially among the peerage. My father arranged a discussion on agriculture."

A burst of laughter came from Aubrey. "Lord Pendleton is forever being consulted, but this may be the first time he was called to tutor."

A rod shot up Freddie's spine, or so it seemed with how he straightened so abruptly. "I've been free of my tutors for some time."

She tightened her grip on his arm, unnerved by the core of anger in his tone.

Aubrey waved the letter. "I meant no offense. Only you are a bit younger than those who usually come to him for guidance."

The strain in Freddie's body eased at the response, much to her relief. "I've taken over a portion of my father's estate to manage. Lord Pendleton was to assess my plans."

"But instead, he sent you running up to London with this letter? I doubt that was your father's intended result."

"My uncle is not going to be pleased at this turn of events, either, Georgiana. It seems you've been deceiving him and your sisters far more than we thought."

From Barbara's pained look, Georgie could tell her cousin felt the burn of their deceit as strongly despite her own secrets only recently revealed.

"Just let us explain," Georgie begged, not wanting to lose the bonds she'd made with Barbara or any of them.

Aubrey raised one eyebrow as he said, "I do believe you're right about the need to explain, and this letter says little beyond Lord Pendleton's wish that I assist Mr. Hathwell in finding you. Perhaps we should call for the carriage and resolve this in more private circumstances."

Barbara nodded her agreement, and Georgie could hardly dispute the need. It would be best to get Freddie gone from here before someone noticed he lacked an invitation to stay.

"I presume you will be joining us, Mr. Hathwell. Or will you be finding your own way out?" Aubrey asked, glancing between Freddie and the broken hedge.

"I will accept your offer. Thank you."

She noticed no flush on Freddie's features, despite the reminder of his method of entry. Or perhaps his focus remained on other concerns. From how Freddie laid his free hand over hers, Georgie gained the impression he didn't plan on letting her out of his sight any time soon, a sentiment she wholeheartedly supported.

Chapter Thirty

With the tension defused, Freddie realized he should have expected such a response if he'd been lucky enough to find her here. It wasn't as though he went to the forest for a secret tryst. Lord Aubrey had no reason to see him as anything less than an interloper.

From the looks between Georgie and her cousin, though, he may have found an advocate in Barbara despite their less than auspicious meeting. She might have been reluctant to champion a farm hand in gentleman's clothing, but surely she would not deny them now with the understanding he had enough land to keep Georgie properly.

If she could convince Lord Aubrey to take their side, Lady Brookway could hardly tell an earl's son his intended was unacceptable. Considering Barbara was cousin to Georgie, if his mother held against Georgie, that would be exactly what she'd be doing.

The third young woman in their group caught Georgie's hand and tugged her to one side as they approached the carriages. Because she came with them, he assumed she had to be Lord Aubrey's sister and therefore Georgie's new friend.

When Georgie let go of him, Freddie tensed his fingers once before releasing her. He could not keep her always within reach for all he might want to, and she had explanations to give to more than just her cousin from the look of it.

A hand on his arm startled Freddie, and he realized he'd been staring after the two of them for some time.

"They'll be back soon enough. Aubrey has called for our carriage."

He aimed an attempt at a smile in Barbara's direction, an effort that failed from her look of barely contained laughter.

She shook her head. "This has all been rather sudden for us. Georgie has become a close friend to more than just Isabella, and yet she allowed us to carry on believing you nothing more than the farm boy Charlotte and Uncle Ferrier thought you."

Freddie grimaced. "There are circumstances that bound us to hiding the truth for so long we were unable to realize when the time had come to share it. Not all parents are as welcoming as Lord Aubrey's."

A look of confusion swept Barbara's face, driving Freddie to elaborate.

"My mother would far rather I marry above my station than below it."

Georgie's cousin let out a sharp laugh and shook her head all at once. "I'm afraid there is more to this than you understand as well. Let me introduce myself since all others have failed to do so. I am Lady Barbara Whitfeld."

Her confusion now transferred to Freddie as he stared at the woman he'd thought a merchant's daughter. Even he knew the Whitfeld name. Lady Whitfeld featured rather prominently in society and so in his mother's planning.

"You're not Georgie's cousin in blood then?"

Barbara, or rather Lady Barbara, put a hand on his arm once again. "I am her cousin just as her father is my uncle. I may not have become nobility through marriage, but my mother did. I'd like to believe Aubrey's family would prove as welcoming as my father's had been, but I'm not the one to test such a belief."

"Georgiana never called you other than her cousin, Lady Barbara."

"I am Barbara to my close friends, and from the look of things, you are soon to be part of that circle. Your shadow has been present long enough already."

She laughed at the image before returning to his comment. "Georgie wouldn't have mentioned it. She puts little weight on titles and nobility as I'm sure you know. Why, she took a long while to forgive me when an ill-thought-out word implied she was less. Don't think for a moment all this can turn her head. She's kept her heart locked away for your coming." Barbara tipped her head to one side. "Though I suppose it might have been easier not to be swayed by the titles when she knew you had one of your own."

"It's a small title with small land. If my Georgie were to be swayed, she's sure to have had enough cause to do so. I should have trusted her better."

Barbara gave a gentle chuckle. "You should have, but had you trusted her more, you wouldn't have come to London after her. She's been pining for all she kept herself busy being Isabella's friend and companion. It's enough you trust her now."

The carriage arrived then, not Lord Aubrey's as he'd expected but rather a crest he had not even his grandmother's description to identify. It drummed home the fact of her station for whom else but Lady Barbara could lay claim to this crest.

His eyes widened as he took in the livery on the coachman and remembered the reach of the Whitfeld name. If Lady Barbara were to introduce Georgie to his mother first as her cousin, Lady Brookway would have to overlook Georgie's common background. She'd never risk offending one of the matrons whose favor she would love to curry.

"How could you not have told me," Isabella said as soon as they moved out of earshot. Before Georgie could answer, though, Isabella shook her head. "No, it was your secret to keep. But what a delicious one."

Georgie half wanted to object as her friend turned to give Freddie a looking over, but instead, she joined in the scandalous behavior. She hadn't had the chance earlier, but Freddie looked exceptionally well formed in his coat and trousers.

"It's so beautiful how he came after you. How he was willing to challenge others for your hand."

"How he walked away, you mean? How he assumed I'd fallen under the glamour of London?"

Isabella tapped Georgie on the arm. "And what was he supposed to think coming upon you in close conversation with two gentlemen?"

A peal of laughter burst from her lips, and as she recovered, Georgie noticed how her love had turned so he could look in their direction despite being in conversation with Barbara. The rude behavior should have shocked her. Instead, it made her warm inside.

Her gaze still on him, she murmured, "He should have trusted me." Turning to face Isabella more firmly, she added, "Besides, they were dancing attendance on you, not me. I had little to contribute to stories of growing up in London, and no experience being one of the peerage."

Just then she noticed the carriage had drawn up next to Freddie and Barbara.

"It seems to me you won't be able to make the second charge for long." Isabella took her arm as they strolled back to join the others. "But I'm sure those gentlemen would have been fascinated to hear the story of how you and Freddie became companions. I know I would."

They reached the carriage before Georgie had the chance to respond with more than a narrow-eyed glare, but Isabella only laughed it off as she climbed in to take a seat at Barbara's far side, leaving Georgie to sit next to her cousin while Freddie and Aubrey took the backward-facing bench.

She thought herself safe for the moment at least until Barbara laid a hand on her knee.

"We'd all like to hear the story, I'm sure," her cousin said, having clearly caught the edge of Isabella's comment. "And how can we help if you keep us ignorant."

Georgie sent an imploring look to Freddie, but he gave an encouraging nod, leaving her little choice but to tell a tale she'd held close for as long as she could remember.

The whole story seemed far too contrived when brought out for their inspection, and Aubrey's amusement brought little comfort even though he could hardly stand in judgment. Her cheeks warmed as she saw what had begun in innocence grow into a betrayal she'd been too close to recognize early enough to prevent. Expressions all around became grim as she spoke of their attempts to win their parents' consent without revealing the whole too soon.

"But Freddie's mother started pressing him to find a titled bride the moment he sought his father's approval and now it's a mess."

Georgie slumped her shoulders as she brought the story to the current predicament, having entertained them almost the whole ride with descriptions of Freddie as an incompetent nobleman. While they'd been laughing, though, the stories only made Georgie aware of how large the gap between their experiences stretched, and how unlikely it was that his mother would be willing to welcome her.

Aubrey sent Barbara a significant look. "And here I thought our tale one for the playwrights. Yours has all the markers of a comedy, and we'll be the ones to bring it to a happy ending, won't we, my love?"

Barbara took on an expression of extreme concentration, her brows furrowed as if angered, as she considered her answer.

Just when Georgie thought to free her cousin of the burden, Barbara's face cleared.

"We'll have to have Freddie's family up from the country for a visit. After all, they'll be neighbors to your best friend, Aubrey. Why shouldn't we want to come to know them better?"

She paused to glance between Georgie and Freddie. "I think for the time being we'll pretend you encountered each other at the Chesterburg affair. As long as we don't state it outright, there should be no harm. Let your mother fall in love with Georgie first, as we all know she will, until there's no objection to the union even once the truth comes out."

Georgie twisted to stare at her cousin. "If I hadn't learned the full of your scheming about Aubrey, I'd be stunned at the workings of your mind."

Barbara gave her a proper smile. "But you'll be happy to employ those workings in your favor, I hope?"

Aubrey laughed loud enough to fill the carriage. "As if you'd give them any choice. I'd guess the wording of the invitation is already bubbling about in your head. Perhaps it's a good thing you were born female. You'd be a terror in politics."

She reached out to tap him on the knee. "I plan to be a terror regardless of my gender. You, my love, will be the voice with which I speak."

He threw both hands up in the air and said with a tone none could mistake as serious, "You see what fate I am left with? Nothing more than a puppet for her to pull the strings."

"And you love every moment of it," Georgie said with the conviction of her own connection with Freddie.

The coachman called down then as they came to a halt, and Aubrey left the carriage first so he could hand the women out.

"Hurry up, Georgie," Barbara said. "I have to speak with my mother to make the final arrangements and write that invitation. After all, we have an excuse of urgency what with Freddie's business in the city coming to a close."

Though caught by laughter, Georgie did not argue as she stepped down and out of the way so her cousin could make haste up the stairs and into the town house.

Freddie came to stand at her side, once again drawing her arm through his. "Can even my mother stand firm against such machinations?"

Aubrey slapped Freddie's shoulder. "If I could not, I'd be willing to lay down a wager at White's you'll have her blessing before the week is out."

Chapter Thirty-One

reddie arrived back at his grandparents' home long after the household had retired. He apologized profusely to the servant who came to the door, much to the young woman's embarrassment, but at least he'd avoided being questioned before getting some well-needed rest.

Lady Whitfeld had been delighted to meet him and enthusiastic about their plan.

"Who would have imagined our little Georgiana could find herself a prime catch out there in the country. No wonder she's shown so little interest despite the gentlemen attempting to secure her attention."

Even the memory of her descriptions made his jaw ache with the force of clenched teeth. He'd been right to hurry. Georgie may have held firm against them for a while, but had he stayed at the manor and waited for her to come back, she have had little reason to hold strong against the weight of her aunt's personality.

Such were the thoughts that preoccupied him still upon rising the next morning, but soon memory of Georgie's hand in his, of her welcoming smile, and the forgiving one shortly thereafter, gave Freddie the strength he needed to face the day.

He'd be seeing Georgie again in the evening, but Barbara had requested time to set about preparing for his parents' arrival. She'd had no doubt at all concerning their response, and from his mother's mentions of Lady Whitfeld, he found it likely as well.

"There you are, dear Freddie," Lady Tamwood said the moment he entered the breakfast room. "I've been eager to learn of your efforts. I hope your delayed return doesn't mean you failed in your attempt to discover her whereabouts."

Freddie slipped into the chair a young servant held out for him.

"No, I didn't fail." He did, however, succeed in hiding his grin as he said nothing more. If his grandmother wanted to hear the whole of it, she'd just have to work a bit.

"You always were a trying boy," she grumbled, recognizing his tactics. "I suppose you plan to eat before you reveal what you discovered?"

Though he'd thought to go to the board and collect his meal, the same servant carried a selection over to him before Freddie could rise again.

"I doubt the patience you so lauded when I arrived has grown any stronger," Freddie said as he accepted the serving.

"Insolent boy. Have out with it then."

He paused long enough to inhale the aroma of freshly buttered scones then chuckled when her cane rapped loud against the floorboards.

"Yes, I learned of her direction, but even better, I found her. I snuck into a party through the hedge to accost Lord Aubrey and there was my Georgie instead."

"You didn't!" The twinkle in her eyes ran counter to Lady Tamwood's shocked tone. "What is it about young people today? We always obeyed the rules of convention in my time."

Freddie aimed a raised eyebrow in her direction. "Somehow I doubt the veracity of your words, Lady Tamwood."

A blush stood out in sharp contrast to her normal pallor, proving him right without any chance at prevarication.

"Go on with your tale, Frederick. We're not waiting on the story of my misspent youth but yours."

He tucked away the reminder to examine his grandmother's history some other time as he'd be sure to learn amusing if not scandalous tales with the dangers of such knowledge long past. Finally giving in, he explained the whole of the previous day's events.

Lady Tamwood gave a chuckle. "Through the hedge. Really, Frederick, the trouble you get yourself into. You could have marched up the door, presented your grandfather's card, and been ushered in without a moment's hesitation invitation or not. But I suppose that never occurred to you when faced with a towering wall of bushes."

"It proved much harder to breach than you might have thought. I'm lucky I didn't tumble through to fall at her feet."

"Now that would have been a sight to see. And with all of this still she forgave you your quarrel and welcomed you with open arms?"

He grinned at the memory. "Not exactly. She gave me a talking to even you would be proud of."

Lady Tamwood tapped her cane again. "Sounds like an enterprising young lady. I look forward to meeting her." She aimed a narrow gaze in his direction. "I will be meeting her soon, will I not?"

"As soon as my parents can be convinced to join us here."

Clapping her hands together as a woman of much fewer years might, Lady Tamwood laughed aloud. "You'll have my daughter up for a visit as well? What a delight it will be to see her. It's been far too long. Half a year even."

Guilt kept Freddie silent, knowing the stretch of time as much his fault as his father's. He'd supported Lord Brookway's reluctance because he hadn't wanted to be parted from Georgie rather than from any real need. Never once had he considered Lady Tamwood's sorrows. This attaining a mature outlook had proved painful at times in ways he never imagined.

"Eat up now, Freddie. You'll need your strength I suspect. How lovely to be present when my daughter learns the whole of what you've been up to." Lady Tamwood clapped her hands together in delight. "I can't wait to see her expression, though I suspect she may surprise you. My daughter might love London, but you've ever been the focus of her attentions, and not for the chance at raising her standing either."

Freddie followed his grandmother's directive even as he hoped she'd be proved right in this. He did not look forward to a life with his mother and wife at odds, and he would take no other than Georgie as his own.

GEORGIE SAT IN THE WHITFELDS' front parlor with Isabella and Barbara for the morning visiting hours. Several young men from the previous events had stopped by or left a card, making Georgie squirm and proving Isabella's statement correct. They'd been just as interested in her company as that of her friend.

She wished Freddie were there, but Barbara had thought it a bad idea. If they were seen together with such comfort between them, it would be hard to quell speculation and harder still to keep his mother ignorant long enough to welcome Georgie. Though her cousin hadn't mentioned it directly, Georgie knew Freddie's involvement in two almost brawls at Lord Chesterburg's party also weighed in the decision.

The first honest smile of the day came on the heels of that thought.

Her cousin didn't know Freddie like she did. Such outlandish behavior came only because of the quarrel between them. He'd been nothing but civilized all the years she'd known him, despite their rough surroundings.

She glanced over to where Isabella conversed with one of the lords who'd come calling. At least her friend could benefit from the visitors, and Georgie gained another chance to enjoy Isabella's company before she returned home.

"A message for Lady Whitfeld," the butler announced, bringing all conversation to a halt.

"Well, bring it over then," Barbara's mother said with an imperious wave.

They all stayed attentive as she broke the seal, though only those present the previous day could suspect at its contents. Barbara had sent a rider out that very night, delaying not a moment longer.

Over breakfast, they'd discussed what events could be canceled, and for which could their party be expanded with three additional guests. Freddie assured them yesterday that the Whitfelds would not be called upon to house his parents, but for them to come to know Georgie, they must spend as much time together as possible.

"It's from Lady Tamwood."

The others turned away, having little interest in the writings of one too old and too disinterested in the goings on of society, but Georgie stayed focused along with Barbara and Isabella.

"What did she say?" Barbara asked at last, breaking the tension and making her mother chuckle.

"Her daughter and Lord Brookway have departed for London already. They'll be arriving in the afternoon. She would be much gratified if we, meaning the Whitfelds and Georgie, would join them for dinner this very night."

Barbara clapped her hands together and smiled, but Georgie felt a shiver of fear ice her back.

She hadn't thought to meet them quite so soon, and not under the watchful eye of Freddie's grandparents. He must have told Lord and Lady Tamwood something for them to include her specifically in the invitation. Would they be welcoming? Or was this an opportunity to show Freddie how little she belonged?

"I wish I could come with you," Isabella said, breaking into Georgie's thoughts. "I'll miss the grand pageantry."

Georgie laughed, seeing the humor in her situation for the first time. "And cost me the opportunity of telling it all to you? I'd never thought my life such a spectacle as it has become."

Isabella glanced down at her hands. "It won't be for long. Pretty soon you'll be off to your home once again, this time secure in your future."

Putting one hand on top of Isabella's, Georgie gave her friend a light squeeze. "I'm not leaving this very day no matter what happens."

A weak smile barely moved Isabella's lips. "A day or two more. And here I'd been counting on you to guide me in my own search for love."

Georgie recognized the edge in what her friend had clearly tried to use as a joke. "What I know of navigating the season is half from your tutoring, and you need no guidance from what I can see. You've been conversing nicely this day with several young men, and you had them all entranced at the party. Much more so than I."

Isabella shrugged. "You make me comfortable with your squirrel faces."

"Are you saying my features are those of a squirrel?" Georgie said with a chuckle. "Should I be offended?"

Isabella slapped Georgie's shoulder. "You know very well that's not what I meant. You have this way about you that makes everything serious turn fun."

Her smile strengthened and the sad moment passed, but Georgie understood what caused it all too well.

"I'll miss you too once I'm gone, but you'll be welcome to visit anytime. As soon as the season ends, you can come to my father's farm. And later to my new home once I'm married. I suspect we'll be spending some time up here in London each year anyway. Freddie always left for at least one visit, and I see no need for the practice to change."

"Perhaps when you return I'll have a household of my own as well."

"That's the spirit. And there's no shortage of acceptable men to choose from either."

A shadow crossed Isabella's expression, but before Georgie could ask about it further, one of the referenced gentlemen rose to make his apologies just as another was announced at the door.

"It seems we'll need to call for some more tea and shortbread." Lady Whitfeld gave a rueful shake of her head. "I'd forgotten what it could be like since Barbara spent so few of her hours at home. Now when Charlotte came out, though, the card holder was always full."

Georgie swallowed against a fierce desire to learn what had happened to her older sister at last. Luckily, her will remained only lightly tested as Barbara laughed.

"You know full well the cards come as much for you as any, Mother. If I didn't rest at home it was for fear of being swamped with company."

"And an inclination for activity over sitting around chatting as we very well know. Lord Aubrey will have hardly a minute to rest once the two of you are joined."

The chance slipped away as mother and daughter bantered back and forth, leaving Georgie none the wiser about her sister's situation and with a vague feeling of jealousy at a relationship she'd lost when she'd been just a child. Perhaps she could gain such a closeness with Freddie's mother, but that hope rested on their ability to build a connection before her common background became an issue between them.

Chapter Thirty-Two

Lady Tamwood had taken things in hand as she always did, giving Freddie's parents barely time to lie down after their journey before the guests would arrive. Freddie knew he should be disapproving for his parents' sake, but he longed to see Georgie, and with his parents' hasty arrival, all chance of seeing her had seemed lost. He only hoped their lack of rest would not turn them against Georgie.

"There now, isn't this delightful," his grandmother said with twinkling eyes as she cast her gaze over the company assembled in her front parlor. "It seems the seating arrangements are unbalanced, however. We shall have to do better come dinner time."

Freddie sent Lady Tamwood a sharp look which she chose to ignore. He'd sat to one side of his mother, an attempt to obscure his closeness with Georgie, and one his grandmother could all too easily undermine.

Lady Brookway scooted to the edge of her chair, all eager schoolgirl in the presence of her betters instead of the composed person Freddie was accustomed to seeing.

"I was delighted to get your letter, Lady Whitfeld. I had not been aware you knew of the Brookways."

She fell silent, clearly unsure if she should have spoken such aloud but driven by the curiosity that radiated from her.

Freddie could easily see where his own exploratory nature came from and only hoped Barbara's mother would go gently.

Lady Whitfeld bowed her head toward Freddie as if expecting him to control his mother, or so he thought until she said, "We had the chance to spend time with your son the other day, and after such a delightful encounter, how could we not want to meet the parents who brought him forth?"

Her eyebrows rose to accompany the question, but Freddie could almost hear the laughter she withheld, as thrilled to be part of a grand escapade as Lady Tamwood when he'd have thought them both beyond such frivolity.

Freddie exchanged a glance with Aubrey and discovered the same suppressed humor on his face.

Only Georgie seemed to share his concerns, her features pinched.

How were they to keep to the plan when their conspirators seemed ready to burst?

"A party?" his mother said, bringing him out of his thoughts. "I'd never have expected Freddie to attend such when he came for business. How lucky for all of us he did."

She sent him a questioning look, and Freddie scrambled for an explanation that would keep up the pretense without an outright lie.

"Oh, he came to London with more than business in mind," Lady Tamwood said, her lips curling into a smile.

"What do you mean by that?" Lady Brookway asked.

Freddie waved a hand behind his mother's head to catch his grandmother's attention, but Lady Tamwood showed no signs of noticing.

"Why only that he came after Miss Georgiana here. Couldn't chance losing her to some London dandy after all."

The whole room fell silent. A discomfort crept in to crush all curiosity and pleasantness, spreading far enough to catch the notice of the older gentlemen gathered at the mantel to discuss politics.

Freddie put up a finger to tug at the cravat his grandfather's valet had tied in the latest style, one that seemed to be choking him.

His mother twisted to face him, but where he'd expected an angry glare, only surprise showed in her features.

"Is this why you were so reluctant to accept my help in finding a bride? And here I thought you were down at the tavern rather than visiting our neighbors. Really, Freddie, you should just have told me what you were up to. I know I haven't been much for going about, but I could have helped you. Certainly we could have done better preparations than jumping on a horse and charging up to London without even a suitable coat to wear."

From the heat that suffused his face, Freddie knew a flush marked his features at her description despite its truth. He waited for her to state her objections and shame both him and Georgie right there, but instead, she turned to Lady Whitfeld.

"Children are forever going about things in their own ways, are they not?"

Lady Whitfeld chuckled. "You could not be more right. With what my Barbara put me through, I can hardly dispute the statement."

Though Freddie hoped his mother would be distracted by such a leading pronouncement, he should have known better as Lady Brookway turned to stare at Georgie.

"You look so familiar, my dear. Are you sure we haven't met before? I don't recall a branch of the Whitfeld family in our area, but with Freddie hardly deigning to leave the country these days I have to assume you come from an estate nearby Brookway. You'll have to tell me how you managed to turn his head. I should have suspected something of the sort, but he's never shown much of an interest in the ladies."

Freddie swallowed a groan at her blunt statement. Lady Brookway had spent too much time in the country herself and had forgotten how to talk around things as they seemed to do in London society.

At least it had distracted her from learning Georgie's family name what with his father and Georgie's having had dealings. The others had kept to the plan to introduce Georgie solely as Barbara's cousin and nothing more.

"I was raised nearby, it's true," Georgie said, her tone soft. "My aunt offered to arrange my coming out since my mother has passed on."

"Oh you poor dear. How gracious of your aunt to be willing to stand in her stead. How are you finding London? It must be a bit confusing what with the lack of a feminine touch in your raising."

Freddie almost laughed aloud at the truth behind his mother's statement, but relief kept him silent. Lady Brookway seemed to consider Georgie's illustrious relatives and current standing of more interest than what she'd left behind, at least when assuming Georgie had been raised on an estate rather than a farm.

His love sent him a mischievous smile when Lady Brookway turned to Lady Whitfeld for a discussion of plans for the visit, clearly finding the tenuous nature of their state amusing.

Freddie smiled back, wondering just what this life would hold for him. Somehow, if the married state could not tame his grandmother, he doubted it would have any effect on his soon-to-be bride.

At least they had achieved their aim.

His mother would come to know Georgie before being apprised of her humble background despite his grandmother's meddling.

THE WEEK PASSED IN A carefully orchestrated pageant designed to show off Georgie's best behavior and appearance. While she appreciated all the work Barbara and her aunt put into ensuring Lady Brookway could find no fault with her, Georgie longed for a quiet day spent at Freddie's side. The constant parties had proved tiring.

She wouldn't have minded the company of his parents either.

She'd found both to be delightful. Nothing like Freddie had described when concerned with his mother's rejection.

"It feels as though we've known you forever, Georgie, my dear," Lady Brookway said as they sat in the Whitfeld front parlor after dinner, for once with no later plans. "And it's obvious you've enchanted my son. I wish we had more time to spend with you."

Georgie murmured a polite response, laughing inwardly at how she'd never imagined them getting along. The sobering thought that Lady Brookway harbored a misunderstanding as the foundation of their connection followed immediately afterward and crushed her humor.

"Surely you'll be staying in London longer now with a reason to linger," Lady Whitfeld broke in, her cheeks flushed from the Madeira they'd just consumed.

Lady Brookway cast a glance toward where her husband stood deep in conversation with Lord Whitfeld. "As much as I, and my mother, would agree, my husband says the estate can't just run itself. This trip was unexpected as it was, so he didn't have enough time to prepare and must get back."

Georgie caught herself before she suggested Lady Brookway stay behind. With his mother gone, surely Freddie would arrange some time for them to spend together without all the London trappings.

Lady Whitfeld looked between Freddie's mother and Georgie before allowing herself a broader than usual smile. "I believe I have the perfect solution. Georgiana, I'm sure your father has been missing you. You could return with them in the morning."

Only half listening before, now Georgie turned to her aunt in shock.

After all their careful plans to bring Lady Brookway around to acceptance, now she was to drop Georgie at her humble farm without warning?

"What a delightful idea. We can talk along the way. As much as I've enjoyed the events Lady Whitfeld arranged, we haven't had enough time to get to know each other. Besides, I'd like to meet your family as well."

Georgie, who had never felt faint in her life, now had heat suffusing her features and making her head spin. What could she say to that without causing the very offense she needed to avoid?

"Of course," she said in a voice barely audible over the pounding of her blood.

"It's settled then," Lady Brookway said with a firm, carrying voice.

"What's settled, Mother?" Freddie turned to face the women, drawing the attention of Barbara's father and his own.

Georgie stared at him, hoping to catch his notice and prepare him somehow for what was to come, but she failed as his mother rose, prompting the rest of them to follow suit.

"Why that Georgie will accompany us back to the country. We'd best get going so she has the chance to pack her things before we bring the carriage round to collect her in the morning."

Over the usual babble of regret at the need to depart, Georgie met Freddie's startled gaze and saw his expression turn to worry.

"And I will join you as well. I've completed what I came to do, and there's no need to linger."

"Oh, how wonderful," Lady Brookway exclaimed. "I'm sure that will make Georgie happy."

Georgie managed a weak smile, but rather than rejoice at this turn of events, she imagined how the strain in his features would turn a pleasant journey into one soured as he worried about how his mother would condemn them at the very end. She had shared his fears when Lady Whitfeld first advanced the notion, but seeing them in another made her want to rebel. This had gone on long enough, and Georgie refused to spend the long hours of a journey from London in the same uncomfortable silence that had marked her arrival.

"I'm grateful for your offer to drop me at the Ferrier Farm," Georgie said into a momentary pause in the conversation. "It will be ever so grand to be home. But if you're longing for your own estate, I can always walk the rest of the way."

The stunned expressions on every face turned her direction made her strangle on a laugh for all the situation could not have been more serious. Even Aubrey and Barbara were drawn in. But better here, surrounded by the support of her aunt and cousin than with her father glaring at the lot of them.

Whatever she'd expected, the smile that lit Lady Brookway's features had never been in consideration.

"Of course. That's why you look so familiar. You are the very image of your mother. How I miss my dear Frances."

The stunned looks transferred to Lady Brookway, all except her husband's. He merely looked solemn.

"You'd have been too young to notice, Freddie," she continued, "But I met Frances Ferrier when we first arrived in the country. She had a true wild side, nothing like your Georgie here, but her heart was as wide as an ocean. She took me under her wing. I was devastated when she died."

Lady Brookway caught Georgie's hands in her own. "I am so sorry I never came to check on you and your sisters. I couldn't face it, not with Frances gone. Lord Brookway brought me news of you after a while, but my silence had gone on too long by then. I thought I'd cause more harm in reminding your father of his loss than I could be of service."

The grief in Lady Brookway's eyes brought forth tears in Georgie's as well, but before they could fall, Freddie's mother tightened her grip once and released Georgie's hands.

"Enough of that. This is not the time to dwell on old pain. It's a time to celebrate. Here I'd thought Georgie a delightful stranger, her familiarity a trick of the mind. Instead, the two of you are well on your way to reuniting two families and healing the wounds my self-absorption inflicted. I cannot wait to see the expression on your father's face when I turn up at his door after all this time, on the arm of none other than his youngest daughter."

Lady Brookway caught Georgie's face between her palms. "How I could have missed this between your name and your features, I do not know. I used to bring berry pies in the hopes of enticing her youngest out of the woods."

Georgie froze, remembering many a time when her mother told her of the delights they'd enjoyed while she stayed hidden. She'd never guessed the baker to be Freddie's own cook.

Lord Brookway came to stand beside his wife, gazing down at her with softened features. "We'd best be on our way then so we can leave promptly next morning. Ferrier will not be pleased for us to arrive so late we roust him from his well-deserved rest no matter how good the cause."

Ignoring convention, Freddie drew Georgie against his side as well, a smile twitching at the corners of his lips.

"What are you thinking about?" she asked him in a low voice.

He shrugged. "I had no idea the history when I used my mother as an excuse to ask after you. No wonder he proved willing to answer. My father must have asked the same many a time."

Georgie failed to smother her laugh at that, no more able to contain her delight with the discovery of his mother as an ally rather than an impediment. Now they had only her father to convince.

As she waved Freddie and his parents into the night, Georgie wondered just how difficult her father would prove to be. Would the connection to her mother ease their path or divert it?

Chapter Thirty-Three

When Isabella arrived well before proper calling hours the next morning, Georgie rushed down to greet her.

"Aubrey told me everything after he returned last night. I would have been over then, but he told me I had to wait until morning. I feared I'd missed you."

Georgie caught her arm and pulled her up the stairs. "I'm ever so glad you did not. I'm still packing, so you'll have to come up. I had no idea how much I'd collected while I was here. Lady Whitfeld and Barbara have been nothing but generous."

She blushed at the chaos of her room when they arrived, but Isabella only shook her head.

"You know they'd be happy to have a maid do this for you."

"One more thing I'll have to get used to once Freddie and I are married, but until then, I'm accustomed to doing for myself."

Isabella dropped to the only spot on the bed not covered in clothing, her melancholy expression deepening. "I can't believe you're leaving after all. And without a word of warning."

Georgie put a hand on her friend's shoulder. "If Aubrey told you the whole of it, you must know I had nothing to do with this plan."

"He told me enough. It must have been terrifying when you revealed the whole truth. I know you'd worked hard to let her assumptions stand."

Georgie sank to the floor, her legs folded beneath her and skirt billowing out on every side. "You have no idea. I thought it would be the end to everything, that Freddie and I would have to head for Gretna Green after all."

"You wouldn't." Even Isabella looked stunned.

She shook her head back and forth slowly. "I would if it meant we could be together," Georgie said, "But Freddie refused the plan."

A dark blush stained Isabella's features, and Georgie sighed.

"I didn't mean to shock you. It's just with everything set against us as it seemed, I wanted to explore all possibilities."

"Georgie, it's a good thing your heart was already claimed when you came here. Otherwise, you would have set London on its ear with your audacious nature, and even the society matrons would have been calling out your virtues. You are an original for sure." She shook her head. "Now get up off the floor and help me with this mess. You'll delay the carriage and annoy your Freddie's parents. Not the best way to start the relationship if you ask me."

"Leave off. You were right when you said I should have accepted help. I haven't the least idea how to pack gowns such as these. They won't do well bundled into a cloth like my normal dresses. The embroidery would take an age to straighten. I don't even know why I'm keeping them. It's not as if the cows will care what I have on."

Isabella laughed aloud, the sound surprising both of them. "You think your future mother-in-law will never call you up to the manor? Or do you wish to tear down the impression of a civilized girl you've cultivated since they arrived."

"My father would be stunned to hear such a description applied to me that's for sure, but showing up in a well-mended dress stained with my work in the fields might not be the best solution." Georgie tipped her head to one side, contemplating the image. "Perhaps she would have recognized me faster had I appeared so."

"I thought you hadn't met before."

Georgie shrugged. "I see Aubrey failed to tell every detail. It appears Freddie's mother and mine had become fast friends. Lady Brookway saw a hint of her long lost friend in my features though she couldn't place it. I'd been much too young to remember her visits."

Isabella clapped her hands together. "How splendid. She can't very well object in that case. If the mother was good enough for her, how can the daughter be any less for her son?"

"Exactly," Georgie said with a wry twist of her lips. She didn't miss the implication. Without the connection, she'd have been less than the dirt beneath Lady Brookway's heels. Freddie had thought the same and look at all the trouble his belief had created. They could have gone to his mother from the start with the same reaction, or a better one since Georgie's origins wouldn't have been obscured.

"Don't go all somber on me now, Georgie. Your dreams are coming true. Doesn't that prove there is little weight to these barriers?"

About to tug on the cord to summon a maid, Georgie turned to stare at her friend. "You can say that when you've dismissed Mr. Ingham out of hand?"

When Isabella seemed about to protest, Georgie waved her words away. "I know what you told me. I also know what I've seen with my own eyes. Don't be so quick to let differences turn you aside when your interest is firmly fixed. You won't find happiness by settling for a more appropriate choice."

"You say so who had everyone thinking you cuddled with a farm boy when instead you'd found the most eligible of gentlemen?"

Though her friend tried to turn the conversation to other matters, Georgie gave her a fixed stare, denying the distraction.

At that moment, Barbara and Sarah arrived with three other maids.

"I thought you might require some assistance if you're going to have time to eat before we leave."

She stopped at the sight of Isabella before her face broke into a welcoming smile.

"You're leaving as well?" Isabella asked without a pause. "Aubrey is not going to be pleased."

Barbara raised her shoulders in a weak gesture. "I've sent a note round, but it seems the best solution. The carriage is large enough for five, and I can help soften Georgie's father, especially when I share the news that Aubrey and I will be joined formally in the winter."

"Lady Whitfeld felt a winter wedding with a ball afterward would dispel the last of the gossip when Lord Whitfeld wanted the banns posted promptly," Georgie added. She might not have known of Barbara's intentions to come with them, but this she knew.

Isabella took a turn at waving the information off. "Aubrey said as much, and she's right. When I think on the words given to explain your country banishment… A ball is a good idea, though with the delay, some will be searching the grounds for a cradle."

She'd clearly meant the last as a joke, but Barbara gave a grim nod anyway. "It can't be helped. All season events have been planned, and it would have the same effect were Mother to add to the list at this late date."

Georgie caught her cousin's arm to give a supportive squeeze. "It will be for the best. No one seeing the two of you together could doubt yours a love match. But it's not necessary for you to follow me back to the country. I can weather my father's disapproval on my own. I know how hard it was to be separated from Freddie."

Barbara covered Georgie's fingers with her own. "We'll have the whole of our lives together. Let me do this if only to make up for my unthinking words and selfish behavior when your father played host to my banishment."

One of the maids coughed then. "Lady Whitfeld says you're all to come down to breakfast. You, too, Lady Isabella. Me and the girls will make short work of this and have you all ready, Miss Georgiana." She said the last with a curtsy more elegant than Georgie could manage.

Summarily dismissed, they filed down to the breakfast room so as not to keep Lady Whitfeld waiting. It would be a tearful farewell on many parts, but Georgie knew she'd be back to visit if for no other reason than Barbara's wedding. Perhaps by then Isabella would have made up her mind and chosen Mr. Ingham as her heart demanded rather than holding out for a title.

Chapter Thirty-Four

ady Brookway spent the whole trip regaling them with tales of Georgie's mother. It turned an occasion Georgie had feared before her announcement into a delight. When a glance out of the carriage window revealed familiar sights, though, the wish to prolong their journey had little to do with her enjoyment.

The coachman had already been directed to go to the farm first.

"It's been far too long," Lady Brookway had said, "And I'd like to support you now as I should have all these long years. Frances would have liked that."

Georgie suddenly wanted to attempt the pretense they'd planned to use on Freddie's parents with her own father, that the two of them had met in London and fallen in love, but she'd promised herself no more lies. What made the approaching confrontation hard had little to do with where her affections lay and everything to do with having deceived her family for more than half her life.

By the time the carriage rolled to a gentle stop in the deepening evening, a tense silence had taken over their company, spreading out from Georgie to envelop the whole.

She could see her sisters gathering outside in her mind's eye, too nervous to look at the reality. Soon her father would amble out to see what a crested carriage brought them this time, though he'd most likely know this crest more than any of them had ever suspected.

The door opened to the sight of the coachman as he offered a hand first to Lady Brookway.

Freddie left next, then his father and Barbara until no one remained in the carriage beyond Georgie.

She gathered her courage and accepted the coachman's assistance from the vehicle. He released his hold as she joined the row of people aligned next to the carriage, the one opposite missing a member.

She should have been on the other side, not stepping down with such grand company when her sisters showed signs of their labors.

Her father's gaze swept the group once before moving toward Barbara rather than Georgie.

"I hadn't expected you back so soon," he said in a statement that held more than a little question. "Were things in London no longer to your taste after some time in the country?"

Barbara laughed and shook her head. Awareness of the difference between her demeanor when she'd left and now showed in her cousins' expressions even though Georgie had grown used to Barbara's joy.

"I have no plans to make the country my permanent home, Uncle. How can I when my betrothed has aspirations to government? No, I came not on my own account but on your daughter's."

Georgie trembled to see her father's face darken, and she waited to receive his glare even as Freddie moved a step closer to her.

"What has Georgiana done this time?" her father barked. "Don't tell me she's run off with that farm hand even now."

"I have not," Georgie said, stepping forward to deny his slander.

Her father turned toward her then, eyes wide and eyebrows raised. "Georgie?"

He stared at her long enough that Georgie remembered how Sarah had prepared her for the journey along with Barbara. She'd grown accustomed to the fancy dresses and having her hair done up with smooth ringlets dangling over her ears, but none of her family had seen her in this way before, and the carriage light shone too dimly to outline her features.

The two rows dissolved as her sisters swarmed forward to greet her.

"Are you sure our disheveled sister is under there?" Jane asked.

"You look like any other fancy lady," Marian said.

Charlotte sent a gentle smile her way. "I knew you had it in you."

Their father brushed them aside to get his own fill of her, catching Georgie by the shoulders. "My sister has done a lot in such a short time, but I'd expected you to stay a bit longer."

Georgie grinned, forgetting Lady Whitfeld's admonishments in the face of her family's surprise. "You thought she'd keep me until she found some lord to take me off your hands, you mean."

He met her teasing with a frown. "I had no wish to be rid of you. Only to prevent you from destroying your reputation and that of your sisters along with it."

She stepped forward once again, this time to throw her arms around her father. "I know you didn't, Father. I am truly sorry for all the worry I caused. I've come to explain everything."

He'd moved to return her hug, but her words made him grow still.

She felt more than saw him take in the rest of their company.

"Lady Brookway. I didn't expect to see you here," he said, tension shading his tone as he stepped out of Georgie's embrace. "And Lord Brookway, you're always welcome. Mr. Hathwell, the same. But unexpected at this time as well."

Georgie fought the desire to move between Freddie and her father, his formality a thin cover for the suspicion now narrowing his gaze.

"Can we not come within?" Lady Brookway asked with a gentle smile. "It's been a long journey from London, after all."

"We'll not keep you," Georgie's father said with a nod toward the carriage. "Thank you for returning my daughter."

"Father," Charlotte cried, shaking her head. "Of course you can come in. I'll put on a pot of tea. Jane, help me prepare a treat. Marian, take them to the parlor."

Georgie waited for her own task, but Charlotte had caught their father by the arm and dragged him off, her furious undertone audible where her words were not. Jane trailed behind the two of them.

Marian executed a lovely curtsy, a clear sign the others had kept up their dance lessons, and said, "Please. Follow me. It's not up to your usual standards, I'm sure, but our parlor is likely a welcome change from a carriage, no matter how well sprung."

Freddie slipped Georgie's hand through his arm, a motion Marian did not miss from the twitch in her mouth, but when he did the same for Barbara, leaving Lord Brookway to see to his wife, Georgie's sister said nothing. She only led them forward, leaving Georgie to wonder how often Lady Brookway had sat in their very own parlor when she'd had little interest in Mother's friends. Did Marian recognize their visitor as Charlotte must have?

THEY'D BARELY SETTLED IN THEIR seats before Mr. Ferrier returned. Red lingered in his cheeks from his daughter's scolding, but he showed no sign of being chastened as he took in the company.

His glare almost made Freddie regret the decision to sit at Georgie's side, but his fingers tightened where they were wrapped around hers, unwilling to pull away like a guilty schoolboy.

"Has my sister failed after all? Did I send my Georgie away only to have some lord take what I'd hoped to deny a farm hand? Was even Lady Whitfeld not strong enough to stand against the city's loose morals?"

Georgie tried to jerk to her feet, but Freddie held her firm as he met Mr. Ferrier's glare. "Your daughter's virtue is safe with me."

Though the heat of embarrassment collected in his cheeks, Freddie kept his gaze steady. He'd never meant to put Georgie in a situation where she had to face the question, but he'd been foolish in his decisions from the start. He would not let her suffer for it.

He'd meant only to defend her, but his gaze dropped as he realized the accusation of loose morals well deserved if not in the way the farmer meant.

Georgie's father paused, and Freddie could see the pieces fall into place as the man looked between them. But when he'd braced for an assault, instead, Mr. Ferrier turned his attention to Freddie's parents.

"Is this the way you raise your son, Lady Brookway? To steal behind a man's back and take what should only be given?"

His mother rose from her chair and moved toward Mr. Ferrier. "There was a time when you called me Louisa," she said, the strain growing thick.

Again, red slashed Mr. Ferrier's cheeks, but from the muscle working at his jaw, he barely contained anger not guilt. "That time has long passed, and you know why."

Where a braver man than Freddie might have stepped back, his mother laid a hand on Mr. Ferrier's arm.

"I do. And the fault lies with me. Don't let old angers and grief blind you to what is happening now. Things would have been much different had I listened to such advice so many years ago."

What she'd hoped to achieve, Freddie didn't know, but the farmer only folded both arms across his chest as he twisted to where Freddie and his daughter sat.

"Are you planning to spin me a tale about meeting in London, then? That you had never seen each other before and yet a firm bond formed in the week since I sold you a horse?"

A small chuckle escaped Georgie at the aggrieved tone coloring the last word, but she quickly smothered it behind her hand. The man had a reputation for weighing his horses above all others.

Freddie kept his own visage sober with effort.

He rose, wanting to meet his future father-in-law's accusations as a man rather than being scolded like a child.

"We did not intend to tell you anything but the truth." Freddie spared a grateful thought for their decision to give up the idea of trying to soften the blow by obscuring the method of their meeting.

"A bit too late for truth if my suspicions are correct."

Without him to restrain her, Georgie also popped up to confront her father, but Freddie spoke first.

"I confess I did meet in secret with your daughter, but it began long before we had mature feelings for one another, and in innocence. She found me in the forest when I had escaped my tutors, and we became fast friends. I have never treated her with less than the respect she deserves even now."

At least his parents did not react poorly, having already guessed the truth of his tutors careful tending, but Lord and Lady Brookway sat still in the face of this pronouncement.

Mr. Ferrier shook his head, though it wasn't until Freddie saw the twitch of the man's lips that he realized what drove the disbelief.

"And here I thought her safe to run wild where only Grannie would wander as long as she stayed clear of hunters. I should tan your hide and send you packing."

Clearly neither his title nor youthful strength intimidated the farmer, a trait inherited by his enchanting daughter.

Georgie snorted, the undignified sound all too familiar if out of place with her fancy appearance. "If you were willing to part with one of your horses, I doubt you'd send him off empty handed this time. Giving over one of your daughters should offer little suffering."

Freddie reached for her, wishing he could have prevented the mocking words. The situation needed a delicate touch.

Mr. Ferrier ran a hand over his head and winced, clearly just as familiar with her nature. "It seems a little late to come for my blessing, young man. You've laid claim to her heart strong enough for Georgie to defy her father for all you swear you left her form untouched."

He turned to face Georgie and the energy drained from him. "To have lied all these years, Georgie. Could you not have come to Charlotte if my counsel seemed of little use?"

Georgie's defiance drained away at her father's words.

The secret meetings had begun in innocence as Freddie stated, a little piece she could claim for herself when everywhere else she went, her sisters had already been. She'd wanted something special, something different, and parlor visits organized by their parents would not have served.

She stared down at her twisting fingers, unable to respond to the hurt in his tone.

Even her mother had not known when Georgie told her everything else. What had seemed simple now bore the markings of a selfishness of the kind to harm others. In all the years she'd slipped away, she'd been laughing at her father and oldest sister not in fun but in mockery even though she hadn't seen it in that light.

Her father closed a warm hand on her shoulder and drew her chin up with the other. "Would that you could put the trust in us we mistakenly put in you."

She shrank away, but he'd stepped back, dismissing her from his thoughts, or so she supposed.

"I'd be a liar if I said I'd never made an error or spoke falsely, and I'm not so much of a fool as to risk my daughter's regard by holding this against the two of you."

Her head came up then.

He looked not at her but toward Freddie. "Tell me only you will love her as we do."

Freddie chuckled.

From the surprise in her father's face, he'd expected that response no more than Georgie had, but she refused to let it shake her trust in Freddie's love.

Freddie held up a hand before her father could protest. "I know what I said, but the innocence of our beginnings denied only maturity to comprehend. My intentions have been honorable from that very first day. I could not imagine a moment in my life without Georgie in it."

She started at his confident statement, no different than when he'd first stated his plan to her under the trees. While she'd been playing games, he'd set his interest and held steadfast despite the pressure to marry another and her angry words. She'd wasted so much time in doubting him.

Georgie slipped her hand into Freddie's as her heart swelled with love. Her gaze locked to his, she said, "I might have been slower to realize, but from the moment I came to understand such things, I knew there would be a place for you in my life."

Her father gave a rueful sigh. "Frances would have known just how to handle this situation, but even I can see the two of you are taken with one another. I'll not stand in your way, and from the company, I'd guess your parents feel the same, Mr. Hathwell."

"Please, call me Freddie."

Georgie's smile broadened at his quick response. Her father would have no trade with standing on titles, but Freddie had been raised to one so might have held on to certain expectations.

"Freddie then."

The glare from her father would have scorched her had it not been softened by a glimpse of humor as he continued, "I know my youngest daughter well enough to be watching the roads between here and Gretna Green if I didn't approve. At least you have more to offer her than a farm hand eager to steal her virtue."

Heat flooded Georgie enough so she knew her visible skin had darkened with the blush.

Freddie tightened his grip on her hand and laughed once again. "I begin to see where she gets her nature."

When she tried to jerk away, he only held firm.

Her father offered nothing more than a shake of his head as she sent an appealing glance in his direction. The idea that he'd be working against her on Freddie's side seemed too amazing to believe, but it brought a smile to her lips all the same.

"All I ask," her father said into the stillness, "is you have an engagement first. A long one."

Georgie found her hand freed as she ran forward to embrace her father. "We're young yet," she said in response, the words muffled against his shirt cloth. "Besides…" She stepped back. "I hear tell Freddie has some land management to perform before we marry."

The chuckle came from Lord Brookway at that, and the two fathers exchanged a glance full of agreement before her father turned back to look at Georgie.

"You always were a wild one," he said. "I should have expected something like this from my little Georgie. It's enough to have no secrets between us at last." His eyes narrowed. "This is the last of the secrets, yes?"

As she nodded, Freddie caught her hand again and raised it against his chest. "At least you need not worry I don't know just what I'm getting into," he told her father.

Laughter came from every side then, her sisters and his family joining in.

Though the humor came at her expense, Georgie welcomed it as a sign her family would do nothing to keep them apart. Freddie's parents had accepted her into their midst, and none of her family would stand against him.

Thank You for Reading

I hope you enjoyed your time spent with the characters in *An Innocent Secret*. Many of those you've met either have their own story in an earlier Uncommon Lords and Ladies novel or will earn their spot soon enough with Georgiana's friend Isabella laying claim to the next one. They are a precocious set of characters with their own challenges and opinions that come together to make these Regency sweet romances a delight.

I love to hear about your experiences with my characters, what you liked, loved, and even hated, so drop me a line in email to:

author@margaretmcgaffeyfisk.com

or use the contact form on:

http://margaretmcgaffeyfisk.com.

And while you're there, if you sign up for my monthly newsletter, I'll share a bit of my writing and publishing journey, fun events, and even snippets or pre-publication stories as a thank you for letting me into your inbox. You can also choose to receive release announcements only, which are split into genre and go out when a new book is available in that genre. Feel free to select as many options as you'd like.

Finally, can I ask a favor? If you're willing, I'd appreciate a review of *An Innocent Secret*. Whether you loved or hated it, your feedback will help Uncommon Lords and Ladies find the right audience. If you choose to review on your website as well as retail and/or reader sites, you can also send me the link with permission to include it on that book's information page, if you're so inclined.

If you'd like to read an excerpt from *A Chance Meeting*, the story of how Georgie and Freddie's friendship began, please turn the page.

A Chance Meeting

An Uncommon Lords and Ladies Short Story

Frederick Hathwell's envy of the farm workers leads him to sneak away from his tutor and attempt to turn a poetic metaphor into reality. Only he knows nothing of the mechanics of fishing, a fact that provokes laughter in a dirt-smeared urchin he discovers at the side of the brook.

Frederick Hathwell, heir to Lord Brookway and the Brookway Barony, stared down at the paper in front of him. The lines of poetry his tutor had set him to copying teased Freddie with their descriptions.

The poem spoke of a river and the man who came to fish as a metaphor for the passage of time. The currents always flowed in the same direction and ever away from the man just as Freddie's first ten years had done.

A giggle from the housemaid brought his head up. His tutor was once again distracted by the lovely Jenny.

Freddie sighed and shifted his gaze to the window.

Shouts rose from below as the farm lads took a break from their labors to play some sort of game. His mother refused to let him join them even on days his tutor spent elsewhere. She said he needed to set his sights on higher company, not pick up the habits of commoners even out here in the country.

She'd never quite forgiven his father for taking her from London where, as the fourth daughter of a viscount, invitations to all manner of high society events poured in. Freddie didn't share her longing for the city. He'd have given anything to be out there in the sunshine.

The discarded crusts of bread from their lunch lay close enough for him to reach from his desk. He picked up one and went to take a bite when the tutor's whisper brought heat to his cheeks.

The man had been secretly courting Jenny for many months now. Or not so secretly since Freddie knew about it. But Freddie had no need to tell anyone just how his tutor occupied the time while he did his assignments.

The hard edge of the loaf cracked in his grip, his frustration taking control when he'd thought it well in hand.

His tutor didn't even glance up.

Freddie looked from the two adults to the bread and back, a plan forming.

He'd kept the tutor's secret. Surely the man would not betray him should he sneak out. To do so, his tutor would have to explain his own inattention.

Careful not to scrape the floor with his chair, Freddie rose and crossed the room. He glanced back once to make sure he hadn't been noticed, but his tutor's attention remained on the fair Jenny.

The sun shone brighter than ever before as he slipped out of the servant entrance and attained the yard. A laughing shout made Freddie pause before he continued on.

If he were to join the boys in their game, word would get back even with the tutor's silence. He had to think bigger than that.

A scrap of rope dangling from the clothes line caught his attention. Freddie cut it off with a knife he'd acquired surreptitiously from the kitchen some days before. The tip had blunted when he used it to carve his name into the underside of his desk, but the length proved sharp enough for this task.

He had rope and bread. A stick would be all he needed to make a fishing rod like in the poem. Though he hadn't been to the brook since his mother learned how their coachman had been taking him there last year, Freddie knew he could find it if he tried.

In this, he proved to be right.

Guided more by instinct than knowledge, he strode to the far field standing against the forest edge. He plunged into a thicket he didn't remember being there and pushed his way through to find the game path they'd always followed. Freddie pulled twigs from his hair and brushed leaves off his shirt as he kept going until he could hear the rush of water.

A laugh erupted from his mouth as he thought of the poem. The current might run from him, but he could catch the brook itself as it lay confined to its banks.

His chest swelled with pride at this accomplishment. He hadn't needed the coachman's help to navigate the forest after all.

Freddie scrambled the last of the distance with inelegant haste, but no one could see or scold him. Now he had become the fisherman, or would as soon as he put his pieces together with the long stick he found just before the worn path vanished into the brook.

He tied the stick to one end of the rope and a piece of bread to the other, then tossed the bait into the water. In moments, he'd have his first fish in hand, something the coachman never allowed him to do for fear he'd fall in.

Nothing happened.

He could see the fish in the current.

He could see the fish eating every last bit of his bread lure. Not a one did he catch.

Freddie had no idea how to get the fish out of the water.

His father inherited the barony just two years ago. They'd lived in London before then, on a property owned by his grandparents, Lord and Lady Tamwood.

Lord Brookway, as his father became, had no time to spare for his son beyond meals and ensuring Freddie made the most of his tutoring. Something simple like fishing had never been a priority if his father even knew the way of it.

Freddie jerked the string out of the water as a fish caught hold, mimicking what he remembered the coachman do. He felt the tug, and his heart swelled with joy, but only the string came free.

No fish. No bread.

A chuckle sounded from behind him and grew to full laughter before he could find the source.

Blue eyes stared at him from a dirt-encrusted face, a tangle of yellow hair standing up in all directions above the rock sheltering the urchin.

Even with his attention, a broad grin remained, no sign of repentance in the mischievous expression.

Freddie drew in a sharp breath, ready to tell this urchin just who he was and what respect he deserved, but something held his tongue.

He tipped his head to one side. "If you find my efforts so amusing, how's about you try?"

"It's your rod."

He shrugged. "It's not doing me much good, now is it?"

The grin grew even wider though he'd have sworn it wasn't possible as the urchin mirrored his shrug.

"I could show you."

Freddie forced his face into a reluctant frown as the urchin offered just what he'd hoped to achieve. "I guess you could at that."

Up popped the urchin and the flash of material around her legs revealed not the infant boy he'd expected but a girl. She couldn't have been more than a year or two younger than his own ten.

Freddie stared at her, taking in long hair the rock had hidden, her simple dress, and the bare toes visible from beneath her skirts.

"Never seen a girl before?" she asked with no sign of shyness or propriety.

He blinked twice. "Not like you, I haven't."

"Well, now you have. Give over the rod, and I'll fix it for you."

She took the stick from his lax hold before he could hand it to her. Then the girl sat on top of the rock she'd been sheltered behind to tug something free of her skirt.

He almost laughed aloud as he realized she raised a hairpin much like his mother wore if of a simpler design. Freddie had a suspicion they had little else in common.

His thoughts proved true a moment later as he watched the girl press against the rock with a swift, confident motion until the pin had bent into a sharp curve. It would never serve to secure hair again.

"You have to have a hook to catch them on," she told him with a tone much like his tutor used to explain some complex element of mathematics. "Otherwise they just enjoy your treat and slip away.

Freddie nodded as if he understood her statement then stared at her open palm in confusion.

"The bread? An earthworm would be better, but I doubt the likes of you would go digging for one."

Her challenge almost had him down on his knees though he had no idea how one found a worm by digging. Only the knowledge that he couldn't stay out here much longer had him pull the last bit of crust from his pocket.

She broke it into three pieces, thrust one onto the pin, and handed the fishing rod back.

"When they bite, you need to pull up and back all fast like. It pins them."

Dubious, Freddie followed her instructions as she told him how to toss the end into the current and move it back and forth. She sank down cross-legged next to him, and they watched the water together in a companionable silence.

Before long, a fish came up to nibble, and he jerked back with a shout.

She fell over as well, laughter taking hold of her again.

"You needn't deafen it," she gasped out after a moment. "It was already caught."

Freddie stuck his tongue out at her in a break of propriety that would have made his mother faint. Then he held up the wriggling fish he'd caught, his grin as broad as any she'd managed.

She wrinkled her nose and shook her head again before taking the rod from him and showing him how to remove the fish.

Freddie couldn't remember an afternoon he'd enjoyed more than this one, not even back in London with the parks and street performers. When he pulled the rod to catch a third fish, his disappointment had nothing to do with the success and everything to do with his empty pockets. No more bread meant no excuse to keep her with him any longer.

"Georgie. Georgie! Where did my troublesome child get to?"

The girl next to him froze at the sound, then she leapt up, ready to run to whomever called.

Freddie caught her arm. "Georgie is you, right?"

She tugged against his hold. "Georgiana Ferrier. I've got to go. That's Mother calling."

He thrust the last fish at her with his free hand.

"You can get it off the hook yourself," she said, her brow wrinkling with confusion.

"No, the fish. This one and the others. Take them with you. I'll only get in trouble if they know where I've been." From the look of her, he doubted her family had food to spare.

Her face softened into a smile that held as much pity as any he'd felt if not more.

"Thank you," she said as prettily as the ladies who'd visited them in London.

He passed the collection of fish up, first pulling the last one from the hook to prove he could.

As soon as she took the fish, Georgie scampered off without ever promising to return.

Freddie watched the flash of her bare feet as long as he could make them out against the gathering dark, but soon he realized just how late it had grown. He'd be missed.

He searched the nearby trees for a spot to conceal his rod and headed back, more determined than ever to make his escape a second time. If luck stayed with him, she'd be just as eager to find him there as he was for her to do so.

The rest of this story is available for free in eBook to anyone who subscribes to my Romance Release Announcements newsletter on my website. This newsletter is only sent out when a new romance title is available. Select the Monthly Newsletter on the signup form as well for a peek into my writing process along with notifications of my releases across all genres.

About the Author

Margaret McGaffey Fisk is a storyteller whose tales often cross genres and worlds to bring events and characters to life. She writes science fiction, romance, steampunk, and fantasy, but will go wherever the story takes her. Foreign Service brat, data entry clerk, veterinary tech, editor, manager, and freelance programmer are among the roles she's lived, giving depth to the cultures and people that form the heart of her works. As her website is titled, she offers tales to tide you over.

She'd love to hear from you through any of the contact points listed on her website, or you can subscribe to one of her newsletters for release announcements, snippets, and other news:

http://margaretmcgaffeyfisk.com/subscribe-to-my-newsletter/

Visit the Author

Website

www.MargaretMcGaffeyFisk.com

Twitter

@Marfisk

Google Plus

+MargaretMcGaffeyFiskAuthor

Facebook

MargaretMcGaffeyFisk

Other Works by
Margaret McGaffey Fisk

UNCOMMON LORDS AND LADIES

(SWEET REGENCY ROMANCES)

Beneath the Mask

A Country Masquerade

SEEDS AMONG THE STARS

(SCIENCE FICTION ADVENTURE)

Shafter

Trainee

THE STEAMSHIP CHRONICLES

(STEAMPUNK ADVENTURE)

Safe Haven

Secrets

Threats

Gifts

SHORT STORIES (eBook only)

Forged

War Child

Curve of Her Claw (illustrated by Star Olsen)

Visit http://margaretmcgaffeyfisk.com *for more information about these and other titles.*

Acknowledgements

My first thanks goes to all you readers who have taken a chance on my ability to tell a tale and have made Uncommon Lords and Ladies the series it has become.

My husband, Colin Fisk, and other members of my family deserve my thanks as well for tirelessly reviewing the manuscript, helping with the marketing text, and providing feedback on the cover art. My friends, including Erin Hartshorn, also helped get this title into your hands.

My support network has encouraged me in numerous ways including listening to plot points, hashing out the back cover text, and helping research various historical aspects to provide as accurate a glimpse of the time period as possible. If any mistakes remain, they fall on my shoulders alone while there are an uncounted number that were eliminated before Georgie's story ever reached your hands.